THE HANDSWORTH TIMES

THE
HANDSWORTH
TIMES

by Sharon Duggal

Bluemoose

First published in 2016 by
Bluemoose Books Ltd
25 Sackville Street
Hebden Bridge
West Yorkshire
HX7 7DJ

www.bluemoosebooks.com

British Library Cataloguing-in-Publication data
A catalogue record for this book is available from the British Library

Hardback ISBN 978-1-910422-20-5

Paperback ISBN 978-1-910422-19-9

Printed and bound in the UK by Short Run Press

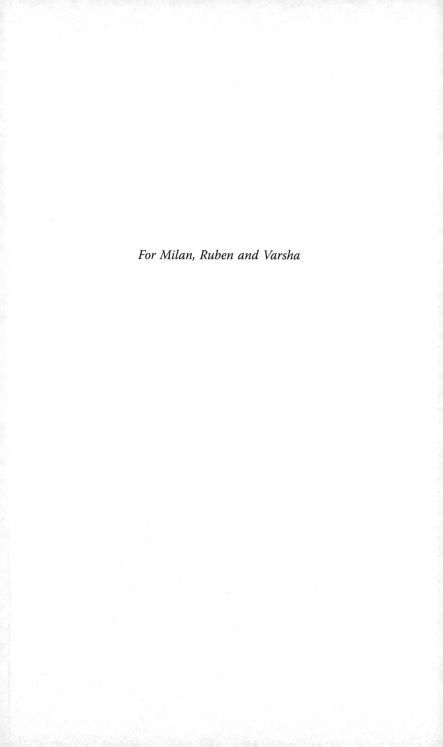

For Milan, Ruben and Varsha

10 July 1981

Chapter 1

Mukesh Agarwal sits alone in the Black Eagle pub, unaware that a riot is brewing or that Billy, his youngest son, is still out on his bike with Joey McKenna and some older boys from Church Street. It is Friday evening, payday, and the pub is full of drinkers downing pint after pint, no thought for the week's shopping or the mounting bills. There is a buzz pervading the smoky air – a good-humoured drone interjected with the occasional belly laugh or uninhibited belch. It is cut through by the sudden crash of doors swinging open and bashing against walls.The banter hushes and drinkers twist their bodies to see a middle-aged man stumbling in breathless, his maroon turban damp around the edge with sweat.

'There is trouble at Villa Cross,' he says. 'Police all around, boys throwing things, smashing cars. It is bad, really bad. I advise you go home before the trouble comes this way.'

The drinkers glare at him, shrugging their hunched shoulders before turning away, obviously underwhelmed by his news. Villa Cross is just a short distance away at the top of Lozells Road, they would have heard the trouble if it was that bad, even above Judas Priest on the jukebox.

Propped up against the red flock wallpaper next to the cigarette machine is a large ginger man with a doughy face. He continues to gawp at the man who has stumbled into the pub and after a moment he speaks.

'Who the fuck are you to advise me anything? You sod off home,' he says, '...and I don't mean to Soho Road.' He continues to mutter indecipherably, spluttering into a cloudy pint of

Double Diamond. Games of cards and football talk continue around him.

Mukesh Agarwal recognizes the man in the turban as Surjeet Singh, a shopkeeper from the Lozells Road; the owner of a small, cluttered concern selling everything from the *Sun* to spaghetti hoops. Singh's General Store is next to the Acapulco Café and just a few doors up from the entrance gates to Hardiman's Sheet Metals where Mukesh has worked, grudgingly, ever since arriving in England over twenty years earlier.

'Oi, Surjeet, saab, come and drink beer with me while this trouble sorts itself out,' Mukesh says, slurring his words as he speaks. Surjeet Singh stares at Mukesh.

'Mukesh, my friend,' he says in their shared Punjabi dialect, 'this is bad trouble, the police have weapons and shields and the boys are throwing firebombs at them, milk bottles filled with petrol. People are going to get hurt. Already the windows are broken in my shop. I had to get out quickly when a group of these hooligans smashed into it; they were taking the cigarettes and sweets. The police are making it worse by calling them bad names, 'black bastards' and other such things, but there are some of our boys mixed up in this too: Indian boys, Punjabi boys, Sikh and Hindu, and Muslim. And they are hitting all these young men with their truncheons, right in front of me. It is a terrible thing.'

Mukesh slides down from the bar stool where he has been sitting since leaving work two hours earlier. His legs buckle beneath him as his feet make contact with the floor. He staggers across the faded red swirls of carpet towards Surjeet Singh and falls into him.

'Sometimes Surjeet,' he replies as Surjeet props him upright, 'these things look worse than they are. Not to worry, I can get my cousin to sort out insurance for your broken windows. Let us go and see this trouble together, I have to walk through Villa Cross to get to home.'

Less than a mile away from the Black Eagle, in Church Street, Anila, the youngest of the Agarwal girls, is reading *Smash Hits* as she sprawls across the bottom bunk in the small attic room she shares with her two sisters. Warm air drapes heavily across the room despite the open skylight. Anila pushes her thick black hair behind her ears, drags her body over so she is stomach down, bends her legs and crosses her ankles towards the sky. She follows the printed lyrics of *Ghost Town* with her index finger, mouthing them silently as the song squeaks out from a paint-splattered transistor radio on the floor beside the bed. 'Boomtown to doom town', the BRMB disc jockey had said just before the song started; the phrase sticks in her head like the Finger O' Fudge jingle.

Nina, the eldest of the five Agarwal children, is cross-legged on the other end of the bed. Her soft, shapeless body makes her seem younger and more childlike than her sisters. She is flicking through the 'Handsworth Times Royal Wedding Lead-Up Special', the second in a series of four.

'How much can they go on about this bloody wedding? It's like there's nothing else going on in the world', she says. 'All that money wasted. I mean, who cares about this stuff around here? It's supposed to be a bloody local paper. It's no wonder those kids in London are lobbing bricks through windows. How they can go on and on about the cake in a local paper when just on the next page it's mentioning one of those Irish fellas starving himself to death in that H Block thingy – he had an aunty on Oxhill Road, apparently. Anyway, it's bonkers, innit?'

As the radio news bulletin ends, Nina glides her fingers over sketches of fantasy wedding dresses – white fairy-tale meringues next to faded photos of royal unions gone by. 'Yuk!' she says, pointing at a particular image, 'That is not how a princess should look, all horsey in net curtains.'

Kamela, the third sister, taller and sleeker than the other two girls, grunts a mumbled response from across the room where she kneels under the bright light of a red Anglepoise lamp. She holds a small compact mirror in one hand, plucking vigorously with tweezers at the tiny stubble beneath her pencil-thin eyebrows with the other.

The girls don't acknowledge their mother, Usha, as she nudges open the attic door with her elbow. She carries a tray of clinking tumblers filled with syrupy Vimto and a plate of yellowing half-moons of sliced apple.

'Have you seen Billy?' Usha says, as she sets the tray down on the nearest surface. 'He isn't in his bedroom. I thought he was with Kavi but Kavi doesn't know where he is... I don't know where he is.' Her voice trembles slightly and Anila glances up; it is a momentary gesture. 'He should have been here for dinner. Where is he?'

The girls shake their down-turned heads. Usha quietly passes each a glass and then she is gone; the faint sound of her tread falls away down the wooden steps, while her disquiet lingers in the room for moments longer. Beyond the wide-open skylight in the attic bedroom a siren screeches by like a nail drawn down the blackboard of the evening air.

Outside the Black Eagle pub the sound of sirens is deafening. A cloud of charcoal-grey smoke rises up above the houses and shops that separate the pub from the Villa Cross junction. Mukesh and Surjeet begin to cough as fumes of burning wood and metal engulf them, stinging their eyes and scratching at the backs of their throats. As they turn the corner into Villa Road they see a crowd gathering up ahead. The onlookers are watching nervously from the periphery as a brick is hurled into the large plate glass window of Woolworths. The window shatters into thousands of tiny crystals and a group of indistinct bodies disappear into the blackness of the store, emerging moments later with pockets full of cigarettes and arms full of fairy wings, socks, sweatshirts and nightdresses. One shadowy body lifts out a wire trolley from the window and passes it to a companion on the street below, before flinging out goods from within until the trolley is piled high with clothes, toys, seven inch singles and six-pack cassette tapes wrapped in cellophane. Anxious voices from the gathering crowd shout out towards the group of boys standing around the broken shopfront.

'Chimmo, Rammi, Walter. You there boy?'

Police officers are everywhere, more than either Mukesh or Surjeet have ever seen in England before. The officers stand in shirt sleeves, a zebra line of black and white. They form a barricade across the top of the high street where Villa Road meets Lozells Road, all the way from the Acapulco Café and across to Mr Lovejohn's cage-fronted optometrists on the corner of Barker Street.

'Lozells is getting brok down,' a voice in the crowd sighs.

'It 'as halways been brok down,' says another, and others in the crowd nod and suck teeth in agreement.

Lozells has long been a broken place. The Lozells Road runs through the heart of it and this is the most broken place of all. Cracks in shop windows are fixed with gaffer and parcel tape. Many shop windows are already boarded over, daubed with the words 'Business as Usual' in jagged spraypaint lettering. Uneven pavements along the sides of Lozells Road bear witness to the nocturnal lives of the drunks and the homeless who sleep in burnt-out cars or in the entrances and doorways which stink of urine and damp clothes, rotten with mildew. Empty bottles of cheap vodka lie discarded next to wrappers of burgers made with cheap meat. At night rancid half-eaten burgers are recovered from filthy bins and devoured by tramps full of bitter expectation after hours of hanging around late-night fried chicken joints and kebab houses. Any rare shoppers with money in their pockets walk hurriedly down the Lozells Road towards bus-stops to the livelier Soho Road and on towards the city centre. But there is another side to Lozells Road – the heart-thumping, roots reggae music that escapes from open windows and doorways all the way down it, bringing it to life. Music is the blood pumping through its arteries – heavy chuga-chuga bass beats and low mournful voices which keep the heart pulsating:

> *My journey is far and so, so hard*
> *So far, so hard and so misty too*
> *I can't see my way, no I can't see my way*
> *But I know Jah will guide me through.*

Velvety smooth words drift out and mingle with the high-pitched birdsong of Indian playback singers and the grating, tinny rattles of Radio One on transistor radios. Combined, the sounds waft discordantly around a soup of smells: over-ripe plantain from Jimbo's Caribbean Market, fragrant coriander, aromatic curry leaves, fresh, cool mint, stale cooking oil and the overwhelming stench of sickly, sweet goat carcasses hanging by their necks on giant butcher's hooks above the blood-stained counter of Taj & Co. Next door to the butchers, Ashoka's Textile House is a vivid rainbow of Technicolor silks and cottons folded over a neon-blue nylon washing line which is nailed to a sun-bleached canopy. The bright fabrics sway in the breeze, soaking up the surrounding odours. The Lozells Road spills over with colour and noise. Tonight the sounds and smells are changing.

'They are destroying our neighbourhood,' says Surjeet as the two men become part of the crowd.

They are jostled by the group as people push ahead to get a better view of the mayhem unfolding in front of them. Mukesh feels a sharp nudge in the back from an anonymous elbow and he falls hands first into the road in front, which is blanketed in tiny shards of splintered glass. Within seconds minuscule droplets of crimson blood appear as polka dots speckling his palms. He wipes them away across his damp, sweat-covered shirt but they reappear in milliseconds. Surjeet pulls him back up to standing position. The men are wedged together, swaying in unison with the crowd. A policemen turns towards them.

'Move along you lot or we will have to deal with you all too. Go home,' he shouts roughly, pushing his shield up against them. 'It's not a bloody telly show. Move along.'

'What is 'appening, officer? My boy is out there... Leroy, Leroy Murray, can you hear your mother? Can someone tell me what is 'appening?'

This voice, which attempts to be heard above the crowd, is that of a small, middle-aged black woman named Violet. The policeman ignores her and stares instead at the growing group of young, mostly black teenagers in front of the barricade. They begin to charge away from Villa Cross down Lozells Road towards Church Street and beyond, arms full of the Woolworth's bounty. Objects hurtle through the air towards the policemen and the crowd of onlookers who step backwards instinctively. Tiny metal Matchbox cars and chunky Tonka toys come raining down towards them alongside broken windscreen wipers, wing mirrors and the more ominous petrol-filled milk bottles set alight with cotton wool stoppers.

At the Villa Road junction traffic is building up behind a stationary overcrowded bus. The upper-deck passengers press their faces to the steamy windows, mouthing muted comments with angry faces towards the crowd. Beyond the bus, an ambulance is jammed; its siren blares out above the noise as it tries desperately to budge through the traffic, unable to push forwards or move backwards. Cars, buses and vans all begin to honk their horns. Around the traffic the golden glow of fire bombs illuminates the sky into a spectacular incandescent sunset. Violet Murray cups her hands over her ears.

'Let the ambulance through,' she shouts, but the junction is gridlocked now. And then, all of a sudden, she screams and her voice is piercing. 'Oh my god, oh no, Lord have mercy,' she cries.

The small crowd of onlookers all turn away from the traffic chaos to see what has caused this startling noise and they see a ball of flames moving towards them: an orange silk lantern floating on air.

'Bloody hell it's a person,' a voice shouts and the crowd is suddenly silent.

The flameball moves closer towards the police barricade but the police move forward to chase the rioters as they run towards Birchfield and the Aston Villa ground. The policemen seem unaware of the human torch burning beside them. Leroy's mother begins screaming again, this time short, shrill screams that burst out of her in quick succession. Others in the crowd are screaming too, joining in the terrible noise until it becomes a constant, ghostly wail. Mukesh covers his face with his hands; the four pints of bitter from earlier press down on his bladder and he strains to hold on.

'Lord have mercy,' Violet shouts again. 'It is no more than a child... Someone help him. Please help him, for god's sake.'

The burning figure crumples to its knees, flames rise up from his waist towards his chest and face. He is close enough for his petrified eyes to meet those of first line of onlookers. Two adolescent girls begin to cry and they bury their faces deep into each other's shoulders as they hold on to one another.

The churning alcohol in Mukesh's stomach begins to rise up towards his mouth, scorching his throat along the way. He takes in a long, deep breath of the smoky air through his nostrils and it halts the acidic bile attempting to rise up through his body. Sobriety hits him suddenly and he too becomes transfixed by the burning boy just a few metres ahead. Without thinking he begins undoing the small, transparent buttons on his work shirt with clumsy fingers. Finally, the damp shirt is undone and he removes it fully before pushing his way through a small gap in the crowd. He strides towards the burning figure.

'Mukesh, what are you doing?' Surjeet Singh shouts after him in English. 'You will get burnt too, come away bhai, the ambulance is coming through now!'

Mukesh carries on without looking back. As he approaches, the boy looks pleadingly into his face and Mukesh stares back, forcing a smile and trying desperately to look calm; a tiny glint of hope flickers across the terror in the boy's eyes. Mukesh recognizes him as one of the older boys from the top end of Church Street. He has yelled at him often for hanging around, smoking marijuana and for wolf-whistling at his daughters. The heat around the boy is intense and as Mukesh gets within a few feet he reels backwards, tripping on a discarded Sindy doll still in its packaging. He forces himself on, inching forward, shaking out the sweaty shirt as he moves until he is close enough to smother the uppermost flames around the boy's midriff with it. The ambulance edges towards them.

Chapter 2

U sha stares out of the living room window into the shadows that rise and stretch along Church Street towards the Lozells Road. The sky is a tangerine glow seeping into an almost opaque blackness where tiny specks of starlight fade away into infinity. Usha's eyes are wide, she avoids blinking. One by one her daughters slip into the room, bored of the attic and intrigued by the sense of unease creeping through the house. They lounge across the rickety settee and sprawl across the floor. Then Kavi hurtles into the room.

'Nine o'clock, Fantasy Island!' he says, switching on the large black and white TV in the corner. 'A plane, a plane,' he shouts in a comedy voice as the opening credits begin to roll. He points up to the ceiling just as the diminutive Tattoo does the same on the screen.

'Not this shit again,' says Nina. 'Isn't it past your bedtime, kiddo?'

'It's not shit, it's bostin,' says Kavi, plonking himself on the floor next to Anila. 'Anyway, it's only just dark, and Billy is still out on his Chopper,' he continues. And then after a pause, 'Even I wouldn't be allowed out this late.'

'He isn't allowed, you prat, that is the point. Can't you see Mom is worried?' says Nina.

Anila glances up at the television from the exercise book where she has completed her scrawl of the lyrics of *Wordy Rappinghood* in blue ink. She looks anxiously at her mother standing in the window.

'Do we have to?' she says.

Usha looks at the four children. All except Kamela are now lying across the faded, rust-coloured carpet. She hates that carpet. She scrubbed it with Dettol at 6 o'clock that morning, just as she does every week-day morning since reading about the incontinence of mice in a copy of *Reader's Digest* at the doctor's surgery two years earlier. The article triggered recurrent nightmares where dozens of scrawny rodents scurry around the house while the family sleep, scrambling through tiny gaps, leaving undiscovered sticky, black stools in large transparent containers of rice and pulses. In one dream the mice sneer at her with the faces of her neighbours, Marie O'Connell and Elsie Meeson, as they dribble urine across the laminated kitchen worktops where the girls butter bread for their packed lunches. So, each morning Usha crawls out of bed and scrubs away the mouse piss before the rest of the household awake. At first the children complained about the damp squelch underfoot and the stench of disinfectant rising through the house, stinging their nostrils as they tumbled downstairs for Ready Brek with jam before school. Usha has banned them from the living room on weekday mornings. On Saturdays she sets the alarm for 5am, giving the carpet an extra hour to dry before *Tiswas*.

'You want some tea, Mom?' says Anila gently.

Usha doesn't speak; instead she stares into the night, watching the last fragments of sunset disappear beyond the sky. An amber glow still flickers over one section of the Lozells Road, just visible from the front room window. Anila looks from Nina to Kamela for a steer, but both stare back at her and shrug their shoulders. The melodramatic theme music signals the end of *Fantasy Island*. It is ten o'clock.

'Go to bed, Kavi, before Dad gets back. It's bad enough with Billy still out,' Nina says.

'Sod off, Nina, you can't boss me,' says Kavi.

'Go to bed, Kavi!' Kamela says, backing up her sister, 'Can't you see Mom is worried about Billy? It won't help if Dad comes in all pissed up and you are still awake.'

'What difference will it make?' says Kavi. 'He'll find some excuse to kick off, like he always does when he's had a drink. He won't be pleased about any of it... you lot still down here, Mom in a daze, Billy missing...'

Anila glares at Kavi as he leaves the room, then she looks at Usha, hoping her mother hasn't heard the word which has remained unspoken this evening, until now. Kavi thuds up the stairs towards the bedroom he shares with Billy. As the bedroom door slams upstairs, a framed photo of Usha's parents topples off the brick mantel downstairs, smashing onto the corner of the unlit gas fire – the glass breaks into three triangle shards.

A renewed silence in the house is broken a moment later by a jangle of keys and a creak at the front door. The girls stare at each other, holding their breath as their father closes the door behind himself. A wisp of smoky air seeps into the living room as Mukesh drifts past it towards the kitchen. Momentarily relieved, the girls let out their held breath in sharp exhales and Nina speaks in a hushed voice.

'Deff this, I am going up... I can't be arsed with a scene,' she says.

'Don't worry, Mom, Billy will be fine, he'll be at the McKennas' house,' Kamela says, following her sister out of the room. Nina whispers over her shoulder into the room as they leave,

'Don't bother saying anything to Dad, let him think our Billy is in bed – he'll be back in the morning before Dad is even up.'

The two girls creep up the stairs on tiptoe. Anila stays fixed on the floor, scrawling in her tattered exercise book and occasionally glancing up at her mother's slender back as Usha continues to stare into the night. Eventually the noises from Lozells Road begin to subside and the night outside appears to settle.

Mukesh heads straight through the kitchen and into the tiny bathroom concealed behind it. He picks up a musty blue flannel from the side of the bath, rinses it under the cold tap of the sink and begins to wipe away at the grey film of ash which coats his skin. The coolness of the cloth is fresh against his scorched skin and he places it flat across the whole of his face for a second until the smell of singed hair rises up from his chest and through the cloth, evoking the bitter stench of burnt flesh. He flings the cloth into the sink, leaves the bathroom and collapses onto a chair next to the small table in the kitchen. He looks around as if seeing his family kitchen for the first time: it is a narrow oblong room of mismatched units, some nailed to the wall, others free-standing. A chipped teapot sits next to the kettle and next to that are jam jars, three in all, filled with sugar, teabags and loose change. Above them are the shelves he built and painted himself when they first moved into Church Street, soon after Nina was born. The upper two shelves are stocked with over-sized plastic containers full with pulses, dried beans and rice; the lowest one is a garish mixture of bright plastic-framed prints and glittering ornaments, all depicting a range of Hindu deities. Mukesh stares at the stack of unwashed crockery sitting beside the sink; the rest of the kitchen is spotless as always. School photos of the children stick to the window frame with drawing pins; a milk pan, full to the brim with thick, mustard-coloured chicken curry, sits on the gas cooker and beside it buttered chapattis are rolled up in tin foil like a Christmas cracker. Mukesh feels light-headed so he holds on to the side of the chair to steady himself and he closes his eyes. The image of the burning boy is imprinted on his eyelids and he blinks several times in succession, trying to dissipate the pixels that make up the image of terror in the boy's eyes but it is set firm in his mind, burning into him as if he is still standing amidst the red-hot flames. He begins to weep. His crying quickly becomes uncontrollable and he starts to rock back and forth, tears streaming down his face, stinging his red-raw skin.

Just after 6.30 in the morning there is a loud, unambiguous knock on the front door. Usha moves towards it slowly with the heavy weight of sleeplessness behind her, aware that she is forcing herself away from the etherealness of night towards the stark reality of dawn. As she opens the door a gentle lilac hue shadows the faces of two young police officers standing in front of her. She closes her eyes and when she opens them again the faces are still there, looking back at her expressionless.

'You might want to sit down,' the female officer says.

'No!' Usha says abruptly. An instinct deep inside her has kept tears suppressed throughout the night but now they well to the surface. She struggles against them with sharp gulps of air, knowing that to succumb would be to open a flood gate.

Anila is jolted from a fitful sleep by the prolonged howl of her mother. It slices through the morning hush of the house and echoes beyond into the street. It is a terrible sound that transcends the parameters of humanity to ally with anguished mothers across the range of animal species. Anila pulls herself sleepily towards the front door and reaches it just in time to catch her mother as she crumples to the floor. They both slump down on the cold linoleum of the hallway – Usha is a heap on her daughter's lap while Anila is paralysed by the weight of her mother across her thin legs. Behind the two slumped bodies, Nina, Kamela and Kavi sit rigid on the stairs. Mukesh hovers above them, dishevelled in pyjama bottoms, looking down on the scene unfolding below him. He shivers and a low groan expels itself from a deep place within him. The sallow-faced WPC looks up at him – his eyes are dark, puffy and ringed by a bluish shadow as if he has been in a fight. She says words that make no sense to any of them: *accident... ambulance... riot... bike.* Mukesh leans against the banister as his knees begin to give way beneath him.

'I am sorry,' she says in a slightly louder voice, 'it was an accident.' She shuffles from foot to foot as she speaks, like a child admitting to a misdemeanour. 'He just cycled out in front of the ambulance. It couldn't stop in time. There was a burns victim on board from the riot, they had to get him to the hospital as soon as possible and your lad... Billy... well they just didn't see him until it was too late. There were no lights on the bike. It would have been very quick they said. He wouldn't have known anything. He had...' she pauses, and then says more quietly, 'gone by the time they got to him. I told your wife that too...' Her words trail off.

'Alone?' Mukesh says, but he says it so quietly no-one hears.

'Shit,' whispers Kamela to Nina, 'what is she saying?'

'Mom won't get through this,' her sister replies.

Anila looks at the police officers as they stand awkwardly in the doorway, neither of them attempting to move closer to the threshold. She is still not completely sure if she is awake or asleep.

Chapter 3

'Billy was born in the lift,' Usha tells her friend Brenda Kelly a week after Billy's death. Brenda dips malted milk biscuits into sweet masala tea, catching the soggy biscuit with the tip of her tongue as it melts into her mouth.

The two women have been friends since meeting some years earlier on the edges of the Bomb Peck, an expanse of waste ground behind Church Street where the children have dens in derelict houses amongst a playground of tyre-swings and climbing frames made out of stained mattresses, discarded factory pallets and oil cans. Like the other mothers from the area, Brenda and Usha had often stood beside one another shouting the kids in for tea as the sun began fading from the sky. One day Brenda broke the silence.

'We ought to have a cuppa sometime, bab. Our kids look about the same age.'

Brenda was the first white friend Usha had made since leaving Lozells Girls School in the 1950s.

Anila kneels silently behind the kitchen door, her ear pressed against it, listening to her mother talk in hushed tones to Brenda in a way that makes her wonder if she really is their mother and not some other mother from some other family. It is the first time she hears her mother talk about giving birth. Brenda manages to coax memories out of Usha in a way she and the rest of the family cannot.

'It was July 1969, almost exactly twelve years ago,' Usha tells Brenda. She describes how the lift in question became suspended between floors D and E of the red-brick Victorian workhouse that had become Birmingham's Dudley Road

Hospital. The building remained shabby and looming decades after its transformation to a general hospital and usually Usha crossed the road when walking past it, afraid it might conceal shadowy malnourished waifs waiting in dark corners to grab her bags of potatoes and cheap white bread.

Billy was born twenty five minutes before midnight. A trickle of hot, bloody liquid seeped from Usha's womb, staining the bed sheets rose-petal pink. She woke to an empty bed and looked anxiously around the room for the snoring body of her husband but Mukesh was still at the pub. Usha pushed off the soiled sheets and piled them in the corner of the room, felt under the bed for her hold-all packed with nightdresses and sanitary pads and scrawled a note to Mukesh.

> *Gone to Dudley Road to have baby. Don't come to the hospital until the children are sorted out. Take them to Bibi's house. Give them cereal first. Kavi prefers Ready Brek but the girls eat anything. There is no Ready Brek. Clean sheets for the bed are on top shelf of wardrobe. I could not reach.*

Downstairs, Usha whispered urgently into the phone.

'Come quickly as possible – the baby can't wait.' And, before she put down the receiver, 'Please, don't use the siren, the children will wake up, the whole street will wake up.' Then she gently placed the receiver down and slipped out of the front door, leaned against the hard brick wall and pulled her shawl around her swollen body, shivering in the chill of night air.

Usha tells Brenda how she was lowered from the ambulance into a waiting wheelchair and abandoned just beyond the hospital entrance.

'Hold on here, someone will be with you in a mo,' the young paramedic told her before disappearing back into the night.

It was a Friday night and the hospital reception was oozing with sickness: urgent-faced orderlies pushed around trolleys of bandaged patients while stiff-faced nurses yelled orders at each other across corridors; meanwhile men, young and old, sprawled across waiting room benches while nervous parents clung on to floppy babies, shifting awkwardly away from the beery breath of the drunks.

'Hello, I'm Sister Olga,' announced a small, neat nurse as she grabbed the handles of Usha's wheelchair. 'And you must be mom-to-be.' She pushed Usha along a maze of lime coloured corridors towards the lifts, talking incessantly on the way. 'Stupid having Labour on the top – all these poor ladies, fit to burst, expected to walk up stairs or wait for the stupid lifts. Labour Ward is on the fourth floor. Floor E1 – why they don't just say fourth floor I don't know. Be there in a tick though – not to worry. What's your name, lovey?'

'Mrs Agarwal.'

'Listen, lovey, it won't be Mrs Agarwal when that baby is pushing itself out of you but if that's what you want I'll just call you Lovey, okay dear? You Injun ladies are so proper sometimes.'

One of the two large lifts was vacant, its doors open wide. Olga pressed the green button marked Floor E as the doors clunked shut behind the two women. Inside, the constant low murmur of the mechanism was welcoming after the din of the entrance lobby and Usha breathed in a sigh of relief, knowing that her baby was only minutes from arriving. But the quiet hum of the lift was broken by a sudden jolt and a loud thud as it came crashing to a halt – jamming in its rickety shaft just moments after it had begun its ascent. The only movement now was the intermittent flicker of the fluorescent strip light.

'Oh my god,' said Sister Olga, her voice rising a level in pitch. 'I don't like these lifts. Not a good time to get stuck now – not with you so close and all. Come on you stupid bloody thing.'

Usha felt dizzy. She wanted to close her eyes and disappear but the burning crush in her belly meant fading away was not an option. She clenched her hot, damp thighs and moaned long and low until the noise echoed off the metal walls. Five seconds passed by before the strip light stopped flickering, plunging the lift into complete darkness except for a tiny hint of illumination from the dwindling display panel above the door. Sister Olga gasped and between the twists and stabs in her belly, Usha yelled at her, 'This baby isn't going to wait for the firemen or whoever else fixes the lifts here. You are the nurse, help me!'

Sweat poured off Usha's swollen body and the limited air around the two women quickly became sticky and humid. Olga removed her glasses and wiped the moisture from her nose with the hem of her skirt before replacing them. Usha gripped her buttocks together, trying to hold back the incredible urge to push out the baby and empty her bowels at the same time. The searing pains were frantic and uncontrollable. She managed to raise herself out of the chair and collapsed on to the floor on all-fours, her bare knees scratching against the harsh matting. In the dark, she felt around for something stable to grab hold of and found Olga's thick, nylon-covered ankles so she squeezed them as tight as she could. Olga gasped just as the baby's head began to appear at the opening of the cervical channel.

'Mrs Agarwal, you alright?'

Olga kicked an ankle free just as the strip lighting flickered back into life. She stepped forward and reaching into Usha's hold-all, pulled out a brushed cotton nightie, the same pale yellow colour as a baby chick.

'Let me go,' she said softly to Usha. 'Hold on to the wheelchair instead – I have to deliver this baby and I can't do it while you're holding me legs.'

Usha did as she was told while a breathless Olga clambered over her and, with only a second to spare, caught the waxy, pink baby in the folds of her apron as it slipped out of Usha's vagina towards the unforgiving lift floor. The women stared incredulously at the tiny creature until Olga spoke.

'Mrs Agarwal, you have a boy, healthy, I think. Here...' She handed the squawking yellow bundle to its mother and the baby stopped crying.

Usha stared into her baby's face. The eyelashes on his left eye were stuck under the eyelid beneath a cluster of mustard-coloured mucus. She licked the tip of her little finger and carefully wiped at the eyelid, flicking away tiny moist crumbs and freeing the long, dark lashes before tracing a gentle finger down the new, wrinkled cheek. The baby opened his eyes for a split second, long enough to meet those of his mother before the stark light of the lift forced them straight back shut. Behind the wheelchair, Sister Olga gagged as the stale air became heavy with the sickly odour of birth and blood. She covered her mouth with her wrist and with the other arm guided Usha back up into the wheelchair.

On Floor E, a small audience of midwives and nurses gathered outside the entrance to the lift waiting anxiously for it to restart, aware that one of their own was stuck inside. When the lift finally shuddered back into action and as the doors clunked open on Floor E, the small congregation clapped and cheered with such enthusiasm that a junior doctor remarked it was as if Apollo 11 had landed for the second time that month. Sister Olga burst into tears as the doors slid open and two nurses rushed to console her, shunting the wheelchair out of the way as Usha sat cradling her new baby – a tiny, sparrow-like creature, still connected to her by the cord. The baby twitched with the noise; he was no bigger, Usha thought, than the bags of lemon Bonbons she bought for the children on the days the Child Benefit arrived.

'That is one helluva story, Usha,' says Brenda when her friend finishes speaking. Usha leans back in her chair, relieved. Outside the kitchen door, Anila has been joined by Kamela. Anila begins to snuffle into the back of her arm as the story concludes.

'I'm never doing that,' Kamela announces. 'It's disgusting all that blood and stuff – no babbies for me, no siree.'

Chapter 4

On the morning of Billy's funeral Usha gets out of bed at six o'clock. She removes the bottle of sleeping tablets from the bedside cabinet and places it under the pillow. Her head aches with a dull pain and, as she silently pulls an old knitted cardigan over her long cotton nightdress, she wonders if she has actually slept at all.

The dawn floods the room with coral-coloured light when Usha lifts a corner of the curtain. The new day adds another space between the life and the death of Billy and Usha feels a familiar hard lump develop in her throat. She sits down on the edge of the bed, sighs, and tries to remember what Dr Selvon had said as he scribbled out the prescription for sleeping pills: denial, anger, guilt, bargaining, depression and finally acceptance. He described the stages of grief to her as though he was passing on a recipe. Beside her, Mukesh stirs in his sleep and the stale smell of tobacco wafts from his sweaty body.

Usha moves downstairs to the kitchen where she sets about cleaning the oven while the rest of the house continues to sleep. Baked-on black crusts cling to the oven walls and she sprinkles Ajax over the interior. Usha kneels on the tired linoleum in front of the oven, smooths down her faded floral apron to cover the lap of her old tunic, and begins to scrub with a rose of wet steel wire. She works up a lather, scraping up and down, side to side repeatedly until the caustic chemicals make the skin on the tips of her fingers wrinkle into tiny bloodless ridges; the white liquid drips down the sides of the oven and collects in a dirty, beige sludge at the bottom. The crusts are difficult to budge so Usha reaches into the nearby drawer and grabs a dinner knife which she wedges under the most stubborn crust then hammers against it with the edge of a wooden spoon, pausing to wipe her forehead with the corner of her apron. As she bangs away at the oven, Nina slips into the kitchen. She pops a slice of bread into the toaster and presses down the kettle switch.

'Nothing gets clean,' Usha says, closing the oven door and wiping her brow again.

'Oh, Mom, it's spotless,' says Nina. 'We aren't living in a hospital, you know.'

Usha turns to look at Nina who stands in the doorway with a slice of unbuttered toast in her hand. Usha's eyes follow the minute trail of breadcrumbs which float down from her daughter's hand, dance in the shafts of early sunlight, and gather at Nina's feet. Nina stares back as Usha rests her ashen face against the oven door.

'I failed him. I didn't protect him. A mother has to be able to protect her children,' Usha says.

At eleven o'clock the hearse and funeral car slide up outside the Agarwals' house on Church Street. Curtains twitch as the low roar of engines moves down the street. Outside the house opposite, Derek O'Connell stops soaping his prized Ford Corsair, places the sponge back in the plastic washing-up bowl beside the car and wipes his wet, frothy hands across his overalls. He stands in silence, head bowed as Usha, Mukesh, Kavi and the girls squeeze into the black limousine.

'I can't look at it,' Kavi whispers to Anila, nodding towards the hearse without raising his head. 'I can't stand that our kid is really in there, all broken up and that.'

'I know,' says Anila. She bends her head towards her knees to halt the swell of nausea careering through her body.

The four-mile journey to the crematorium is made in silence. On arrival the family are ushered out of the car and they follow the small coffin into the pale-blue rotunda ahead of them. Inside the simple brick building sunbeams stream through stained glass windows, flooding the hall in unexpected patterns of colour and light. The family all squint as they enter.

'Blimey, it's like Villa Park on a Wednesday game with all the floodlights on,' Kavi says. Kamela nudges him with her elbow.

People pour in behind the family and all but the front two rows of utilitarian benches are soon filled with the white robes and saris of community elders, some already wailing and snorting into large cotton hankies. Usha's parents sit directly behind her alongside her only brother Ravi and his wife Shashi, who have travelled from Luton that morning without their children. Bibi, Usha's mother, places a hand upon her daughter's left shoulder and her father does the same to her right. Towards the front of the hall, two old men murmur disapprovingly as the family take their seats on the first bench, staring unashamedly at the uncovered heads of the teenage Agarwal girls.

Sitting alongside the elders are a number of West Indians, mostly middle-aged Jamaicans in their muted Sunday best, beads of sweat shining across glistening ebony faces. There are fewer white faces: Elsie Meeson from across the road, some of the O'Connell family and one or two others from the shops along Lozells Road. The white people are dressed in thick, black fabrics in spite of the warm weather, their garments accessorized by flushed faces and damp armpits. The Agarwals are dressed in black too, all except Usha in traditional white, punctuating the front row like a blank space between words in a sentence.

The ceremony is short, comprising a few perfunctory words from the presiding vicar followed by a few more in Sanskrit from Mr Mishra, the Hindu priest from the nearby Heathford Road temple. He chants hypnotically in monotone and mumbles indecipherable verses which all seem to begin and end with the words '*Om*' and '*Shanti*'. Usha and Mukesh stand side by side with Mukesh on the aisle-end of the row. Usha leans into Nina who, in turn, leans into Anila, Anila into Kamela. At the other end of the row, Kavi is the bookend stopping them all from toppling over in a heap. Each of them stares ahead, meeting the gaze of no one. There are no eulogies and the service is abrupt, ending suddenly as heavy maroon velvet curtains close around the coffin, concealing its descent into the chamber below. Usha gasps as the curtains close, leaning even harder into the sobbing girls to prevent herself from collapsing onto the hard, stony floor.

As the mourners leave the confines of the crematorium hall for the stifling heat of the graveyard, Mr Brown, Billy's maths teacher, appears flustered at the doorway. He searches out Mukesh, pushing his way through the mourners, and hands him a card from Billy's classmates and Billy's end of year report.

'We thought you would like to have this,' he says nervously. Mukesh nods at him.

'Bloody hell,' Nina says.

'Too right,' says Kavi. 'What good is that now?' He snatches the report from his father's hands and tears it open, 'It doesn't sound anything like him,' he says. 'I bet they didn't even know him. I bet they wrote it after he... after the accident.'

The mourners begin to shuffle about awkwardly as Kavi continues his rant.

'Billy hated school. He didn't even want to do the Eleven-Plus. He wanted to come to the shit school with the rest of us. The grammar school is full of posh white kids from the other side of town, that's what he said.'

'Shut up, Kavi,' Kamela yells across the mourners, 'it isn't the time.'

'I bet they have a special report for dead kids,' he continues. 'How can we tell now if it's true, eh? And what the fuck does it matter anyway when all that's left is a broken up body turned into a pile of ashes? What is it all about then? Shit all, that's what.' He screws up the paper in his hand and tosses it to the ground.

The mourners lower their heads. Only Usha and Mukesh stare directly at Kavi, their faces grey and desperate. Mr Brown steps backwards and stumbles on a wreath beside a fresh grave.

He looks around, checking the quickest route away from the mourners, then turns and begins to walk quickly. Kavi shouts after him, 'You didn't even know Billy,' and then turning to the crowd of startled mourners, 'None of you even knew him. Where are his bloody friends? Where are Jacko, Joey and Bal and that weird kid from the Peck? They didn't even get told about today, I bet.'

Usha walks away in the opposite direction.

'I am sorry, Mom,' Kavi shouts after her. He begins to run from the mourners who stare on helplessly. He runs past the headstones and the wilted flowers, pulling the neck of his tee-shirt up over his nose and mouth to avoid the stench of rotting leaves and decay that rises up from around the graves. He runs out of the gates and passes Mr Brown scuttling towards the car park. 'Wanker!' Kavi shouts towards him and keeps on running, down Sandwell Valley and Hilltop towards Rookery Road, past the fragrant vegetable shops where he knocks over a tray of ginger roots and trips over them, crashing into a newspaper A-board outside the newsagents. Forty-five minutes later he is breathless and wet as he staggers into the open gate at the end of the alleyway which runs down the side of the house in Church Street. The back door is wide open and Kavi stumbles in and crumples onto the kitchen floor. He begins to cry.

Brenda is in the Agarwal kitchen preparing cheese cobs and bowls of Ready Salted crisps for after the funeral. She stops what she is doing when Kavi appears and kneels down beside him. She strokes his damp hair as she would a puppy and wipes away the sweat dripping down around his forehead and neck with a tea towel.

'There, there, bab, let it all out,' she says. 'Go on, bab, it's good to have a proper cry.'

Kavi clutches on to Brenda's purple smock top, crying and coughing into her lap until that too is damp. He stays fixed there, comforted and enveloped in Brenda's embrace like a much smaller child, unable to pull himself away until the sound of cars arriving at the front of the house just a minute or two later disrupts Brenda's gentle maternal purrs and forces him up. He darts out of the back door and conceals himself in the bush at the end of the garden, away from the strangers who have returned to the house to stand in the cramped hallway and living room, making small talk whilst eating the cobs Brenda has made. Sweat and snot mingle with tears in streaks across Kavi's face and he pulls off his tee-shirt to wipe the secretions away before flinging it to the ground. He searches in his trouser pocket for the two-inch-long nub end of a cigarette rescued from the ashtray next to Mukesh's bedside earlier that day. He wipes away more snot with the back of his hand and lights up the cigarette, blowing out bitter smoke.

Chapter 5

B illy's ashes sit in a brass urn locked away in Usha's yellowing melamine cabinet next to her side of the bed.

'He might as well be sat on top of the telly,' Kamela says to Kavi as they all stand around to watch as the urn is placed there by Usha.

In the days that follow, a succession of older Indian women from the temple come to the house dressed in the white saris and salwar kameez suits they wore to the funeral. They sit in the small living room glancing at the framed family photos and collection of cheap ornaments and statuettes that line the mantelpiece. When Usha leaves the room to prepare masala tea the quiet is broken by Punjabi whispers under the breath.

'Such a shame! Too many girls to worry about and all so modern. It will be difficult to find suitable husbands for them, especially with this trouble.'

'My husband would be ashamed to let me live with such ragged old curtains where guests will sit.'

'They are old perhaps but she keeps the house clean at least. Look, even the photo frames are shiny.'

'Maybe, maybe. It is a terrible thing to lose a child so young. What was she thinking, letting him ride around on a bicycle in the night-time like this?'

'Hush now. You can't control these children born here. And so many children to keep in order. Poor woman.'

As she prepares cloves and cardamom for the tea, Usha reminds herself to sweep beneath the settee and dust along the curtain rail before more visitors arrive the next day.

When she returns to the front room the older women say, 'Thank you, beti' and put their arms around her shoulders. They wail loudly between gulps of hot, sweet chai and their uninhibited noises pierce through the house past Kavi's room, where he lays with his head buried under the pillow, and up to the small attic room where Anila, Kamela and Nina drown out the noise from below with the jangly banter of Peter Powell on the radio, the volume turned up to full.

On the sixth day after the funeral Usha addresses Mukesh. It is the first time they have spoken directly to one another in days.

'Brenda's husband Eugene, Mr Kelly, said we can use his van tomorrow,' she says.

'Brenda, Eugene... why do we have to ask favours from these people?' Mukesh replies, slurping hot tea from a saucer.

'We didn't ask – Brenda is my friend, and she wants to help us. We help each other. Besides, we have to take Billy to the sea... she knows that the funeral isn't finished until the ashes go into the sea. I told her this before.'

There is a pause.

'She says Rhyl is the nearest place. It is in Wales and Eugene said we could borrow his van.'

'What are these people, Irish?'

'What does that matter?'

'All bloody foreigners here, at least we have this in common,' says Mukesh.

The van is a rusty white Transit. The space in the back is sucked up by the expanding bodies of the four teenagers as they jostle for leg and elbow room. Each of them is dressed in at least one article of white, as requested by their mother. Kavi shares a spare tyre as a seat with Anila.

'Shit,' Kavi says as black oil from the wheel soils the edge of his white PE shirt.

Nina and Kamela sit opposite, perched on a blue metal toolbox, trying to prevent the oil stains from marking their cheesecloth tops. Usha sits in the front passenger cab staring blankly ahead and clinging on to the black and gold urn while Mukesh, unused to the van, drives nervously, leaning forward over the steering wheel and keeping his eyes firmly fixed on the grey parallel lines of the M6 ahead.

Along the sides of the motorway, monotonous steely landscapes drag by, blending into one long, horizontal line of spewing chimneys and bland industrial buildings separated by stretches of flat, drab Midlands countryside, uninviting even in the vivid July sunshine.

Two hours seem like six in the van but eventually the family emerge past a sign to Mold and into Wales. The children sit up from hunched positions and scramble for a glimpse of this new country through the windows in the back door. It is a transformed view: a gently undulating landscape of vibrant pea-green hills set against a backdrop of majestic trees and punctuated by creamy sheep, like buttered popcorn roaming high on the sloping banks above the dull hum of the dual carriageway.

Mukesh continues driving, meandering through the splashes of colour until they reach Rhuddlan, a small town of indistinct beige bungalows topped by a castle ruin. Mukesh pulls the van to a stop in a neat little cul-de-sac as they enter the town, marked by a red X on the map by Eugene. The children shift about in the back, stretching out their legs and swapping places between tyre and tool box. Usha continues to stare blankly out of the front passenger window, unaware of the crinkled, white faces peering back at her from behind dull lace curtains. After a minute or two of trying to make sense of the map, Mukesh slips the van into reverse and screeches backwards out of the cul-de-sac. He continues to drive through the high street, closely following Eugene's route, and before five minutes have passed by they are leaving the town through the other end.

The light is different on the north side of Rhuddlan. The sky is a clean, crisp blue and the sun seems brighter than the sun above the motorway. Usha relaxes her shoulders for the first time on the journey, sensing that the sea is now not too far. Anila breathes in a loud, exaggerated breath of the unfamiliar sharp, salty air. One by one each of her siblings does the same. After a few minutes they pull off the main road and head down a slip road. Mukesh pulls the van up on to a muddy lay-by next to a faded caravan park sign and one by one the children climb out of the back of the van, stretching their arms and legs back into life. They have emerged next to a small meadow, deserted except for a cluster of butterflies flitting about wild, cerise-coloured flowers which seem shockingly bold against the bleached summer grass. To the far side of the meadow is a clump of trees obscuring the view beyond.

'I think the sea is just past there,' whispers Nina, pointing towards the trees. Her sisters both nod enthusiastically. The smell of the sea is strong now, like the fishmongers at the Bull Ring market.

It takes longer than they anticipated crossing the meadow. They make their way down a narrow, partly concealed footpath and eventually reach the trees to find it is not the sea which is hidden behind but a wide river mouth, joined on the far side by a thin tributary. Long branches cast unexpected shadows on to the river bank and Usha shudders, pulling her white shawl tight around her diminishing frame. The family walk slowly and instinctively towards a small clearing beneath an overhang of trees, where it is cool in spite of the strength of the midday sun. It is here the Agarwals stand, all six of them side by side, in silence for a sombre half an hour on the deserted bank of the River Clwyd, throwing handfuls of vermilion rose petals after a trail of grey ash which snakes its way down the silvery river towards the faint sighing of the sea. When the last red petal has finally drifted out of view, Usha rummages in her shoulder-bag and pulls out cans of Cherryade and packages of cheese sandwiches wrapped in tin foil. The children eat, heads bowed as lumps of thick dry bread and cheese stick in their throats, difficult to swallow without swigs of metallic pop.

After an hour back on the road Anila breaks the silence.

'Do you think we should go back to school? I mean it's going to be the last week of term by the time we go back. What d'ya reckon?'

'I can't be arsed with that,' says Kavi. 'They'll all be pretending to be sorry for us like they really give a shit. I won't be able to stand it. And anyway, it'll be weird doing normal stuff without Billy. It won't feel right.'

'No-one will be going anywhere not until after the Kriya. It isn't thirteen days yet!' Mukesh says abruptly. He has to shout above the whirring of the traffic to make himself heard.

'What the fuck's that?' Kamela asks the others. Nina shrugs her shoulders.

'S'pect we will light another fire and eat more rice balls,' Anila says.

Chapter 6

Anila stares through the front room window as great slanted sheets of rain slide down and drench the street outside. This day, which started leaden, has descended into a black gloom and by mid-morning it is more akin to a winter's evening than this high summer's day. It is the sixth of August; not even a month has passed by since Billy's death and Anila wonders whether anything will ever be normal again. As the lightning begins to throw great shapes against the sky Anila steps back into the room, pauses a moment and then, not sure what to do with herself, begins to wander around the house.

Five rooms make up the whole of each of the terraced houses on Church Street: two up, two down plus the add-on bathrooms with flat corrugated tin roofs. Some, like this one, also have an attic at the top of the house, accessed by a slightly curved wooden staircase hidden behind a door on the narrow landing. It is to the top of the house that Anila first heads.

In the attic, Nina is reading the latest copy of *My Guy*.

'These blokes all look the bloody same, skinny and white. I mean they look alright and that but why don't they ever have Indians or Jamaicans in these photo-loves too?' she says.

'Cos the moms won't let the Indian boys do that shit – what about respect, beta?' Kamela says in an exaggerated Indian accent from the other side of the room. 'And as for the Jamaicans, they are too cool to do that stuff – and imagine what those gora parents would say if they found their Annabel or Tracey ogling some hunk of a black man? They'd close the crappy magazine down, that's what!' She pauses to catch her breath then continues speaking. 'So what'll it be, Nina... Pop

Muzik or D.I.S.C.O? Ooo I know, let's have that Chip Shop Elvis one that Anila nicked from Villa Cross Woolies the other week, I quite like that one.' Kamela stands up and moves towards the red Dansette turntable; as she does so a small pile of seven-inch singles falls from her lap to the floor.

'Be careful, won't you?' Nina snaps at her sister. 'It's taken us ages to get all those records together.'

Neither Nina nor Kamela notice Anila in the slit of the doorway before she turns and slips back down the narrow stairs.

Kavi's and Billy's bedroom is just big enough for two single beds and the tallboy wardrobe next to a south-facing window which overlooks the scraggy garden. Kavi lies on his bed with his face to the wall. John Lennon's *Woman* plays faintly from a crackly radio concealed somewhere in the room. Kavi doesn't notice Anila either as she hovers momentarily in the doorway picturing John Lennon lying cold on the pavement outside the Dakota building whilst she stares at Billy's made-up bed. After a moment she disappears down the landing to where Usha and Mukesh have the biggest bedroom, a cheerful, sunflower-yellow room at the front of the house with a large street-facing sash window. On a more typical summer's day the windows are flung open and the curtains fill with warm breeze and billow like the sails of a boat. Today the curtains in the front bedroom are drawn and the room is almost in total darkness.

Anila continues to move around the house detached, just as all the Agarwal children have been since the funeral. Sometimes the siblings brush against each other on the way up and down the stairs, other times they sit quietly in rooms together, knees touching, eyes averted, occasionally shifting their legs or arms as Usha cleans around them. Only Mukesh leaves the house on a regular basis, to drag himself to work or to buy coriander, ginger root and rice from the Indian grocer on the corner of Anglesey Street or fish fingers from Fine Fare as directed by Usha. The short hallway with its windowless landing is where silence is most gloomy. Once it was a space where a symphony of chatter, laughter and bicker melded together in an almost tuneful clamour, but this has now faded away and instead the hall and landing provide an empty chasm through the core of the house.

As Anila walks down the stairway to the bottom floor she notices a tiny loose edge of wallpaper and flicks it with her fingers. The action loosens it more, so she pulls at it until it tears a straight white strip all the way to the lower hallway ceiling. At the foot of the staircase a growing pile of the *Handsworth Times* remains unread by the front door. Usha sweeps around the newspapers each morning but she ignores the layer of powdery dust which gathers around their edges. Anila glances at the headline on the uppermost paper – the words that continue to dominate are 'UNREST' and 'TRAGIC' but she refuses to linger on them too long. Some earlier editions of the paper include a photo of Billy supplied by the school. His unkempt black hair flattened down with rapidly applied spit rubbed into palms just seconds before a blinding camera flash. In grainy monotone, Billy looks gawky as the flash startles him into a wide-eyed glare. The photo fails to capture his essence – his sparky youth and the laughter in his eyes. A small globule of saliva is visible on the fringe above his left temple, reflected in the sheen of the photographer's lamp. The newspapers with the photo of Billy have been placed face down and buried in the pile, and Anila knows her mother won't want to disturb them for fear of coming across the images of her boy, full of the life he no longer has.

After wandering through the other rooms, Anila makes her way to the kitchen where Usha is on her hands and knees scrubbing at a turmeric stain on the lino near the sink. Anila watches her for a moment before speaking.

'What are you doing, Mom?'

Usha replies without looking up.

'Cleaning this subji stain, it is where you father dropped his plate the other day after dinner.'

They both know the plate was not dropped but flung down by Mukesh in frustration when the food failed to fill the empty gap inside him – he'd said it wasn't spicy enough but they all knew it was something else. The anger episodes were becoming more frequent since Billy had died. Anila stares at her mother as Usha pushes the scrubbing brush forwards and backwards, backwards and forwards in a rhythm.

'Stop it,' Anila suddenly shouts. Her voice quivers.

Usha looks up startled.

'Just stop it,' Anila says again. 'Stop bloody cleaning things that don't matter. Cleaning won't make Billy alive again. It just makes me feel like we are all dead too, like you are trying to clean it all away. It's all you do, you never talk. No-one talks in this bloody house. You just clean. Can't you see the house is fucking spotless?'

'Anila, that is a horrible thing to say.'

'It's like we are all corpses in the same house, no talking, just existing. It's driving me bonkers.' Anila slumps down to the floor and starts chewing at her stubby fingernails, pulling off a piece of loose skin with her teeth and then licking the tiny drop of blood that appears with a disproportionate stinging pain.

Usha wipes her hands on a tea towel tucked into the waistband of her trousers and stands up. She moves towards Anila and places one hand on her daughter's head. Anila continues to look towards the floor and to gnaw at her fingers; her body is tense and the muscles in her neck and shoulders tighten until they hurt. After a wordless moment, Usha turns her attention back to the stain, kneels down and starts scrubbing away again. Anila looks up, cleans her dripping nose with the back of her wrist and glares at Usha.

'Bloody hell, Mom, don't you give a shit about any of the rest of us? Billy has gone, I am still here. We are all still here you know, stuck inside this miserable place... this miserable little existence.'

Usha pauses and without looking up she mumbles, 'I have to clean Anila. I have to keep the house clean. It's all I can do.'

The sound of the rain momentarily amplifies and a crash of loud thunder echoes off the corrugated bathroom roof before the noise dies down to a more steady, less distinct beat.

'No you don't,' Anila says. She picks herself up, flings open the back door and teeters on the threshold for a fraction of a second before stepping out into the rain – knowing that if she stays in the kitchen she will say something awful to Usha. The wind hits her in the face, numbing the throbbing in her head as her heart begins racing. She thinks of her mother, just a few steps away on her hands and knees, pushing the scrubbing brush back and forth like a robot. She wants to run back in, grab Usha by the throat and shake the private sufferings out of her. Instead she clenches her teeth and emits a loud, long moan towards the ominous grey sky above. Her voice is barely audible above the heavy pelt of the rain which envelops her until her hair and clothes are drenched. Raindrops run down her cheeks and mingle with her own tears creating flowing rivulets across her face. When she is completely soaked, Anila re-enters the house, shivering uncontrollably. Murky water drips from her rain-sodden clothes onto the kitchen floor and creates a brown water trail as she moves past her mother and reaches for a small towel hanging on a cupboard handle nearby. She wipes her face and flings the towel to the floor. She leaves the kitchen, taking the damp of the day with her through the living room and up the stairs. Usha picks up the discarded towel and soaks up the water on the kitchen floor before returning to scrub away at the stubborn turmeric stain.

Chapter 7

On Bank Holiday Monday, Bibi arrives at the front-door unexpectedly. Nina lets her in and allows her grandmother to pinch her cheek and give her a tight squeeze before the older woman disappears into the kitchen and pulls the door closed behind herself. Nina hangs about in the hallway, listening as Usha greets her own mother. They talk in Punjabi and Nina can understand just enough to make out the gist of the conversation. After a few minutes, Nina pops her head around the living-room door and reports to her sisters.

'They're going to stay with Uncle Ravi in Luton for a while, Aunt Shash is having another babbie, it sounds like. She's chucking up all the time and can't cope with the other kids so Bibi and Nanaa are going to help out. They're going for a month or something.'

'I wonder if she knew she was up the duff at the funeral,' Kamela says, doodling spectacles on the faces in photographs in an old newspaper.

'What difference does that make?' Anila asks, lifting her head from the TV listings in the weekend's *Handsworth Times*.

'Indian people are just so bloody weird sometimes,' Nina announces as she pops her head around the living room door a second time.

'We're Indian too, you know?' Kamela says, 'Even if we do forget sometimes.'

'We don't forget, Kamela, we just choose not to remember until we have a good enough reason to. Anyway, listen – Bibi just told Mom that Billy's spirit will have entered the new baby that Aunty Shash is having and he'll be reborn as our cousin.

39

That's why her and Nanaa have to go and look after her now instead of being around for Mom.'

'Bollocks!' Anila says and returns to the listings.

'Bloody hell,' Kamela sighs, shaking her head. 'That'll make everything alright then, I suppose. Perhaps we should be celebrating?' She stands up, claps her hands together and peers out of the window to the street from behind the nets, 'Honestly, it's like we've never left the medieval age around here sometimes.'

When the back gate bangs shut fifteen minutes later, Nina gently opens the kitchen door. The stillness unsettles her but the quiet of the room is broken by a distant howl of a baby in one of the adjacent gardens. It takes Nina a few seconds to see her mother standing in the shadows of the bathroom entrance.

'You alright, Mom?' Usha doesn't reply. 'Bibi and Nanaa will be back before you know it.'

'Yes, perhaps,' Usha says, breaking her own silence before picking up a basket of wet washing from the table and heading down the side return.

'Anyone want to come out? It's lovely and sunny out there. C'mon Kamela, Anila, we can have a fag at the Bomb Peck. I don't want to go on my own and I'll go mad stuck in here – we've hardly been out the house in weeks.'

'Yeah, okay then,' Kamela says unenthusiastically.

Anila rouses herself from her prostrate position on the carpet, 'Go on then, I'll come if you've got any ciggies. Can we get back for Jim'll Fix It though? There's a special on for the bank holiday.'

'I don't know why you want to watch that soppy rubbish,' says Kamela.

'Everyone watches it and anyway, it's Billy's favourite, I want to watch it for him,' Anila replies sullenly.

'You're as bad as Bibi, saying stuff like that.'

'Piss off, Kam.'

Nina grabs her youngest sister's arm, 'C'mon on, we'll be back loads before then – we're only going for a fag. Let's see what's going on out there in the 20th century, shall we?'

Outside, the sunshine is striking and all three girls blink rapidly to adjust their eyes. The street is full of activity: games of football, rope-skipping in threes and fours, car and window-washing and the occasional doorstep conversation. Directly across the road the O'Connell twins play two-balls up against the wall between their own house and Elsie Meeson's. They chant as they play.

'Matthew, Mark, Luke and John, next door neighbour carry on.
Next door neighbour got the flu, so I pass it on to you.'

Marie O'Connell sits on her front doorstep close by, smoking and watching the children as they play. She nods at the Agarwal girls and they nod back.

'Remember when we used to play that?' says Nina.

'Seems like we played it yesterday,' replies Anila.

Further down the road, Gary O'Connell lurks on the street corner with three other boys, all of them around a similar age.

'Have you seen his tattoo?' Kamela asks, gesturing towards Gary. 'It's a massive horrible swastika on his arm. Think he's trying to tell us something?'

'Idiot – we should give him one of those calendars from the temple with the Indian swastikas on, that would really mix him up.'

'He used to be nice to me when I was a kid,' says Anila.

'You're still a kid, bab!'

'Piss off, Nina.'

'I used to fancy him when I was in fourth-year before he shaved his head and became a thug. He tried to snog me once at a school disco.'

'Yuk, Nina, that's vile. Look at him with his stupid drainpipes and braces, and his ridiculous mates – look at that one wearing a Harrington in this weather – bloody idiots!'

A car turns sharply into the street from Nursery Road and Gary and the other boys have to move swiftly to avoid it hitting them. The car windows are all wound down and a familiar Northern Soul song blares out. The group of boys on the corner raise their arms up high and each sticks up two-fingers towards the driver, except Gary O'Connell who gives a Nazi salute. The car-driver shakes his head and laughs and, as he passes Nina, Kamela and Anila, he turns the music lower, slows the car, puts his head out of the window and wolf-whistles.

'I fucking hate blokes sometimes,' Kamela says and the girls turn into the alley out of sight.

The girls make their way to the Bomb Peck, find a shaded spot beneath a silver birch on the edge of the waste-ground and sit down on the uneven ground beneath it. Young boys play cricket with a tennis ball and a plank of wood directly in front of them and beyond that, towards the opposite end of the Bomb Peck, a group of shabby, dreadlocked men huddle around a ghetto blaster. The music is deep, rootsy reggae like they play at the late-night blues parties in the back streets of Handsworth and that seeps through open windows as a soundscape to the darkest of summer hours.

'Are you all going to be okay when I go to Leeds next month?' Nina asks as she stares at a young cricketer; he reminds her of Billy. The sisters all light up cigarettes and scan the scenes around them, eyes darting about to clock any unwanted attention or unsettling activity.

'What do you care?' Kamela says eventually.

'Of course I care, Kamela.'

'You're going whatever, so what's the point even asking?'

'I'm just not sure Mom is too happy about it, what with Billy and that.'

'Don't be daft, Mom is proud of you. I've heard her saying so to Brenda. It's a big deal around here to even think about university, never mind getting a place, and Mom and Dad allowing you to go – it's massive. I wish it was me,' Anila says.

'It might be you in a couple of years, Nils.'

'Well, it won't make much difference to us around here if you go or not, except me and Anila can have a bit more space in the bedroom when you take all your shit with you.' Kamela speaks light-heartedly and Nina replies in the same spirit.

'You're so friggin' charming, Kamela. Anyhow, I know you'll miss me really – go on admit it,'

'I'll be glad to see the back of you!'

At the far end of the Bomb Peck, towards Brougham Road, Gary O'Connell and the other skinheads appear. They play football with a tin can and spit nervously in the direction of the group of black men with the ghetto blaster, seemingly careful to maintain their distance. One or two of the Rastas turn and glare at them but soon lose interest. The skinheads circum-navigate the Rastas and instead lurk around the much younger boys playing cricket.

'They better not come near us,' says Nina, shuffling herself further back towards the tree as Gary and his friends begin hissing at the cricket players. They pick on one particular boy, the wicket-keeper who is about ten years old and has a handkerchief-covered top-knot on his head. Two of the skinheads shove the boy from one to another and as they do so the top-knot wobbles precariously.

'Leave him alone,' the other young cricket players shout but the skinheads continue to taunt the boy until he begins to cry and then they sneer and grab at the handkerchief, pulling loose the top-knot in the process.

'Yeah, leave him alone, you dickheads, pick on someone your own size,' Kamela yells.

'Don't bother, Kam, they're not worth it,' Nina says, but Kamela ignores her and is on her feet and heading towards the skinheads with Anila trailing behind her.

'Oh bloody hell,' Nina sighs before stubbing out her cigarette and standing up.

'Piss off, Paki cows,' one of the skinheads shouts as Kamela approaches them, hot-footed by her sisters. The skinheads turn their attention to the girls and the young wicket-keeper grabs the opportunity to escape, scooping up his handkerchief from the ground and running away as fast as he can. Some of the other boys do the same, dispersing in all directions, but one or two of the less daunted ones hang around on the periphery to watch the confrontation unfold. Kamela walks straight up to Gary O'Connell.

'You idiot, Gary, you used to be alright once – what do you think you're doing picking on little kids? Even your mom and your sisters are ashamed of you these days,' she says.

'Do you know this bitch?' one of the other skinheads says. Gary shakes his head.

'Listen, we've known him and his family since he was running around in a nappy with the rest of us on Church Street so don't bloody pretend to not know what I'm talking about, Gary,' Kamela continues. 'In fact, he used to fancy my sister over there, didn't you?'

'Fuck off, Kamela,' Gary says turning scarlet.

'Yes, shut up, Kam,' Nina adds, embarrassed as the skinheads all turn to look at her.

'Let's go,' Anila says but one of the skinheads picks up a brick and holds it out towards her threateningly. She takes a step backwards.

'Leave it,' Gary says, and the others gawp at him.

'I'm not letting some Paki bitch talk to me that way even if you are,' says the Harrington-wearing boy to Gary as he shoves him aside to stand face to face with Kamela. She doesn't flinch, instead she stares directly at him as he snarls at her.

'C'mon, Kamela, leave it,' Nina says, grabbing her sister's arm.

'Yes, come on Kam, they're just idiots,' Anila adds, grabbing Kamela's other arm.

'Oi, rasclaat baldheads.'

A holler comes from the distant side of the Bomb Peck and all four skinheads and the Agarwal girls turn to see a short line of Rastas stomping towards them.

'Fuck this,' Gary says, and starts to walk off.

'You wanker, Gaz,' the Harrington skinhead says.

'Exactly!' Kamela adds mockingly.

'Bitch!'

As the Rastas get closer the skinheads glance at one another, unable to hide the panic in their eyes. The boy with the brick allows it to tumble out of his hand.

'Go on,' Kamela says gesturing towards Gary, 'run away after your mate, back to your mommies and daddies before the big, bad, black men come and get you.'

The skinheads begin to run towards Gary and Kamela sniggers, ensuring it is loud enough for them to hear. She then turns to the approaching Rastas and raises a thumb towards them. The man at the front of the line nods reassuringly and changes direction, back towards the spot where the reggae music is still pumping out.

The girls light up fresh cigarettes and watch as the skinheads retreat into the distance and some of the young cricket players begin to emerge from behind trees and crumbling walls to resume their game.

'Let's get back, Jim'll Fix It will be on soon,' Anila says.

The girls head towards the alleyway that runs between Villa Street and Church Street and as they approach they hear a rustle behind a hedge of flowering bindweed in an abandoned garden adjacent to the arched entrance.

'What's that?' Nina says and the others shrug their shoulders as they all instinctively link arms again. As they get closer, Nina points out a dark silhouette at the edge of their path and within seconds a bulky figure moves out of the shadows and into view.

'Ah, it's only an old bloke, probably the tramp that sleeps on the bench back there,' Nina says, gesturing towards the Bomb Peck, and the girls carry on walking.

'You didn't really fancy that idiot did you, Nina?' Anila asks, but before Nina can respond the old man is directly in front of the girls, opening his ragged coat and revealing himself to them. Anila screams. Nina grabs her hand and all three girls push past the man, knocking him sideways into the hedge.

'Dirty old bastard,' Nina shouts behind them.

When they reach the other side of the alley and are in the open, the girls lean with their backs against the wall of Elsie Meeson's house and catch their breath.

'Oh my god, did you see it?'

'It was horrible... You're right, Kam, some blokes are so disgusting!' Nina says and all three girls start laughing. 'C'mon then, let's get home,' she continues when they have composed themselves. 'There's too much going on out here and anyway, we don't want to miss Jim'll bloody Fix it.'

Chapter 8

Kavi can't work out how the scent of a dead person can still exist, hanging in the air weeks after they have been burnt like an old box on a bonfire. How can it cling to clothes and waft out unexpectedly as if that body might still be alive, existing in the threads of the fabrics, trapped, invisible and without a voice? He thinks of his brother floating around, lost in space, alone and scared like Major Tom in Bowie's *A Space Oddity*. He slams the wardrobe shut. It is ten weeks since Billy died.

Beyond the bedroom, the house stinks of Jeyes Fluid and bleach. In the kitchen, Usha is scrubbing the inside of a saucepan with a Brillo Pad. Pink soap suds ooze from the wet steel wool scourer and lurid froth bubbles across her bright yellow Marigolds. Her hands look like they should be on the cover of *Never Mind The Bollocks* – garish, Day-Glo punk hands – Kavi thinks as he brushes past her. She doesn't look up. Beyond the cleaning products and the smell of sorrow that hangs about her like a shadow he detects a very faint hint of the coconut and cold cream he remembers from when he was young enough to bury his face in her bosom. He leaves by the back door, glancing at the back of the house which is wedged between other houses, stuck in the middle of a row of tiny red-brick dwellings on Church Street. The houses have one long zigzag roof and the same washing-filled back gardens – scrubby lawns and wild, unkempt bushes toppling over cracked brick border walls, marking out small stakes of territory.

Kavi makes his way through the narrow alley between the Argawal family house in the centre of Church Street and the Farooqis' next door. He walks quickly towards the Lozells Road, avoiding piles of dog shit and discarded litter along the way. There is a dull ache in the pit of his stomach that somehow seems to be connected to the empty day that stretches ahead of him. Kavi crosses Lozells Road after reaching the top of Church Street and glances through the glass windows in the intricately carved wooden doors of the Royal Oak pub. Inside he sees the faces of jobless men sitting in groups of two and three, drinking cheap ale from chipped glasses. In the snug area of the pub at the side of the larger room, he sees older white women in faded clothes clustering around glasses of port and lemon, putting the world to rights. As Kavi kicks a crumpled Coke tin across the street, he hears a sharp sucking of teeth behind him.

'Hey Kavi, man, what you doing hanging about here? You not going to school?'

It is Marcus, the older brother of a boy in his class.

'Don't ignore me, man.'

'Fuck off, leave me alone.'

'Listen, man, we all know you been through some shit yeah, but you going to get yourself into some serious trouble talking like that. I was just being friendly like, you know.'

'Yeah... alright, sorry. I'm just not in the mood, okay?'

Marcus is suddenly side by side with Kavi. His short afro juts out from beneath his red and black tam hat and he smells strongly of patchouli oil.

'So, how's them pretty sisters of yours doing, man?' Marcus says cheerily.

Kavi glares at him. Marcus's body has teetered over an edge between adolescence and manhood and Kavi is a much younger child next to this wiry, square-shouldered boy.

'Look man I'm going down the Acapulco. Clive'll be coming in a bit, after school and that. Wanna come? I got a bit of weed in my pocket – we can have a toke in there – you look like you need to chill out.'

Kavi shrugs his shoulders; he has nowhere else to go. He follows Marcus up Lozells Road towards Villa Cross, pulling his jacket collar up around his face as they pass Hardiman's factory.

Inside the Acapulco the air is heavy with smoke. Kavi breathes in the familiar, muddy scent of marijuana as they enter: it is an ubiquitous smell in the cafe and some days the whole of Lozells smells like this. As the pungent smoke rides up his nostrils an undertone of cooking odours – chilli and juniper berry – travels down his nasal passage, burning the back of his throat. He splutters out a dry, hoarse bark and has to bend double to suppress the cough. An old Rastafarian man stands behind the counter and when Kavi coughs he turns and stares, flipping his thick, waist-length dreadlocks away from his face and over his shoulder. He fixes bloodshot, glazed eyes unflinchingly on Kavi and Kavi wavers on the threshold, allowing the cafe odours to dissipate into the street.

'Shut that bloody door,' someone shouts from the back of the room behind the pinball machine.

Marcus grabs Kavi by the elbow and ushers him to a Formica table at the far right of the cafe, away from the main window. The table is stained yellow with tea and coffee spills. The door swings closed behind them.

'It's alright man,' Marcus looks directly towards the Rasta at the counter, 'he is a friend, the one whose brother was killed in the riot,' he adds and Kavi winces. The Rastaman nods respectfully in their direction, turns back to the crossword on the counter and slowly stirs his black tea with a dinner knife.

'I shouldn't be in here – you don't want one of us in here,' Kavi says when they sit down.

'Don't listen to that shit – this cafe is for all of us. There isn't a colour bar, man. Look around.'

Marcus rolls a spliff. He tears a strip of cardboard from the edge of a Swan Vesta matchbox and curls it tight into a roach and shoves it into the narrow end of the joint. He lights the opposite end and draws on it, sucking in his face until it is so gaunt his cheekbones protrude as if two ping-pong balls are stuck up into the sides of his cheeks. He blows a huge plume of smoke behind him and passes the joint discreetly across the table to Kavi.

'Listen Kavi, man, Clive said you haven't been back to school this term. Does your mom know? It's been nearly a month now since school started up again, man.'

'It's none of your business, Marcus.'

'What do you do all day, Kavi... kick cans around? Hang around the record shops? Ain't going to bring your brother back.'

'Don't talk about my brother,' Kavi says as his face turns a shade of purple.

'Look Kavi, man, I have brothers too, including a baby one, and I can only imagine how hard this is for you but you have to go on living. Make the most of your life.'

'Make the most of it – make the most of what? What have we got here in Lozells or even in Handsworth? What have I got to look forward to, or you? Bloody teachers who decide we are thick before we even open our gobs just because our dads have an accent? And then what, the dole? A dead-end job like my dad who is already miserable enough for the whole family? Fuck off, Marcus, there is nothing here for me.'

'Exactly – that is the point,' Marcus pauses to sip his stewed tea. 'Get a grip Kavi man, your brother wouldn't have died that night if there was no riot – and there wouldn't have been a riot if they hadn't forgot about us, leaving us to live and die in shitholes like this. Leaving old women like my nan to sit in the launderette all day 'cos she can't afford to have the gas fire on.'

Kavi hands back the spliff across the table. He feels giddy.

Marcus continues speaking.

'He wasn't just unlucky – THEY let that happen to him. If you want to get justice for your brother you better stop feeling sorry for yourself and set about trying to change things.'

'What, like throwing a brick through Woollies and nicking all the paper plates and other useless shit?'

'No, like standing up to be counted, man. Like joining the fight against those white baldhead bastards that are allowed to march past our houses and spit in our faces and tell us to go home like we have less right to be here than they do, or worse like the ones in suits and uniforms who decide we aren't up to their stinking jobs as soon as they see us. Like not just hanging around getting stoned and moaning about it all.'

After a long pause, Kavi replies,

'Nah Marcus, it's more complicated than that. It's not just a black and white thing. Look at my dad, do you know who he hates the most? People from somewhere called Mirpur, where our next door neighbours come from. He can't even bring himself to look at them because they come from some village less than fifty miles from where he was born, which just happens to be in Pakistan. He is more racist than any of them. And whatever you say, you black guys don't like us Indians. You think we have it cushy cos we work fifteen or twenty hours a day running crappy little shops that make no money. In a place like this everyone hates each other 'cos we all need someone to blame.'

Kavi gets up to leave. Marcus keeps talking.

'When they say us black guys are pissed off with you lot – that is just divide and rule, man, and that Mrs Thatcher is making it all worse now by taking what few jobs there are away from areas like this so we turn on each other. We have the same enemies, Kavi – the system that allows this to happen and makes us feel so fucking useless. We have more important fights than fighting you skinny Indian dudes. You get it? We are all in this shithole together and some of us want to change that situation.'

Kavi stands up and heads for the exit, swaying as he walks.

'Grow up, Marcus,' he says as he tugs the heavy door open.

Marcus's voice rises in volume,

'Look, we are making a group, Handsworth Youth Movement, young people standing together against the Pigs and against the fascists like in other places – Brixton, Liverpool, even some of your guys up in Bradford, man. My uncle works in the factory, he is a shop steward and has got us some Union money to photocopy leaflets and that. Come to the meeting next week. Here,' he says handing Kavi a crumpled leaflet from his pocket, 'we are going to organise ourselves so we can make them listen to us.'

'Nah,' says Kavi from the doorway, turning the leaflet over in his hands, 'not for me, I got my own battles to deal with.'

Outside the Acapulco, Kavi screws up the leaflet and tosses it to the ground as a police car screeches towards Wheeler Street Comprehensive. The school bell has just rung the end of the school day.

Chapter 9

Hardiman's Sheet Metals has had a presence on Lozells Road since the latter days of the Industrial Revolution. The main section of the building is Victorian and is the only part of the original structure remaining. It houses the makeshift canteen, toilets and offices all leading off dirty, grey halls. Originally the factory engaged in moulding metal into corrugated sheets for the new industries which were springing up all over England's rapidly developing second city. However, since 1905 almost all the contracts agreed by the company have involved the huge Longbridge car plant on the other side of Birmingham. Hardiman's was renovated in the 1950s, as part of the huge post-war expansion. Now the factory floor comprises windowless concrete blocks where over 400 men labour on assembly lines, welding stations and presses, each involved in his own section of work, never quite sure how his bit of metal will connect to the person's next to him.

Mukesh began on the assembly line at Hardiman's the year he came to England. The job had been lined up for him by a contact of his father's younger brother before he had even arrived. He soon moved on to a more sophisticated machine where his job was to form small metal rectangles into coils and cones. For Mukesh, the action of guiding metal through elongated rollers on this new machine evoked childhood memories of playing in the courtyard of his grandparents' house in their village on the edge of Jullendur City. Dadhi-Ma would squeeze excess water from Baba Ji's shirts by feeding the garments into the rollers of a mangle whilst he and his brother ran around her barefoot and mischievous, pulling at the clothes. For nine years he approached the forming machine with a reluctant anticipation brought about both by the monotony of the work and the random nostalgia it provoked. For the subsequent ten years, Mukesh's role was to operate one of the factory's huge soldering irons and, since 1979, to oversee the new apprentices as they got to grips with the heavy machinery. The time after Billy's death was the longest interruption to this routine he had had since beginning work at the factory in 1960.

The beginning of Autumn is cold, not the Indian summer that has been promised. The foggy air in the morning hangs heavy and Mukesh has to drag himself away from the warm, musky smells of the bed long vacated by Usha. The bedroom is as cold as the bitter morning outside.

'Bloody woman,' Mukesh says, cursing Usha for not switching on the gas fire.

He rubs his brow with his thumb and forefinger and makes his way down the stairs, shivering in his vest and pyjama bottoms, his body still clammy from a restless sleep. He stumbles through the kitchen towards the bathroom, all the while propping his head up with the heel of his palm.

'Anyone seen my bag?' Anila hollers through the house from the top of the stairs.

'Do you have to shout so loud all the time?' Mukesh yells back up to her. 'No bloody peace and quiet in this house.'

In the bathroom, Mukesh stares at the stranger in the mirror. His once handsome face is now worn thin and his deep set eyes sag around dark rings of sleeplessness. Behind his reflection he notices eruptions of blistering paint in the doorway.

'Everything falling apart,' he mutters, staring at his crinkled reflection.

He runs his dry fingers across the brittle scratchiness of the night's stubble, wondering how the path of his life has swerved in this direction. He remembers his optimism and the sense of adventure felt on the boat from Bombay to Liverpool almost

22 years earlier, when a pretty, red-haired waitress singled him out from all the other young Indian men with the same Raj Kapoor hairdos and shouted, *'Hiya Elvis,'* each time he passed her by in the canteen. When she spoke directly to him the other passengers turned and gawped, sniggering at his embarrassment as he shuffled away. Now in the cold bathroom in Church Street, the same waitress appears to him as a grainy daydream, she stands by the flaky doorway, winking flirtatiously at him with the same cocky smile across her face as when he imagines her late at night as he pushes himself into the yielding body of his wife. Mukesh shakes away the vision and begins scraping at the black shadow around his chin with a used razor. He finishes his morning ablutions by clearing his nostrils, holding each one down in turn and blowing out great globules of blood-tinged snot into the sink with the other. In the kitchen, Usha mixes Ready Brek in a bowl and gags at the sounds escaping from the flimsy door of the bathroom.

Mukesh arrives at the factory later than usual that day, with only a few minutes to spare before the bell rings. Small groups of men gather in front of the chained gates – fathers next to sons, uncles and brothers side by side. A drone of voices fills the air and the noise seems more heightened than usual. Mukesh glances around at his colleagues, sensing the unease amongst the men but he avoids eye contact and instead wills the day to be uncomplicated. The buzz of the voices around him brings to mind the noise of the many honey-bees Kavi and Billy caught and trapped in jam-jars one summer as a game. They only released them when Mukesh insisted they do so, but by then the bees were frantic and the boys had to stand far back and throw stones to dislodge the lids or break the glass to free the creatures without getting stung. Mukesh had clipped their ears that day and the boys had sulked for hours, making him wish he'd let them be with their childish games, however cruel they were.

Johnny Isaacs, a wide-eyed handsome man, barely beyond adolescence, stands next to Mukesh at the factory gates. He is deep in conversation with Amrit, the short, stocky shop steward, well-liked for his geniality and fairness.

'They are taking the piss, man,' Amrit says loudly. 'We have to get all the men to join us. You have to get the Jamaicans and other West Indians to join us, Johnny, they listen to you, they knew your dad and they trust you. We all have to fight this together... once they cut the tea break they'll be cutting dinner next. What they're really doing is cutting wages, innit? It's their way of doing it, thinking we won't notice, like.'

'Nah man, I don't even drink tea, man. I ain't bothered really, so long as there is time for a fag. Just want to hold on to the job, got a babby on the way and that you know,' Johnny replies.

'Don't be stupid, Johnny. We have to stand together or they just take the piss out of us.'

Amrit turns to Mukesh.

'What about you, Mukesh, yaar, you going to join with us? Can you survive without ten minutes for a nice little drink in the afternoon?'

Mukesh turns and walks away, ignoring the sound of the sucking teeth behind him. He heads towards some large metal bins at the side of the factory entrance, fingering the small hip-flask in his pocket.

'He needs to pull himself together or he is going to be the first out of here,' Amrit says to Johnny.

'Must be hard, man, losing your boy like that – not so easy to pull yourself together,' says Johnny. Amrit nods.

Amrit and Johnny are amongst a small group from the factory who had gone to Billy's funeral. When Mukesh returned to work the day after the mourning period Johnny patted him on the back, mumbling condolences and kind words but Amrit and some of the other men avoided him, lowering their eyes when he passed by, unsure of what to say. Mukesh prefers it this way. More recently some of the men joked about his clumsiness around the machinery.

'Mukesh, you smell like a pub at last orders,' Amrit tells him one morning after pushing him into the toilets out of earshot. 'You need a break from soldering. The men are worried you're going to hurt yourself... get burnt, or worse still you will hurt someone else.'

Two days later Mukesh is called into Hardiman's office.

'Assembly line, Agarwal. There's been complaints from the men, you're going to get hurt or hurt someone else. Can't take the risk, like. Not with you teaching all them young 'uns. It'll just be temporary, mind, until you can refocus, you know what I mean, mate?'

But Mukesh doesn't know what he means, except that from then on he spends each day placing small metal casings over the bolts on uniform metal sheets repeatedly. He doesn't tell Usha about the demotion.

Mukesh unscrews the hip-flask, takes a long swig of the fiery whisky and licks the few dribbles that linger on his lips before returning the flask to his pocket. From the other side of the bins, the noise of the men rises like a wave as Hardiman's shiny black saloon pulls up to the factory gates. Ruddy-faced, Hardiman squeezes himself out of the front passenger seat into the swarm of waiting men. Colin Boyle, an older worker at the factory, shouts out from the small crowd towards him.

'We can't work for nothing you know, Boss.'

'Plenty fitter, younger men that'll be queuing at the dole office for good jobs like these, Boyle,' a stern voice replies. 'I'd get to work if I were you and nip this complaining in the bud.'

The reply is not from Hardiman but Stan Bedford, Hardiman's brother-in-law, second-in-command at the factory and driver of the car. Hardiman and Bedford enter the building, slamming the heavy steel door behind them. The men follow them and queue like a line of ants at the entrance.

'Bloody fools, all this nonsense just for tea-breaks,' Mukesh mutters to himself before joining the clocking-in line.

Chapter 10

When September is at an end, Nina leaves home.

'It's university, Mom, just like you wanted.'

Usha stares at her blankly.

'I will be back most weekends, honest,' Nina continues, and they both nod, convincing neither themselves nor each other.

Usha reaches for her daughter's hand and squeezes it tight, stroking the back of Nina's soft fingers with her thumb.

'Will you eat properly, beta?' she says. 'Promise me you will look after yourself.'

'Of course I will, don't be all daft, Mom.'

Nina disappears towards the stairs to pick up her hold-all and rucksack. Usha breathes in the lingering scent of her daughter as she passes by and then moves towards the living room to slip on her old fashioned dogtooth coat and grab her handbag from the settee.

'I can't take a day off work for this,' Mukesh had said earlier that morning, even though Eugene had offered them the use of his van again. 'Already, there has been too much time off this year. They are not happy about it.'

'Your son died, you didn't go on holiday,' Nina says loudly as her father leaves the house. He doesn't say goodbye. 'Well fuck you too,' she mutters under her breath as the front door closes behind him. Outside, Mukesh leans against wall and takes in three long, slow breaths to steady himself before he moves on.

The bus journey to Digbeth Coach Station is a slow and silent one. Usha grips Nina's hand tight, thumb and forefinger clasped around her wrist as if the young woman is a toddler. Mother and daughter stare at the colourless day out of the dirty bus window, watching the dreary streets of Birmingham whizz by under relentless drizzle. At the station, Usha pushes money into Nina's hand – some of which was left in an envelope marked 'Nina' on the table next to where Mukesh sleeps. Most of the money had been slipped to Usha previously by her own parents when they came to say goodbye to their first grandchild, telling Nina how they couldn't be prouder of her and gifting her a list of Hindu surnames so she could seek out others like herself at university. The rest of the money has been saved up by Usha by scrimping on food shopping so there would be more loose change from housekeeping for the jam jar, now concealed under the sink. Nina untangles herself from her mother's embrace as Usha begins to weep.

'How can empty become emptier?' Usha mutters. She kisses her daughter's damp hair and watches as Nina disappears around the side of the coach towards the baggage hold. Nina boards and finds a window seat. She waves at her mother through the grime-covered window and Usha waves back. Usha wipes away the tears that now flow relentlessly down her face.

As they left the house Kamela had shouted her farewell to Nina for all the street to hear.

'Escaping from the shithole – you are the lucky one. Not trapped in this nightmare anymore, clever clogs. Wish I could see the faces of those shitty teachers when they find out you've actually gone to university just like the posh white kids from the Grammar... this'll show them.'

Anila, who is standing at the door behind Kamela, simply says,

'Make the most of it, Nina.'

'Too bloody right I will,' Nina replies.

It is these words that echo in Usha's head as she walks back through the damp towards the Bull Ring bus-stops. She blows her nose, wipes her face with the palms of her hands and strides ahead towards the bus marked Handsworth.

Chapter 11

One day in November, Mukesh staggers into Church Street at ten past five. It has been a long day at work with tensions building across the factory floor and Mukesh feels his head throb with the quagmire of jumbled-up conversations about tea breaks and strikes which have accelerated over the past few days and have overtaken football talk to become the main topic of conversation amongst the men. As he turns into Church Street, Mukesh fixes his mind on the bottle of whisky that is hidden behind the tea-bags and tins of boiled chickpeas in the small cupboard above the cooker. Further up the street, Kamela and Anila stand chatting in the doorway of the O'Connells' house, directly across the street from their own. They see their father in the distance.

'Shit, he is pissed again, look Kam, he's wobbling around.' Anila quickly passes over a half-smoked cigarette to Debbie O'Connell. 'We better go in, he looks in a right mood. He didn't see, did he?'

'Nah, he can't even walk straight, he isn't going to see a fag from that far.'

The girls slip across the road to the alleyway and enter the house through the back door, quickly disappearing up the stairs to their room. In the bedroom, Anila fiddles with the record player, placing the needle part way along the groove on the LP. She turns the volume up to full and the dum, dum dum-dum dah dah of *Brand New Cadillac* cranks into action, bouncing off the sloping walls and drowning out all other sounds. Anila starts dancing, hypnotised by the rhythm. She moves around the room, twisting up and down to the beat, mouthing the lyrics and singing particular words louder than others.

... balls... daddy... ain't coming back... cadillac...

'You're mad... this is shit,' her sister shouts across the room as she flicks through *Jackie* magazine.

Anila carries on moving and singing along to the music.

'Balls to you... Big Da...'

Suddenly, the door bursts open and slams against the frame of the bunk beds – a tiny crack appears in the white paint of the door.

'Can't you hear when your father is calling you?'

Anila pulls the needle from the record, mumbling expletives under her breath as it scratches across the vinyl.

'Sorry, we couldn't hear you,' says Kamela still looking at the magazine.

'No one can hear anything with that bloody horrible music on,' Mukesh says. He shouts at the two girls without looking at them. Instead he looks around the room at posters of Che Guevara, The Specials and Adam Ant which cover the walls and it is as though he has stepped into a stranger's house. Then, without warning he lunges towards Anila and grabs her by the ear, twisting it tight until the blood runs out of it. Her face turns a deep shade of scarlet.

'Get off, Dad,' Anila screams as the pain rips through her body. 'What you doing?'

'I saw you, Anila, smoking like a dirty kuthi in the street!'

Before she can struggle free he drags her down the flight of stairs into the bedroom where Usha stands over the bed pulling out sheets and towels from a pile of washing to fold and add to a growing stack.

'What the hell are you doing, Mukesh? Have you gone mad?' Usha shouts, dropping the linen.

Kamela is right behind her sister, tugging at her sweatshirt and grabbing at her father's arm, but before she can pull Anila free Mukesh has let go and is in front of Anila with a raised hand. He brings it down in a hard, sharp slap against her cheek and she lets out a tiny whimper. Then, without warning, a gush of hot urine flows through her knickers and collects in a steaming puddle on the brown carpet below her. Anila stares at the pool of liquid on the floor, transfixed by her own reflection in this putrid mirror.

'You drunken fool,' Usha screams at Mukesh, 'you have lost one child, Nina couldn't wait to get away and now you are pushing the others away too.' Usha puts her arms around Anila's shoulders and leads her out of the room. Kamela follows.

'Everything falling apart,' Mukesh whispers as they leave. He sits down on the edge of the bed and covers his face with his hands. When the footsteps on the stairs fade away, he feels for the hip-flask in his pocket. He unscrews the lid and licks up the remaining few drops of whisky that he can shake into his mouth. The smell of urine begins to permeate the room and Mukesh begins to sob. He squeezes the cold metal of the empty flask until his knuckles are taut and white.

Chapter 12

'Mukesh is sinking,' Usha says to Brenda as they sit at the kitchen table drinking sweet, milky masala tea.

Spring is fast approaching but the sky is the same unfaltering lead grey it has been since before the arrival of the New Year some weeks earlier and the air is still thick with winter. Snow fell ceaselessly throughout December and January, keeping the family confined to the house for most of those months. The children spent long stretches of the day in their bedrooms, reading old magazines, listening to weather updates on the radio or just lying on beds trying to keep warm under blankets. In the evenings they reconvened around the gas fire in the living room to watch unfunny sit-coms and boring period dramas, too cold to make the effort of familial communication. February is midway through and it seems as if the snow will return after only a short respite. There is a sharp, icy chill running past the two women as they chat, even though Usha has put gaffer tape around the edges of the sash window and has left a gas ring burning on the stove all morning.

Brenda darts her eyes around the small, gloomy kitchen – it looks different, emptier perhaps. It takes a few seconds for her to realise that Usha has removed her gaudy Hindu calendar and the strange little altar of plastic garlands, miniature framed pictures of brightly-clad deities and brass bowls of sugar offerings that usually sits on a shelf above the worktop; any remaining items on the shelf are now covered over with a pink gingham tea-towel.

'What do you mean, sinking?' Brenda asks.

'Drowning. I mean drowning, like he is moving his arms and legs but cannot swim.'

'In grief you mean? In sadness? That's understandable, bab, it's only been a few months, it doesn't just go away and people react to death in different ways.'

'No Brenda, I am drowning in sadness. He is drowning in whisky.'

A tiny stream of tea dribbles out of Brenda's mouth, down the side of her matt pink lips and collects in a droplet on the table top. She begins to laugh, not a small giggle but a full-blown belly-laugh. Usha stares at her, fixing on her animated powdery skin and the bright pink streaks of blusher across her friend's cheekbones. She touches her own face; the skin is bare except for a thin film of Ponds cream.

'Sorry,' says Brenda. 'It's just I had a picture of him at the Grove Lane baths with his stripy pyjamas on splashing about in the water like a sinking kitten.'

Usha cups a hand over her own mouth as her shoulders begin to silently but rhythmically rise and fall until a rasp splutters out of her pale mouth and becomes a soft giggle, punctuated by high involuntary notes like a chirping bird. The sound spills out into air around them, warming it like an early breeze of a new spring. Eventually, Usha wipes her streaming eyes with the knuckles of her index fingers and sits back on the stiff, wooden dining chair. She catches her breath.

'Not done that since school,' says Brenda. 'The last time was in biology when the teacher told us about the facts of life and I thought she was having us on.'

Usha composes herself. Her face contorts in the same way it does each morning as she opens her eyes after yet another night where Billy still exists full of life in fitful dreams and episodic bursts of sleep. After a short pause she speaks in all earnest.

'I still didn't believe these things even after I got married. It took until the third baby before I realised the connection.'

The women laugh again together, and this time Usha doesn't try to suppress it.

'You think I am joking?' she says. 'I was barely a teenager when I arrived in this country and was married to Mukesh before I reached my twenties. I hardly had a chance to hear the stories that went about the playground.'

Silence dispels the lighter air.

'Anyway,' says Brenda, 'it's a rollercoaster – grief. No wonder he's drinking a lot more. We all deal with it in our own ways. It was the same when my mother died.'

But Usha knows this isn't true; losing a child is a very different thing to losing a parent. Brenda knows it too. The two women sip their tea quietly. After a moment Usha starts speaking again. This time the words roll out as though she can't stop them – as though a floodgate has opened. Brenda listens, watching her friend's face intently, gripped by the words.

'When we were first married he used to scream out in his sleep. I never knew what it was all about. They were loud screams – repetitive and distressing cries like a wounded animal needing comfort from its mother. He had been howling in his sleep like that every night since our first night of marriage. I thought I might go deaf from it.'

'Did you ask him about it?' Brenda asks.

'I had never slept in the same room as a man before – it is stupid but at first I thought maybe it is just what men do – they are so different from us. My brother Ravi used to talk a little in his sleep when he was small so I just thought it was something to do with men. Anyway, then I realised that was silly and thought instead that maybe he was remembering a past life in his dreams. You know? Some kind of trauma from another existence.'

Brenda raises her eyebrows.

'This can really happen, you know? I know it is ridiculous to you white people but it was even on the BBC. Anyway, it's what we believe.'

Brenda nods, bemused. She is only vaguely familiar with the concept of reincarnation and any talk of it brings to mind the image of a tin of sweet, condensed milk.

Usha continues to speak.

'Then, when his friend from the village came to stay with us from India one winter and Mukesh was out at work, he asked me if Mukesh still had the nightmares about his dead brother, as though I knew what he was talking about. I made him tell me what he meant. I never knew Mukesh even had a brother, he never told me – no-one had spoken about him and I just assumed they couldn't have more than one child. Anyway, Mandeep, that was the friend's name, told me that the three of them, Mukesh, Naresh, the brother, and he were inseparable as boys. They spent every day together playing cricket after school and in the holidays they played it tirelessly, extending the same game, carrying over scores for days on end.' Usha continues to tell the story to Brenda just as Mandeep had told her.

The final summer that the boys spent together was even hotter than usual in the Punjab. The sun beat down so hard it felt like all moisture had been wrung from the earth – the grass was scorched and shrivelled and felt like a coir mat beneath their feet. The sky was a permanent shade of cobalt blue and the fields had turned from a luscious green to such an intense straw yellow that the young friends found it hard to look straight ahead without screwing up their eyes tight and blinking like they were seeing daylight for the first time. Their sun-blackened legs ached, while the soles of their feet and the flats of their palms were hardened by the endless climbing, running and kicking of those hot days. Naresh had taught the younger boys how to climb an old shisham tree like monkeys. He cupped his fingers into a step and then heaved the smaller boys on to the most accessible lower branches. The tree's mid-height leafy branches had become their favourite den. From here they threw stones into the school yard behind the garden, hitting the brightly coloured educational murals on the exterior walls of the schoolhouse.

'I think Naresh was just a year or two older than the other two but Mukesh looked up to his brother like he was a god,' Usha explains.

'It sounds wonderful,' says Brenda, 'just how childhood should be. What happened then, to Naresh?' she asks.

'Once at a village wedding, Mukesh bet Naresh he couldn't eat six adult portions of ras malai – you know the sweet you ate at Nina's birthday party? You said it was like eating sugary cheesy sponge, remember? Anyway, Naresh won the bet but later that evening his stomach bubbled until he threw up pale green vomit all over their bedroom. The stale smell of milky sick lingered in their room for so long that after a few days their father dragged the beds up onto the rooftop and the two boys slept in the open air from then on.'

'You'd freeze to bleeding death if you slept on a roof out here,' Brenda interrupts. Usha ignores her and carries on speaking. Her words become more urgent.

'That's when it happened. Mukesh was just nine years old so Naresh would have been eleven, like Billy. One night in his sleep, Naresh rose from his bed and walked like a... how do you say it? A zombie, across the rooftop. Mukesh woke when he heard a noise but by the time he was awake enough to realize that the shadow moving across the rooftop was not an illusion but his sleepwalking brother there was nothing he could do. He yelled at Naresh to wake up and his screaming woke the rest of the house but it was too late – Naresh had somehow managed to climb on the balcony wall and before Mukesh could get to him he had fallen.'

'Friggin' nora,' says Brenda, gripped by the story. She covers her mouth with her hand and Usha ignores her.

'Mandeep lived on the other side of the small village but he said even he was awoken by the howl that pierced the village that night. It wasn't just Mukesh screaming but the dreadful moans of the father and mother when they saw their first born son broken to pieces like that. Mandeep says that their mother never got over it – she couldn't bear to see Mukesh's face as he reminded her of Naresh too much. I think maybe they blamed him for not saving his brother. After that, Mukesh was sent away to live with an aunt in Ludhiana, a big city over thirty miles away. He stayed there for ten years, working in the fields and on the railways until he managed to save enough money to come to England.'

'Bloody hell,' Brenda says, 'so that is what the screaming at night is all about?'

'The screaming stopped the night Billy died,' Usha says. Her eyes are glassy with tears now, 'I don't think even screaming can help him with this nightmare.'

Chapter 13

'You were always the beautiful one,' Anila says to Kamela. 'All the boys fancied you at school!'

The fraying, tartan photo album is open on Anila's lap as she flips through faded images set behind protective transparent sheets. She sits in a dark corner of the attic bedroom, her movements measured like the gestures of an actor in a film being shown in slow motion. Across the room, Kamela darts around in preparation for the day ahead, one minute rummaging through a drawer of clothes, the next plucking her eyebrows over the table lamp.

'It's a wonder you have any eyebrows left,' Anila says glancing up at her sister.

The bright light of the lamp leaves purple floaters – thread-like fragments that dance in the space in front of Kamela's eyes as she skips over to peer across her sister's shoulder. It takes a few seconds for her retinas to readjust. Images of Usha and Mukesh stare back at the girls from the plastic pages of the photo album – blurred, monochrome figures, only vaguely familiar, like distant relatives from a far off era. The soft-focus faces gaze innocently at the photographer; they are young, unmarked by the passing of time, untainted by the tragedy of loss.

'Look at this one', says Anila pointing at a wedding photo. 'Look at all his wavy hair – how much Brylcreem is in that? And that sharp suit. He looks like a Mod. Did they have Mods in India?'

'It's not in India, stupid. It's Antrobus Road, Bibi and Nanaa's house, they got married in the front room, remember? Mom is stunning, and so young.'

The young Usha is beautiful. Huge, almond-shaped eyes stare shyly into the camera, the lids are slightly lowered. Her head and shoulders are shrouded in a delicate embroidered chunni and she is resplendent even in black and white. Both bride and groom wear garlands, Usha a fresh flower necklace and Mukesh a shiny heart hanging down across his suit and tie from a twinkly tinsel and beaded chain.

'You look just like her,' says Anila, 'and I look like him.'

'He was quite a handsome bloke back then, alright for someone fresh off the boat.'

'Yeah, but I don't want to look like a bloke, do I? Even if he is my dad.'

'Well you don't help yourself do you, Anila? You could do something with that hair and let me do your eyebrows. You've got lovely thick hair – I could straighten it with the iron so it's like mine. Maybe if you wore a skirt or a dress sometimes...'

'I'm not talking about clothes, Kamela. I am talking about what is handed down to us that we have no choice about. His big nose, bulbous eyes, shape of face and that.'

Kamela pulls out a colour image of her own sixth birthday party.

'Hey, look at this one,' she says.

In it she stands with Nina and Anila, staring out eagerly towards the camera, birthday excitement sparkling in all their eyes. The Agarwal girls are beside a covered dining table, red and white gingham topped by the centrepiece – a luminous pink and peach coloured iced birthday cake. In the background, Usha is in purple paisley against a wall of psychedelic green and orange swirls. Her hair is backcombed into a high bun on the top of her head and she holds a plump, moon-faced toddler dressed in navy and white on her hip. The photo is vivid, streaming out different hues from every centimetre as if the world had only just discovered colour, each shade a nugget of gold panned from the bottom of a dull riverbed, glinting against the drab of greyscale tin.

'It was when Baba-ji and Dadhi-Ma were here from India. It was the day Baba-ji died. It is the first thing I can ever remember,' Kamela says, turning away from the photo.

'I don't remember,' says Anila, disappointedly.

'You weren't in the room, and anyway you weren't even five by then. They had only been here a few days and then she had to go back on her own with his dead body. He just did it without warning, dropped down dead on the cold kitchen floor – it was the worst thing ever... until Billy. It was just after this picture,' she says pointing to another image on the same page, 'Dad, made me line up with them McNamara twins in the kitchen door so it looked like we were outside.'

Two identical pink-faced girls scowl into the camera. Frilly, pastel party dresses fill the frame and the twins wear their hair in pigtails – straw-coloured Qs jutting out like symmetrical jug handles from the sides of their heads. Kamela stands rigidly between them, her arms straight down her sides and her long, dark hair falling forward from a lowered head.

'They lived next door for a while. Mom was trying to be friendly by inviting them but they didn't like me. They called me names, Paki and that, and their mom sprayed me with Glade air freshener once when I put a foot over their kitchen step. Those dresses got splattered in blood when he fell over. He cracked his head on the sink. It was a mess, blood everywhere, and them two screamed and screamed like we were torturing them. I only wanted to be friends but they were spiteful. Jealous, Mom said.'

'You were Baba's favourite, you were everyone's favourite. I do remember that he was always cuddling you, giving you sweets and that. Nina still says that you got all the sweets when we were little. Everyone likes a pretty little girl.'

'I always think of him on my birthday.' Kamela's voice changes, 'I didn't like him. I didn't want the sweets. I didn't even really care when he snuffed it except for the mess at my party. I'd never had a birthday party before. I felt sorry for Mom having to clean it up. And for Dadhi-Ma having to travel home with

71

a corpse. I thought she would have to put it in the seat next to her on the aeroplane. Stupid, or what?' Kamela pauses and walks back to her own bed. 'You know it isn't always good to be the pretty one,' she says while carefully drawing burgundy lipstick across her mouth.

'I only remember as far back as Billy,' says Anila. 'Like everything started and ended that day. Before that everything seems all made up, like it exists in these photos but not in real life, if you know what I mean? I wonder if things would be different if Billy hadn't died.'

'Like what?' Kamela asks impatiently, still unsettled by the photographs.

'Like not so bloody boring. Like Dad not being rat-arsed all the time and Mom not in a constant daze, cleaning like there's no tomorrow... and Nina maybe phoning occasionally or even coming home once in a while and Kavi, well, Kavi being a bit more, you know, interested.' She goes quiet for a moment and then says, 'It's strange without Billy – it's like there's a space that needs filling but we can't fill it without him.'

'Get dressed, Anila, stop being all miserable, things carry on and we have to carry on with them. Things change – bad things happen but you have to make it all better yourself – no one else will.' Kamela checks her lips in the compact mirror and wipes around the edges with the tip of her finger before rubbing them together, puckering into the mirror and slipping it under her pillow next to the tweezers.

'What, like you?' Skiving college to hang around town all day,' Anila says. 'Don't think I don't know. I saw Debbie O'Connell and she said you had hardly been in since Christmas.'

'Sod off, Anila. Anyway, get a move on or you'll be late for school.'

Kamela leaves the room with her canvas satchel flung across her shoulder.

'Where do you go?' Anila shouts after her. 'Is it a boyfriend or what?'

'Fuck off, Anila!' Kamela says, slamming the attic room door shut behind her.

Anila is dressed and on her way out the front door less than ten minutes after her sister leaves the house. It is unexpectedly warm for March, especially after the long winter, and the sun startles her, scalding the back of her neck as she pulls the front door shut. Directly across the road Elsie Meeson stoops to gather up silver topped milk bottles from her doorstep. A burning cigarette end hangs from her crinkled lips.

'Morning,' she shouts towards Anila. Her voice is husky, weathered like her sloping body. She is the oldest resident on the street. 'Almost seventy-odd years I've lived on this street,' she tells anyone who will listen, 'Ever since I was a babby. Not like this then, proper English then. Clean like. Proud we were of this street, even if we only had an outside bog.' Mrs Meeson wears a lilac candlewick dressing gown, scruffy like the curtains that hang in her front window. 'Some fella on the radio says it is going to be a bloody hot summer again, like '76. Right up your street, you lot, innit?' She glares at Anila. 'Can pretend you're back at home and that, can't you?' Her tone is deadpan and Anila ignores her – it is an old cliché and Elsie Meeson says it every spring.

Anila heads up towards the bus-stop at Villa Cross, already having decided to miss school and head to the Bull Ring instead, to window shop and hang around the library where she can pretend to be studying if anyone sees her.

At the number sixteen bus-stop, half a dozen girls lean against a cracked windowpane on the side of the shelter. They each have a lit cigarette and a cloud of collective smoke rises over heads dissipating into a thin white vapour. Anila watches unseen as Kamela stands just ahead of the group and reaches in her satchel for her own cigarettes; she lights up and nods at the girls seemingly in recognition. The girls do not nod back but instead suck their teeth and throw cutting looks in Kamela's

73

direction. Anila sees her sister shrug her shoulders, turn her back and look up the road for the bus. Next to Anila an old man is wrapped in a dirty mackintosh. He spits a globule of thick, green phlegm into the gutter, missing her shoes by a couple of centimetres and she steps back in disgust. Ahead of her the girls snigger and whisper under their breath into their circle. The bus arrives and the tallest girl pushes past Kamela, jutting a sharp elbow into her ribs.

'Hey', shouts Kamela, 'that hurt.'

'Good', the girl hisses, 'that's for looking down your nose at us. You Paki girls are all the same like that – think you're so nice, cha!'

Anila pushes her way to the front of the queue in time to hear Kamela respond,

'What you going on about? Watch where you are going, can't you?'

'Alright', says Anila just as the bus arrives, 'what's going on?' All the girls turn to look at her and at that moment the bus doors slide open and Kamela jumps on in front of the others.

'Grow up you silly cow', Kamela says, looking back at the girls. She grabs one of the few vacant seats on the bottom deck. Anila sits in the only other remaining empty seat. It is diagonally behind Kamela.

'What the hell was all that about?' Anila asks.

'What the fuck you doing here, Anila? You should be at school!' Kamela replies. The middle-aged man sitting next to her looks from one sister to the other and shakes his head. Kamela turns to him and snaps, 'And you can stop bloody looking too.' The man moves seats and Kamela shifts herself to the aisle-side to deter anyone else from taking the vacated seat.

Anila speaks to the back of Kamela's head, 'If you don't go to college, why should I go to school? It's all messed up anyway – the teachers don't care about us so what's the point? Anyway, I want to know what you do all day in town.'

'Sod off Anila', Kamela says.

74

Kamela jumps off the bus as it pulls into a stop on the outskirts of the city centre, just before Chamberlain Square. Anila tries to squeeze past a pregnant woman so she can also make her exit, but before she can manoeuvre through the tight space the bus pulls off again. Instead, Anila alights at the next stop just a few hundred metres up the road and searches the throng of people for Kamela. She doesn't see her, so heads in the direction of the familiar Our Price Records at the top end of New Street. After half an hour or so, Anila thinks she catches a glimpse of Kamela up ahead on The Ramp. She quickens her pace to catch up but her sister disappears into the crowd. A few minutes later Anila catches sight of her again, this time in the shop window of Boots the Chemist slipping a pile of lipsticks discreetly into her bag, unnoticed by the security guard or shop assistants. For the next ten minutes, Anila continues to observe her sister unseen, watching as she dips in and out of shops, acquiring unpaid for items along the way until finally she stops outside the Wimpy bar, glances at her watch and looks up and down Corporation Street anxiously. Anila steps back into the shade of the C&A entrance to watch and before long another girl arrives and she and Kamela hug as they greet each other. The girl is petite, her hair is spiky, bleached blonde and she is dressed in black in spite of the sunshine. Anila doesn't recognise her but, with nothing better to do to pass the time, she waits until the two girls head off and continues to follow them as they walk back towards the library via the main road. They stick to this route until they reach Paradise Circus at which point they begin submerging into the myriad of graffiti-covered underpasses that tangle beneath the Ringway. Anila keeps enough of a distance to remain unnoticed. The girls walk in the cool of the James Watt Underpass with Anila trailing behind quietly. The hustle-bustle of the world above-ground comes to a sudden, gloomy halt once they are in the depths and for a few seconds it is silent and seemingly empty apart from Kamela and her friend. Anila is bemused as the two girls appear to hold hands and edge towards the wall. The blonde girl looks around and Anila retreats to conceal herself in the shadows before Kamela also glances in both directions of the underpass. The two girls embrace as they did at the burger bar earlier but then that embrace becomes something more intimate and they begin to kiss. Anila gasps. She closes her eyes but the scene ahead remains the same when she opens them a second later – two girls, one her sister, kissing like the men and women in the *My Guy* photo-loves. She is stunned but before she can gather her thoughts there is a shout from behind.

'Oi,' the voice says, 'you filthy bitches!'

Anila about-turns as two of the girls from the earlier bus-stop incident run towards Kamela and the blonde girl, passing by Anila as if she doesn't exist. Kamela's friend begins running too, in the opposite direction. Anila stares at Kamela who seems frozen to the spot. Her sister stares back directly at her, she appears to be in a state of fixed panic.

'Dirty slags,' the voice is yelling down the underpass. The other girl joins in and it becomes a chant as they head towards Kamela.

'Run! Shit, Kam, bloody peg it!' Anila screams but it is too late.

'Leave me alone,' Kamela shouts at the girls who have cornered her. They are right up against her now. They push her between themselves like a ball and finally slam her against the cold, spray-painted wall. Anila sprints to try and reach her sister, but before she gets close enough to intervene Kamela has crumpled to the ground and the girls are running towards the exit of the underpass. Anila tries to pull Kamela up to a standing position but as she lifts her sister's head she sees a wide red slash across the side of her face. Anila's hand is covered in blood. She looks around for help as the echo of the two girls fades down the long, dark subway; the noise is accompanied by a pungent odour of urine and damp chalk and other smells Anila cannot place.

'Bloody hell,' says Anila as she holds a barely conscious Kamela in her arms.

'Swear you won't tell.' Kamela says weakly.

'About the girl? You and the girl?' says Anila.

'Yes,' says Kamela and she closes her eyes.

'I swear.' Anila whispers but Kamela's body is limp and Anila knows she doesn't hear. She props up her sister's bloody face against her own chest and she waits, unsure of what to do.

A copy of *Seventeen* magazine lies next to the bed. Anila picks it up and flicks through the glossy pages of flawless white faces towards the 'Dear Jenny' section at the back. The made-up misery of others distracts her for a moment or two but the problems are those of people that don't seem to exist in her reality, or in any reality really. It is nearly 6am. She closes the magazine and watches as Kamela tosses and turns in the bed across the room. Anila buries herself into the peacock print pillowcase and pulls the bed covers taut over her head.

Chapter 14

A layer of thin dust covers the bottle green window sill of the classroom. Anila runs her index finger along it until her fingertip is coated in charcoal grey powder. She has an urge to lick her finger but she resists. Outside the window, beyond the school gates, a group of young men gather around the lamppost. A rather scruffy hatch-back car pulls up to the side of the small gathering and more young men emerge and begin unpacking a series of bulky items from the boot. From a distance, the men are indistinct in shades of khaki and taupe as they mill about, chatting to one another, seemingly jovial yet focussed on their task in hand. Anila watches the men and is mildly curious about the commotion they instigate until she becomes distracted by a pigeon in the middle distance. It is mangy and limps across the playground with one leg bent awkwardly beneath it. Anila wills it on as it somehow manages to struggle towards the thin border of hedgerow which provides the only hint of green in the concrete playground.

'Anila, Anila, Miss Agarwal!'

The voice is that of the English teacher, Mrs Tatton and as it rises in volume Anila is jolted out of her reverie.

'Where are you Anila? You're certainly not with Piggy and Simon and the rest of us, are you? You won't pass your exams staring out the window the whole lesson. Page 151, read it out, now.'

Anila thumbs through the pages of the tatty paperback in front of her. It takes a few slow seconds to find the page.

'*Simon's head was tilted slightly up.*

His eyes could not break away from the Lord of the Flies hung in the space before him.'

As Anila reads, there is shuffling and giggling all around her – just as there is every class.

'Don't know why I bother,' Mrs Tatton mumbles under her breath.

Anila reads louder in monotone, her listlessness enveloping each word.

'What are you doing out here all alone? Aren't you afraid of me?'

The shrill sound of the school bell cuts the reading short and the noise level in the class rises to a din as the children clamber over chairs, jostling for bags and coats. Mrs Tatton turns to the wall and, with her back to the class, fumbles in her handbag and pulls out a packet of Embassy No.1's. Anila closes the book with a sigh and straggles behind the other pupils out of the door.

The group of young men outside have set up a trestle table by the wrought-iron railings. Laid over it is a red sheet daubed in black letters, the words read SELF DEFENCE IS NO OFFENCE. The shock of the words make Anila shudder – it is a thrill she does not recognise. The letters appear to be jumping out of the cloth and make for a bold splash of colour against the steely, impenetrable landscape that surrounds the school buildings. Anila is drawn towards the banner, pulled in like a paperclip to a magnet as she becomes part of the throng piling out of the iron gates away from the confines of the school grounds. As Anila joins a small group of others heading towards the trestle table, the men begin to chant.

'Here to stay, here to fight.
Handsworth Youth with all their might!'

There is little difference between the ages of the men and that of some of the older school children and as the two groups move towards each other they blend into one amorphous crowd with only the variance in the uniform to set them apart. The chanting dies down and the men quickly shove leaflets into any receptive hands. The majority of the men are black but there are a few Asians too and Anila recognises at least two of the men including Aazim, a boy Nina's age from the top end of Church Street, and Marcus, the older brother of Kavi's friend Clive. Marcus nods in her direction and makes his way over to where she stands at the edge of the trestle table.

'Alright,' he says grinning, 'how is your brother doing?'

'So, so,' replies Anila without meeting his eye.

'I saw him not so long back, kicking cans, hanging out on corners on his own. Your mom know he is skiving all the time?'

Marcus speaks in a sing-song voice, part patois and part broad Brummie like most of the younger West Indians around Handsworth.

'None of your business really, is it?' Anila shrugs.

'You're a feisty one, ain't you?'

Marcus smiles gently as Anila looks up, meeting his eyes for just a fraction of a second before she quickly averts her gaze.

'What's this all about then?' Anila asks, snatching a leaflet from Marcus's hand and staring down at it.

'We are organising ourselves. Had enough of bloody Pigs stopping one of our youth every five minutes. The Government is ignoring the people of Handsworth and we don't want to take this shit anymore, man. There are no jobs for us, no money and now they are allowing the NF to come into our areas and cause trouble – we need to organise or there will be another riot like when your Billy...' He stops short of his full sentence.

Anila stares at him coldly and flips over the leaflet. On the back is a rough pen and ink drawing of twelve black fists punching into the air. Anila likes the image. The ink of the photocopier is still smudgy and a dark residue seeps into the crevices of her fingertips.

'Come to the meeting, we need some girls... maybe you can bring your mates, gobby ones like you? It's West Indians and

Indians together. Bring Kavi – I tried to get him before but he wasn't interested, man.'

An old man limps by. He walks past the school each day just as the school gates open and the children spill out around him. He barks at the small crowd with words that spray out a shower of saliva.

'You lot should join the bloody army instead of hanging around here... you're a bloody waste of space, the lot of yous.'

'Cha!' Marcus mutters and winks at Anila. She walks away still holding the leaflet.

Chapter 15

K avi strums the old guitar he bought for fifty-pence at a jumble sale two years earlier. It is still out of tune. He tries to perfect the chords to *Layla* after it plays out on the Mike Read Breakfast Show.

'You shouldn't play that shit, Kavi. That bloke was racist.'

Nina is standing by the doorway of his bedroom. Kavi looks up and scowls.

'What you on about, Nina? Sod off back to your fancy friends at that crappy university of yours,' he says.

'I'm being serious, Kavi. He's a wanker that bloke. He said some proper shite things at the Odeon on New Street – you won't remember – you were too young and that – but everyone talked about it at school the next day. He called us wogs and niggers and said we should listen to Enoch Powell and go back to where we came from – stupid prat – doesn't he know that most of us would only have to get the number 83 back to Dudley Road Hospital? Anyway, it was all over the local news at the time.'

'God, you are such a pain since you started uni, Nina.'

'I'm just saying! Listen to something good – The Specials, UB40, The Beat or whatever. Just not that racist git.'

'Piss off, Nina, all your hippy black and white unite, rock against this and that crap isn't for me. I like that song, and I like David Bowie too and isn't he supposed to be racist as well?'

'He used to be good, I suppose. He said sorry, didn't he, for that? Said he was on drugs and it made him a bit mad, off his head and that. Not that it's an excuse but at least he realised he was being a dickhead. Not like the other bloke – he never apologised!'

'Study that at uni, did you? I don't need one of your lectures, Nina. I like what I want to, so there. Anyway, what do you want? I thought you were out of here.'

'I'm going back tomorrow, Kavi. That's why I wanted to speak to you. You and Kam, well, Anila says you never go out the house anymore. Is that true?'

'None of your business. You don't really care about here when you are with all those students. They're the sort that think they're clever talking about people like us as though we are weird creatures in a zoo for you all to look at and discuss. I bet you don't even tell them you're from Handsworth, do you?'

'Look Kavi, I can understand why Kamela doesn't go out but you haven't got an excuse and all I'm saying is you should be seeing your mates, playing football and that.'

'No excuse? You might have forgotten, Nina, but see that bed over there?' He points at Billy's bare mattress, strewn with his own discarded clothes and school books, 'Well,' he says, 'there isn't anyone to sleep in that anymore. Billy has gone... dead! I don't want to go out and pretend to be interested in football and shit when all I can think about is how he was here and now he isn't.'

'It's been ages, Kavi. If you don't want to go out fine, but can you at least try and get Kamela out? She needs to get out or she'll go mad up in that bedroom. She might go for a walk with you – just to the Bomb Peck or something. I've tried and so has Anila but she might feel safe with you, you being a boy and that.' She pauses for a response but Kavi ignores her. 'And by the way, there isn't a moment away from here when I'm not thinking about you lot – just because you leave a place doesn't mean it leaves you, if you know what I mean?'

Kavi picks the guitar back up and plays the opening riff to *Layla*.

'Bloody hell, it's Howard Hughes,' Kamela declares as Kavi arrives in the attic.

'What you on about, Kam?' Anila says, looking up from her schoolwork.

'Nothing, just you two should read a bit more, you know, something other than the Handsworth Times.'

'What, like those crappy magazines you nick from Lavery's?' Kavi says. 'Anyway, I know who he is, I'm not thick, I saw a thing on BBC2 and you can bloody talk – you've hardly been out this room for weeks. I just want a fag. Either of you got one? There aren't any long enough nub ends – you two have had them all or Mom's been and cleaned up already.'

Kamela hands Kavi a cigarette from the half empty packet she had slipped away from Mukesh's bedside table as he lay in a deep sleep the morning before. When her father awoke, he yelled through the house accusing Usha of throwing his cigarettes away to spite him. Kamela felt neither guilt nor remorse at this and instead pushed the edge of the chest of drawers against the door, teetered on the bed, lit up and blew out smoke-rings through the open skylight.

Kavi mutters a desultory 'morning' to Usha as he passes by her whilst she is in the midst of dusting behind the television set. He goes out the back door and stands in the shadows of the alleyway smoking his cigarette and looking out onto Church Street. Across the road, Elsie Meeson is banging on the O'Connells' front door. Derek opens it, naked from the waist up with a half eaten sausage in his hand. Before Elsie Meeson can utter a word he disappears back into his house and shouts loud enough for the whole street to hear.

'Marie, it's the old bag from next door for you.'

'Soz, duck,' Marie says as she arrives at the door.

'Don't soz me, lady! I'm sick of you gyppos making all that noise all the time. I can hear you all night shouting at each other and your brats screaming away. Well, I've come to tell you to keep it down or I'll be going to the council about yous. And that lad of yours, can you tell him to keep it down when he comes in from his nights out boozing too? Sick of it I am. Couldn't sleep a wink with all your noise.'

'Now hang on you, just 'cos we're Irish doesn't make us gyppos, right.'

'Bog Irish, that's what you are. Tell that lad of yours to go and get a job, and that lazy old man of yours too. And tell them to stop nicking the milk from my doorstep while you're at it. I know it's your lot – thieving gyppos, that's what you are.'

Kavi moves closer to the alleyway entrance so he can get a better view of the women brawling. Up and down the street heads poke out of windows to witness the disturbance; some of the more brazen amongst the neighbours step out of their front doors and stand cross-armed watching as the commotion unfolds. Further up the road, Joey McKenna and the other boys stop their game of street-football to heckle and clap as the women become more heated.

'Hey, don't you call us bloody names, you old bag.'

'My grandson, Martin, is the same age as your lad and d'ya know where he is? Well, I'll tell you – he isn't in the bloody pubs spending dole money on pints of Ansells. No, he is out in the Falklands defending our queen and country, like your boy should be. Shameful it is! Well hopefully Mrs Thatcher will sort you lot out – send you back to Ireland so you can scrounge there instead.'

'Sheep are the only thing getting defended in the bleedin' Falklands as far as I can see,' Marie O'Connell says.

Derek joins his wife on the doorstep. 'Maggie bloody Thatcher? It's because of her there aren't any jobs,' he says. 'Do you think we want to sit around all day twiddling our fucking fingers without two pennies to rub together? Do you think men like me want to be idle? No we fucking don't. Soul-destroying it is, not the bloody holiday you think it is.'

Elsie Meeson drops the flickering end of her cigarette on the O'Connells' doorstep and turns away.

'Yeh, sod off back to your hole, you old slag,' says Derek and then he addresses the rest of the street. 'Show's over you nosy bastards,' he says before pushing Marie down the hallway and slamming their front door shut.

'All the usual fun and games around here then,' Kavi says to himself as he stubs out his own cigarette and emerges from the alleyway into the early summer sunshine. He makes his way up towards St Silas' and Joey McKenna nods in greeting but Kavi ignores him. Instead, he veers left before he reaches the church and heads down the alleyway towards the Bomb Peck behind the houses on the west-side of the street. As he nears the waste ground, a voice behind him shouts his name. He turns to see Joey McKenna running to catch up with him.

'Kavi, Kavi, stop a sec will ya?'

'What do you want, Joey?'

Joey is fourteen years old or thereabouts, a year older than Billy and a year younger than Kavi.

'I haven't seen you for ages, on the street or even at school and that.'

'And?'

'I mean, since your Billy passed away and that last year, you've hardly been around.'

'What is your point, Joey?'

'Look,' says Joey proudly, pulling out a small transparent bag from his back pocket. 'Fancy, a spliff?'

'You're a bit young, aren't you? Where did you get that?'

'Nicked it from my cousin, Tony. Don't tell and you can share it with me.'

The two boys sit between a large tree and a crumbling brick wall and smoke the joint that Kavi prepares with Joey's grass and Rizla papers. They smoke in silence, passing the joint from one to another until Joey speaks.

'Your Billy was my best mate, Kavi.'

'He wasn't your best mate. You just think he was now because he isn't here anymore.'

'I was with him that night. You know, when the riot happened.'

'I don't want to know,' Kavi says, but Joey carries on speaking.

'I mean, I didn't see it or anything, I couldn't have stopped it but I was with him before it happened. We were on our bikes, just messing and then we turned the corner and there was this riot and shit happening so we just went down the first road we could and then we got split up and then...'

'I don't want to know,' Kavi says. He stands up but feels dizzy and sits back down.

'I haven't told anyone. I shouldn't have let him go off in the dark on his own. It's been six months or something and I haven't told anyone.'

Kavi stands up again, this time more slowly, steadying himself on the wall as he rises.

'Nine months!'

'What?'

'It's been nine months, Joey and I don't want to know about your shit. Who cares if you feel bad? Don't mention our Billy again, ever. Not to me, not to anyone.'

Kavi walks away, leaving Joey smoking the remainder of the joint. He walks past a bench where an old man lies beneath a blanket of broadsheet newspaper. As he passes by the bench, a blob of grey pigeon mess drops from the sky and lands on the area of newspaper covering the man's head. The man stirs, grunts and a ragged arm drops towards the ground.

'What a depressing shit-hole it is out here,' Kavi says aloud as he makes his way across the abandoned gardens and derelict houses towards Church Street and home.

'I'm bored,' says Anila, closing the book in front of her. 'I can't be arsed with exams. It all seems so pointless.'

'You're clever at all that school stuff, Anila. You'll be okay. You might even get into a university or a poly like Nina and get out of this place. Not like me – one art 'O'level and all that. I'm stuck here. Probably end up getting fixed up with some accountant from West Bromwich if I'm lucky.'

'Give over, Kamela. Nina is right, you need to get out. You can't stay locked in here scared of everyone. Those girls, well, don't let them stop you from being who you are.'

'Oh Anila, you are sweet, bab, but you haven't really got a clue have you?'

'Don't be patronising, Kam. I know more than you think – and I do read books and stuff, about all sorts. I know the world isn't as straightforward as people think. That, you know, it's all a bit mixed up – like that Martin Degville and the weirdos that work on his stall in Oasis market and Phil Oakey, Marc Bolan and that.' She is careful to avoid any direct reference to the moments before the attack in the underpass.

'Is that what you think, that I'm a mixed-up weirdo? Well, if my own sister thinks that then what hope have I got around here? Leave me alone, Anila.'

'I'm sorry, but, well, it was a shock seeing you that day. I mean it isn't normal is it? It's not as bad as two blokes together though, like in the Naked Civil Servant thing we saw on the telly, but it is still strange, you've gotta admit. I mean, what would people say?'

'Shut up, Anila.'

Kamela sits on the edge of her bed, with her back towards Anila. Anila tries to think of something to say.

'I'm sorry Kam, maybe I don't understand but I can try.'

'You're not helping, you know?' Kamela says, shuffling back around. 'Don't talk about it – it was just a mistake, a phase or something.' Both girls go quiet. 'Do you think I should go to the doctor?' Kamela says after a few moments have passed.

'The doctor – no way. He'll tell Mom and she won't be able to cope with that. You'll grow out of it, Kam. They say in Sex Ed. that everything can get confused at our age – hormones and that.'

'Suppose so... hope so! Don't talk about it again, Anila.'

The girls return to their books and away from each other. After a minute, Anila speaks again.

'It's so boring since Billy died – nothing to look forward to.'

'There wasn't before either, remember?'

'I know, but it has made it seem more obvious – you know, everything being a hassle, it all seems sort of, I dunno, magnified, like white people hating us all and blacks hating whites and Indians and Pakis hating each other and no jobs and stuff – it's so boring. Bloody hell, Kamela, when you start thinking about it, it's no wonder you and Kavi are not bothering to go out the house.'

'Don't take the piss, Anila.'

'I'm not, I'm being serious. I'm sick of it all.'

'Don't you think enough has happened with the rioting all over the country and a war on now, and people bloody starving to death and what with Billy and Dad and the trouble at the factory and that? What else do you want to bloody happen?'

'I'm bored of it all being miserable. I just want something to change. There's nothing wrong with that is there?'

'Well go and bloody change it then. Just leave me out of it. I have had enough of trying to make sense of what is going on out there, never mind in here.'

Anila replies more somberly.

'I miss Billy. I think I see him sometimes in the street, but it always turns out to be someone else.'

'I miss him too,' Kamela replies softly while fiddling with the transistor radio on her bed. *Ebony and Ivory* crackles out from the small speaker and she turns it off again immediately. 'Put something decent on the record player, Anila, will you? And turn it up loud!'

Chapter 16

Mukesh tumbles out of bed as he stretches his arm into the darkness to stem the loud ring of the alarm clock on the bedside cabinet. His body thuds to the floor and he knocks the side of his head against the edge of the cabinet, a glass of water topples over, cracking as it hits the surface; the cold water drips onto Mukesh's bare arms.

'Bloody bugger,' he mumbles under his breath and begins to feel about in the pitch blackness under the bed. As his fingertips touch the stiff leather of his hip-flask he breathes a sigh of relief and clutches tightly on to it as he pulls it towards him.

Usha is already wide awake, even before the disturbance in the bedroom. She turns over in the bed, curls up into a small ball and squeezes her eyes tightly shut. She tries to block out the sounds of her husband fumbling around in the dark but she cannot. Mukesh pulls on his work clothes noisily, making no effort to be quiet. She waits for him to leave the room before stretching out into a more comfortable position. The room is still in the shadows and yet again the sun has failed to break through the thick, grey clouds of dawn. She lies on her back, eyes open, looking into the darkness, wishing the day to be over before it has even begun.

When he is dressed, Mukesh slips the hip-flask into his trouser pocket and heads to the bathroom, taking a swig on the way. He pauses to top up the contents from the bottle of whisky hidden deep behind the tins in the cupboard next to the cooker. After a few moments he closes the front door behind him and heads for the factory, leaving the rest of the household seemingly asleep.

The ground is covered in a coating of dew and Mukesh's feet slip and slide beneath him. He takes another small swig of the whisky, it burns the back of his throat but does nothing to steady his feet. His empty stomach rumbles deep and hollow and he tries to remember when he first found he needed the whisky so early in the day, when it became more necessary than a hot cup of tea in the morning or it became the first thing he thought of on waking up, but he cannot. He craves another swig before he reaches St Silas' Square and he looks around before pulling it out of his pocket; most of his work colleagues live in these streets.

Hardiman's is a short walk from the house but this morning, after a night of vivid dreams and fitful sleep combined with the precarious path underfoot, Mukesh is slower than usual. He stops to rest a moment, leaning against the brick wall of the nursery school on the corner of Wills Street. He pulls his jacket tight around himself and lights up a cigarette with shaky hands. As he walks, images of the previous night's dreams invade his mind, appearing and disappearing like flickers on the television. The dreams are all of his children: Billy's face is that of the burning boy, flames melting his flesh like candle wax; Nina is running down a busy road, dodging traffic, without so much as a backwards glance; Kamela lays in a pool of her own crimson blood, her face in shreds like torn fabric; whilst Anila swims in a bath of urine and excrement, the shit sticking in clumps to her skin and hair. The images of Kavi are the ones he wants to block out most of all: in them Kavi's face merges with his own as his son staggers about, filthy and drunken like the tramps that sleep in the doorways of the Lozells Road or on the benches around the Bomb Peck.

By the time Mukesh approaches the factory gates it is already past 8.55am and the hip-flask is almost empty. It takes him a few minutes to notice the line of men beyond the first set of gates blocking the doorway to the main part of the factory.

'Hello yaar,' Amrit shouts jovially towards him. 'Good you can join us. I was thinking you would just stay at home this morning.'

The seventy-plus crowd begin a slow hand clap as Mukesh gets closer and he turns around to see who they are clapping for. As he does so he notices other men arriving with placards and faces he recognises from the factory floor carrying piles of an unfamiliar red-top newspaper.

'What is going on, Amrit, why is no one working?' The words slur out on a wave of whisky breath. Amrit's face drops.

'You don't remember? We have been talking all month about this one day strike. Don't tell me you have just come to work as usual, Mukesh?'

Another voice from the crowd says,

'Too pissed to take any notice that's what's going on there.'

'Really, Mukesh? Did you not remember?' Amrit says in disbelief. 'Even from Friday? It is only three days ago and we have been talking of this for months. They are finding ways to reduce our pay by taking away our break-time. There have been ballots, letters from the union, posters – all sorts of things. It is all the men talk about. This is a big deal, Mukesh. They are exploiting us and changing our conditions without discussion.'

'I don't talk about tea-breaks,' Mukesh mumbles. His head is fuzzy and he is beginning to feel nauseous. His stomach rumbles loudly.

'Well fuck off home then you useless shit. We are all in this together and if you are not with us then you are against us!' The words are yelled by an anonymous voice from the back of the crowd.

'No,' says Mukesh stubbornly, 'I will lose money if I don't work. I need to feed my family.'

'You can't go in,' Amrit says horrified. 'You would be crossing the picket line. Mukesh, do you know what this means?'

'It doesn't mean anything, Amrit. You carry on with your children's games, I need to earn money. This is an English thing:

strikes... tea-breaks... pickets... not for us Punjabi men – we work to feed our families.'

The crowd begins to boo and Mukesh looks around at them, staring defiantly into the first set of eyes he meets. He takes out his hip-flask and blatantly pours the liquid into his mouth as he begins to push his way through the jeering crowd. As he turns the handle on the steel doors that lead into the factory the jeers increase, dominated by a chant of 'Scab. Scab. Scab.'

Mukesh stumbles into the reception area of the factory floor. He looks through the interior windows to the machine-room and notices three or four men towards the furthest part of the room, each has his head lowered and is operating his machine in silence. Mukesh raises the flask and shakes the last small drops of whisky into his mouth. A sense of panic creeps up through his body as the liquid runs dry.

'Agarwal, what are you doing?'

The voice comes from directly behind and Mukesh jumps at the sound of someone unnoticed so close.

'Mr Bedford, sir. I am here at work, not like those lazy buggers outside.' His words stammer out.

'Is that booze, Agarwal?' Bedford snatches the flask and raises it to his nose. 'Whisky, you bloody fool. Are you drunk, man? You are in no fit state to be in this factory, Agarwal.'

The other few men on the floor look up towards Mukesh and Bedford. Mukesh stands with one arm outstretched, his hand flat against the wall for support, but he still sways backwards and forwards like a jittery child.

'You can't come to work drunk, Agarwal, you bloody idiot. My god, who in hell is drunk this early in the morning? We have cut you some slack the last few weeks but this is not acceptable. You are completely pissed, man. You can't operate machinery in that state.'

'Cut some slack,' Mukesh repeats, he has never heard the term before and he repeats it a second and third time under his breath.

'Go home,' Bedford says, his pink face turning bright red. 'I am suspending you. This is a disciplinary now. Do you understand?'

Mukesh doesn't understand and he stays fixed with his arm against the wall as though he is having a casual chat with Bedford at the Barton Arms or the Royal Oak.

'Get on to your union rep. We will be in touch. Go home, Agarwal and don't come unless we tell you to.'

The men on the factory floor turn back towards their work as Bedford slams through internal doors towards the management offices. Mukesh, still perplexed, trips as he leaves by the doors he has entered just a few minutes earlier. Bedford's words have not yet sunk in.

Outside, the men don't notice as he staggers behind them and heads for the side-gate into the back alley. Just as he is about to slip through the gate a hand lightly touches him on the shoulder. It's Johnny.

'What's going on, brother?' Johnny says.

Mukesh pauses before blurting out a reply.

'Suspended, suspended and sent home like a naughty schoolboy.' He is shaking as he speaks.

'Shit man,' says Johnny, visibly shocked. 'Let me buy you a cup of tea or something. Sober you up before you go and tell that nice wife of yours, eh?'

Within a few minutes the two men are sitting in an otherwise empty cafe around the corner from Hardiman's, sipping steaming cups of over-brewed tea and milky coffee. Mukesh is grateful for the fried egg sandwich Johnny has ordered for him but it does nothing to alleviate the nausea which churns in his stomach.

'What you going to do, brother?' Johnny asks.

'I don't know… everything is falling apart, Johnny,' Mukesh says as his eyes begin to well up with tears.

'Oh shit', Johnny mutters to himself as Mukesh begins to weep silently. 'Got to be going, the others will notice I am not there,' he says more audibly before standing up to leave. 'Go on home, Mukesh. You're no good for nothing today, brother.'

After Johnny leaves, Mukesh dozes in the stiff cafe chair. The middle-aged waitress behind the counter shouts across to ask if he wants another cup of tea, Mukesh jolts himself awake and glances at the wall-clock above the woman's head – over two hours have passed by. He shakes his head at the woman, she 'tuts' and returns to the *Handsworth Times* on the counter.

Mukesh leaves the cafe and makes his way to Lozells Road and onwards to Church Street. As he approaches his turning he notices the landlord of the Royal Oak pub sticking a poster in the window – it is opening time already. He enters the pub without hesitation, as though this was his destination the whole time.

'Mukesh, what are you doing home so early?' Usha asks as Mukesh stumbles through the back door close to 4pm that afternoon. She is chopping cauliflower at the kitchen table in preparation for the evening meal.

'Go to hell', Mukesh slurs back. Usha is alarmed, he has never been in this state so early in the day before.

'Mukesh, what is wrong? Why are you home? Have you been drinking?'

'Go to hell I said... and I will follow you. That is where we are all heading to.'

He moves closer to where Usha is standing and she takes a step backwards. The stench of alcohol is overwhelming. He stumbles towards her, knocking over a stack of washed dishes next to the sink; two plates crash to the floor and smash into pieces. Then, without warning he picks up the colander of freshly cut cauliflower from the table and tips it on the shards of smashed crockery.

'Mukesh, what are you doing? That is our dinner. We don't have money to waste throwing food away.'

'I make the money, I can waste the money, working every day, morning till night and even then they don't appreciate it.

They all slowly, slowly go away... and we are left with empty stomachs.'

'Be quiet Mukesh, you are not making any sense – the children will hear you. They will be upset.'

'Upset,' Mukesh slurs, 'I am upset – no one cares that I am upset. I am bloody upset. All this time in this stupid country, working in that stupid factory, abandoned by my children, suspended by the factory and you, with your Jeyes Fluid and Squeezy and bloody English friends... What about me? Who cares about me in all of this? I don't even belong here.'

'Suspended! Mukesh, you are drunk? Go to bed, sleep it off so you can go back to work tomorrow.'

Usha kneels down to clear up the broken crockery with a dustpan and brush. She picks out most of the cauliflower florets, checks each piece and puts them back in the colander to wash.

'Can't you bloody hear me, Usha? Suspended! No work until they tell me to come back.'

Mukesh kicks the remainder of the crockery and cauliflower across the lino floor before staggering upstairs towards the bedroom. On the way out of the kitchen he grabs the half empty bottle of whisky from the cabinet.

Mukesh sits on the edge of the bed and lights a cigarette. He throws the flickering match into the washing basket by the door without thinking and within moments a cotton sari blouse begins to smoulder as the match flame ignites the fabric. Oblivious to the small fire growing in the corner, Mukesh rests the cigarette in the bedside ashtray and lays his head against the pillow. Almost immediately his eyes close and he slips into a drunken sleep – once again the burning face appears and is transformed to the visage of Billy; his boy melting away into liquid – a dissolving face without eyes.

Kamela is lying on her bed listening to the inane banter of a radio deejay as the acrid smell of burning cloth travels up the staircase towards her attic room. She edges open the door with her foot to investigate the smell and the gap is just wide enough for her to see a smoky haze seeping up from the landing below. She jumps up and heads down the stairs. As she reaches her parents' bedroom, flames are beginning to flicker above the rim of the basket towards the wardrobe and the curtains just beyond. She grabs a damp towel from the back of the door and stops the fire before it manages to spread beyond the buckling plastic criss-cross of the washing basket. Mukesh sleeps on, tossing and turning and moaning as the smoke gathers around him in a cloud. Kamela waves the towel above him, dispersing the smoke until all that remains of the fire is the bitter odour of burnt plastic mingling with the stench of beer and whisky emanating from Mukesh's sleeping body.

'Bloody idiot,' Kamela thinks as she watches her father lying on the bed in a restless slumber.

She grabs the bottle of whisky from the bedside table and opens the window wide before leaving the room. Once back in the attic she leans against the closed door, takes a large swig of the whisky and savours the strong, burning sensation in her mouth before shoving the bottle deep under her bed.

Chapter 17

Most dry days Anila walks the longest way home she can after school. Today as she walks she thinks about her conversation with Nina on the phone two days earlier. It is the first time since the Easter holidays that her sister has phoned, and this time it is to tell Usha that her grant instalment hasn't arrived and could she send her something? Anila answers the phone.

'How you doing, Nils?' How distant her sister sounds, Anila thinks.

'Oh, you know – same old, same old. Kavi doesn't go to school still and Kamela still doesn't go out and Dad is just hanging around like a bad smell now he's been suspended. I think Mom is going mad just cleaning around them all the time.'

'Blimey, is she still doing that? I don't know how you put up with it and all, Nils. Come and visit me. I could send you some money for the train fare when my grant comes in – after your exams I mean. There are some great parties up here.' There is a pause before she speaks again… 'I've been meaning to tell you about someone I met at one,' she says. A conversation about boys is a first for the sisters.

'Nina – have you got a fella? Or maybe, it's a lady-friend,' Anila says jokingly. 'You students get up to all sorts I've heard.'

'Don't be disgusting, Anila. God, what the hell have you been reading? Anyway, shut up and let me tell you. I was a bit drunk, like and… there's no one else in the room is there?'

'No, go on spill the beans… is he Indian or what?'

'You can't tell anyone, Anila, okay?'

'Just tell me, go on what's he like? What's his name?'

'Imran.'

'Imran! What, like the cricket player?' Anila bleats.

'Yes.'

'But that's a Paki name isn't it?'

'Paki is a racist term, Anila, I thought you knew better.'

'Nina, are you going out with a Pakistani bloke? Oh shit, Dad will kill you... and Mom. He's not from round here is he?'

'No, Leeds. Oh, Anila, he is bloody lovely though and really clever. He's in the year above... and it has kind of got serious if you know what I mean.'

'Bloody hell, Nina, you haven't, have you?'

'Haven't what?'

'You know – done it with him – with a Paki bloke from Leeds?'

'Shut up Anila. Grow up and stop talking like some idiot from Handsworth. There is a whole world out here and it's one where it doesn't matter which side of the bloody partition your ancestors came from. For goodness sake, at least he isn't black.'

'You sound like a Handsworth idiot now, Nina. You know as well as I do that a Muslim boy is worse than a black boy to some people around here – we all know what Indians and Pakis think about each other and that. Anyway, go on, what was it like – did it hurt?'

'Anila, just get Mom to phone us will you? Room 401 remember. I've got to go. Don't tell anyone, promise?'

'Yeah, yeah.'

A few weeks have passed since the young men with trestle tables were outside school and now Anila finds the leaflet with the black fists screwed up in her pocket. She reads it over and over again and examines the illustration of the fists closely. She thinks about Marcus calling her feisty, it isn't a label she has had before but something about it makes her feel good. Anila switches her mind to Nina living a new life in a different world, away from the Agarwal family in some far off northern town. She imagines the boyfriend, Imran, as if he is some hero from a

Bollywood film, twirling Nina around by the hand on a tropical beach. Anila is embarrassed by the naffness of the image she has conjured up but then, unexpectedly, her imaginings move into daydream and Imran transmogrifies into Marcus, and she into the girl. Marcus is pressing his lips to her wet mouth, his body is pushed up against hers and they are naked. Her hands feel the spikiness of his short afro; his hands explore parts of her body which are unexplored even by herself. They are no longer on the Bollywood beach but down the back alley off Carpenters Road where she stops to have a sneaky cigarette on the way home sometimes. She shakes her head to get rid of the daydream. A dull menstrual ache in the pit of her stomach is followed by the sensation of moisture between her legs. 'Shit', she mutters, wondering if she has time to slip home and use the bathroom before the meeting on the leaflet starts – it is at 5pm that day.

Anila tries to enter the meeting hall at the back of St Silas' Church quietly but stumbles over a discarded bucket by the entrance as she rushes to escape the rain that has just begun to fall. Almost thirty young men are already crammed inside the small, dank, windowless room. Most of the men are Jamaicans and other West Indians but many are Asian too and some turn to look at her after her noisy arrival. She stares back, surprised to see these young men gathered together; the only place she has seen young Asian men gather in such numbers before is at the sprawling weddings that pack the temples, gurdwaras and school halls of Handsworth at weekends and where men, young and old, congregate in clusters along corridors, eyeing up the girls. It is a different kind of eyeing up she senses now.

Anila has arrived just as the first speech is building to a climax. The crowd jostle for space at the front of the room, patting one another on the back, nudging each other like schoolboys before a football match. The speaker is standing on a plastic chair at the front of the room. The chair wobbles as he shifts about on it. He is a small, scrawny young man with blue-black hair cut short in a crop close to his head. His eyes are eager, shining out against fine facial features – he is like a raven, Anila thinks. Kash Ram, she hears someone whisper as the speaker begins to talk. His voice booms out strong.

'It is my belief,' he says, 'that when people are attacked, they have the right to act in self-defence. The nature of that defence depends on the nature of the attack. I believe the defence of Black people – and remember brothers we are all black here whether our origins are in Africa or in Asia – who are menaced by the threat of fascism makes the organisation of defensive groups like this one an absolute necessity.'

Anila is instantly transfixed by the man. She has never seen or heard anyone like him. He is not a bit like the images of the white, spiky rock stars that cover her school books and adorn her wall or the young West Indian and Indian boys that are her neighbours and her fellow school pupils. Kash Ram is barely in his twenties, he is small and the same shade of brown as she is, yet he is articulate and confident like a much older, more important person. The crowd in the room begins to holler and cheer as the speech draws to an end. There is a palpable camaraderie enveloping the room.

'We cannot allow the police to continue to hound us like dogs for no reason whatsoever while they allow racism to breed like a disease around us, encouraged by politicians. Remember brothers, we are here to stay, here to fight. Handsworth Youth with all our might.'

These particular words resonate like a mantra.

Anila breathes in sharply, she is stirred up in a way she doesn't understand and doesn't quite know how to control. She steps closer to get a better view of the man on the chair. More of the small congregation become aware of her and there is mumbling and shuffling around the room. Kash Ram pauses, sensing a shift in the atmosphere. He scans the room for the cause of it and rests his eyes on Anila, she is the only girl in the room.

'Hello,' he says. 'Good to see you here. Welcome to the Handsworth Youth Movement, may you be the first of many sisters to join and fight alongside us in this struggle.'

Anila feels a hot blush rise into her face as he addresses her directly. Now all the men turn and stare at her. She moves backwards into a corner and leans against a pillar, partly obscuring her view of the room and it of her. All but a couple of the men turn back to face the front of the room.

'Hey,' Marcus sidles up to her. 'You made it,' he says. 'Well done, man. You should have dragged that brother of yours along too.'

Marcus is dressed in khaki, army surplus mostly, punctuated at either end by black boots and jet black hair. Anila blushes again, this time at the thought of her earlier fanciful musings but nevertheless she is relieved to see Marcus's familiar face in this crowd of strangers. He stands beside her for the rest of the meeting and she can feel warmth radiating from his body; he smells like incense sticks. Kash Ram's continued speech is distracting and Anila finds herself bemused as the crowd participates in waves of cheers and shouts of bitter protestation, spontaneously sharing stories of police brutality and experiences of racist encounters. Anila concentrates on what is being shared around her whilst still aware of the warmth and smell of Marcus beside her. Two young Indian men intermittently glance over their shoulders towards her and whisper in unashamed disapproval – she knows it is because she is standing next to a black man.

Three further speakers take to the chair and each repeats the same message with intense and vociferous passion. Towards the end of the fourth speech the metal legs of the chair have begun to buckle. Anila absorbs little about the second, third and fourth speakers but Kash Ram sticks in her head and she wants to replay his speech over and over, like she does with certain songs she has taped off the John Peel Show. As the meeting closes, a heavy, dreadlocked Rastaman presses play on an oversized ghetto blaster decorated with spray paint and stickers. A familiar reggae rhythm cranks up, it is a tune by local boys Steel Pulse, known to all the local kids and often heard booming out from open car windows and shop fronts around the area like an anthem. The men at the meeting nod their heads in time to the music, mouthing the lyrics as they pile out of the meeting room.

> *'Handsworth shall stand, firm – like Jah rock –*
> *fighting back*
> *We once beggars are now choosers*
> *No intention to be losers*
> *Striving forward with ambition*
> *And if it takes ammunition*
> *We rebel in Handsworth Revolution'*

For Anila, *Handsworth Revolution* is a soundscape to the faded Victorian Handsworth Park which she often walks through in the lighter summer months with her siblings and her mother, to visit Bibi and Nanaa on the other side of Handsworth. The park sits like a green heart at the centre of the area, its wide tree-lined arteries clogged with the residue of the ragged life-blood pulsating to this same beat. The opening bars of the song cause a pang of nostalgia and a momentary headache as Anila thinks of Billy mischievously running on ahead when they last walked across that park together, this music playing in the background. After a moment, she begins nodding her head to the music in the same way as the others that leave the meeting, and the song, although familiar, begins to sound brand new, as though she is hearing it for the first time.

Usha is washing greasy plates with a worn yellow sponge when Anila slips in through the back kitchen door after the meeting. It is just past seven in the evening.

'Hi, Mom,' she says, flopping into a kitchen chair. 'I'm knackered.'

'That's nice, roti is in the oven.' Usha tilts her head backwards towards the oven while her eyes remain fixed on an oily rainbow across the froth of soap suds in the sink. She speaks as though she is talking to herself.

'Not hungry,' says Anila. As she heads out of the kitchen Usha says,

'What about food, Anila?'

'I said, I'm not hungry. Didn't you hear? Or were you too busy with your washing up?' She immediately feels guilty for snapping at her mother in this way but the moment has passed and it is too late to take the words back, and she is fairly certain her words didn't even register with her mother.

Upstairs, Kavi is lying on his bed strumming his guitar. Anila barges in and perches herself on the side of the bed. Kavi plucks at the guitar strings without looking up.

'Did you go to school today, Kavi?'

'Nah.'

'What'd you do all day? You need to go to school you know, more chance of a job and that.'

'No Anila, no jobs, no point, no school.'

Kavi turns to face to the wall. Anila ignores his lack of interest and speaks hurriedly. She tells him about the meeting, about Kash and Marcus, and about the urgency to organise and be part of this group.

'You've got to come to the next meeting, Kavi. It's all young blokes like you. Probably some of your mates and that.'

When she stops for breath Kavi speaks, still facing the wall,

'Not for me, Anila, no point. No point in very much really cos, you know, we just drop dead in the end.' He turns back, over and looks straight at Anila as he says this.

'Shit Kavi, that's so miserable.'

'True though, ain't it?'

'Billy wouldn't want you talking like that.'

Kavi sniggers.

'And that's so stupid, like. Billy's not here and we don't know what he would have said or not said because he isn't here. Point made! You go to your meetings and stuff but it won't make a difference to me. And I'm not going to school because it's shit. In fact, it all shit out there.'

'You are nearly sixteen, Kavi – who knows what will happen in the next few years? You have your whole life ahead of you. You can't just give up.'

'Stop trying to be so wise, Anila, life is going to happen, yeah, and right now I don't see how it can be anything other than shit, for me at least.'

'Yeah, but Kavi, the thing is I think there is a way to change it.'

'Not interested, Anila. No bloody meetings are going to make things any better for me. Billy is dead – and the best I've got to look forward to is the same as Dad, working in bloody Hardiman's, having babbies and being stuck in Lozells for the rest of my life.'

Anila stares at her brother, pitying him but clinging on to her own new-found optimism. His face has the same bitter twist in it as the old man who walks past the school scowling at the kids as they hang over the fence swinging their legs. She leaves him to mope on his bed and climbs the wooden stairs to the attic where Kamela is gently smearing pale green face mask on to her hands. The room smells of cucumber and sour milk. Anila stares at her.

'It was free in the magazine,' Kamela says, by way of an explanation. 'Didn't want to waste it, like.'

Anila lies on her back on the bottom bunk, her arms folded behind her head. She closes her eyes and goes over the meeting in her head. Her thoughts linger on Kash Ram – his animated face is a vivid picture and his strong, stirring words ring in her ears as she drifts off into a daydream.

'We will refuse to be discriminated against.
We will rise up and show them we are not weak.
Together we will succeed.'

Chapter 18

Kavi lies across the long settee in the living room. The television mumbles out the banalities of local human-interest stories as the early summer sun streams through the spotless window, illuminating the screen to a practically unwatchable state. The living-room door is open, as are the kitchen door and the back door leading from the kitchen to the garden. A faint waft of singed fish fingers permeates the room. Kavi's stomach rumbles.

'Mom,' he shouts at the top of his voice, 'is there anything to eat?'

Mukesh sits in the armchair next to the window in the same room as Kavi. He raises his eyes over the top of the copy of the *Handsworth Times* he has been reading for over an hour.

'You are a lazy bugger, Kavi. Why don't you make your own food instead of watching this rubbish television all the time?'

'You can talk,' Kavi mumbles, but the rustle of the paper prevents Mukesh from hearing his son's backchat.

In the kitchen, Usha stands in the open back doorway. She listens to the familiar rhythms of *The Clapping Song* and *Skip To My Lou* as they trickle towards her from gardens further down the street. The singing is accompanied by the fresh, lively sound of young girls giggling. On the street in front of the houses, Joey McKenna and another boy race their Chopper bikes from St Silas' Square to the bottom end junction with Nursery Road. Usha watched them for a moment earlier as she put a bag of rubbish out for the dustbin men to collect. The boys were wearing capped-sleeve tee-shirts and they gripped the handlebars tight, backs against the uprights, legs akimbo, freewheeling down the hill, whooping just like they had many times before with Billy in tow.

'Furr...king nora, whahayeee...'

They are still whooping now.

Usha leans against the back door frame to steady her sleep-deprived body as she listens to the sounds around her. The day is startlingly light after the long grey days that have preceded it. The sky is a crisp and stark blue and seems as though it has been freshly painted onto the world.

Kamela enters the kitchen and stares into the blank space, not noticing her mother at the back door. She has hardly been out of the house since the attack in the underpass a few months earlier. Her scar has faded and now resembles a small knotted rope across the edge of her cheekbone quite close to her ear. To conceal the scar she keeps a tress of hair pulled forward, twirling it habitually with her thumb and forefinger. She opens the biscuit drawer but finds only crumbs and a broken edge of a digestive at the bottom of an airtight Tupperware box. Back in the living room Kamela shoves Kavi's legs off the settee, making room so she can sit down.

'Get off, I was here first,' Kavi snaps at her.

'Get off yourself, you lazy sod. All you do is sit on the settee all day.'

'And what about you? All you do is look in the mirror, picking at your scabs and feeling sorry for yourself.'

'Fuck off, Kavi, you are so cruel these days. Anila is right – you are just cruel and bitter and instead of doing something to change your life, you just sit around having a go at everyone else.'

'Kamela, do not use this kind of language in my house.' Mukesh shakes out the paper and lifts it from his lap where it has lain as he snoozes. Kamela gives him a dirty look. Both children ignore him.

'You fuck off, Kam. At least I can go out if I want to. At least I'm not scared of stepping out the front door.'

Usha stands at the back door listening to the bickering which has now drowned out the external sounds of a sunny day. She returns to the kitchen, pulls on her rubber gloves and begins to rub at the steel pots and pans she has pulled out from the back of a cabinet. She thinks about Billy as she washes, remembering him as a toddler, pulling at her legs for her attention while she stood at the sink or the cooker.

In the living room, the bickering continues. Kavi has increased the volume on the television and the theme tune to *Pebble Mill at One* blares out.

'You wouldn't understand, Kavi – not that you are bloody interested – it's not my choice,' Kamela shouts above the din.

'Yeah but you are just letting them win by staying in the house all the time.'

'Yeah, well I'm gonna go out in my own time. Anyway, take some of your own medicine,' she says as she clips Kavi across the side of his head with the heel of her hand.

'Ow, you cow! Fuck off out my space.' He clips the top of her head back, careful to avoid her scar.

'Your space?' Mukesh says, edging the newspaper down a few inches, 'Actually, this is my house and you are disturbing me. Can't you see I am trying to read the newspaper?' He raises the newspaper back up to obscure his face.

The siblings begin to shove each other – Kamela prods Kavi with her elbow, he flicks her bare arm with his thumb and middle finger.

In the kitchen, Usha stares at her own grey reflection in the dishes she has been washing and then, without thinking, she pulls off the rubber gloves and flings them to the floor before marching into the living room.

'Shut up all of you. Shut up, shut up, shut up. I can't hear myself think, I can't hear anything except your voices swirling around in my head.' Kavi, Mukesh and Kamela all stare at Usha as she continues her outburst. 'Actually, you are in my space all of you. Kavi, you should be at school, Kamela, you at college and as for you...' Usha turns and stares as Mukesh cowers behind the newspaper. She pulls the newspaper out of his hands, screws it up and throws it to the floor. 'You,' she continues, 'you are no use whatsoever. All you do is drink and shout and sit around. Why aren't you crawling back to that factory to ask for your job back? Have you no shame? What kind of example are you to these children?'

'I am still being paid some of my wages,' Mukesh says meekly. 'Anyway, I have to wait for the tri... tribun... union thing in a...'

Usha interjects before he has time to finish. Kavi and Kamela stare at her, both are speechless.

'I can't stand it anymore. I can't stand you all lying around doing nothing, waiting for me to cook you food and clean up afterwards. And with what? There is no money, Mukesh. I have to scrabble around for discounts at the shops and wait until it is almost closing time so the vegetables are cheaper. I have even spoken to Brenda about getting some work in the sewing machine factory. Have you no shame?' She repeats the question directly to Mukesh. 'All you do is spend what little money the factory gives you on whisky and cigarettes when I can barely feed the children. It is embarrassing.' Usha pauses for breath before carrying on. 'I can't stand it. And none of you even think to help with the housework. It is like something has died in each of you... and in me too,' Usha sits on the arm of the settee. Her voice becomes softer, 'I miss him so much,' she says. Kamela links her arm through her mother's arm as Usha carries on speaking, 'This is stupid – I cannot allow this to carry on,' Usha stands up, shaking her arm free. She turns to Kamela, 'Kamela – you are going back to college on Monday otherwise term will end and you will never go back. You have already missed too much. Kavi, you are going to school even if I have to drag you there myself.' She then turns to Mukesh again, 'And you,' she says, 'well you know what you have to do.'

'I'm not going,' Kavi says and he walks out of the room slamming the door behind him.

'I will try,' says Kamela gently.

'Thank you, beta,' her mother replies.

Mukesh says nothing.

Usha leaves the living room, picks up the gloves from the kitchen floor and throws them into the sink.

Chapter 19

On the first anniversary of Billy's death, Usha cleans out the wardrobe where Billy's clothes still hang as if he might walk in one day and reach in to grab a tee-shirt or a pullover from the back hangers. Kavi sits hunched with his back against the wall, hugging his knees close to his chest, watching as his mother gently removes the clothes, folds each item and delicately places it in a neat pile on Billy's now coverless bed. The faint smell of an ephemeral life seeps out, pervading the room as the clothes are disturbed. Usha lingers on Billy's favourite garments, running her long fingers across the fabric and allowing fleeting memories of Billy to waft through her mind as if he only ever existed as part of her own being. Kavi stares blankly as Usha weeps, burying her nose into the musty wool of a misshapen Dennis the Menace jumper which she had knitted in stolen moments for Billy's eleventh birthday. It has hardly been worn. Kavi pushes open the sash window, letting a damp breeze flush out the final sensorial elements of Billy from the house. Usha folds the last faded tee-shirt and places it on top of the small pile on the bed. And then, task completed, she cups her hand over her trembling mouth. Her startled face is like that of a small abandoned bird. Kavi looks on helplessly.

Anila walks out of the school gates for the last time. All around her high spirits resound off the hysterical and sentimental goodbyes.

'See you at the baths in the holidays.'

'I'll phone you when we get back from me Nan's caravan.'

'Or-right – let's meet up to on the Ramp this Saturday.'

'You going down the Springford Disco this Friday? See yous there if you are.'

Flour and eggs are tossed in the air. They combine with the summer drizzle and descend, clinging temporarily onto blazers and hair, before plopping to the pavement in clumps of sticky glue.

Anila drifts past the shirt-signers, ignoring the conversations about keeping in touch and meeting up. She walks on towards Soho Road, beyond Lozells and into the heart of Handsworth without as much as a backwards glance. Her destination is an old warehouse on the corner of Grove Lane. It is ten weeks since her first encounter with Kash Ram and the other men from the Handsworth Youth Movement. She has been to every meeting with the group since then and it is to them that she now heads.

Over the last few weeks the meetings have become more regular, particularly in the period leading up to the end of school. They now take place at least once, if not twice, a week. Slowly new people begin to attend – some because of the leaflets they hand out on the corner of Soho Road or outside the local libraries, others because they have heard about Kash on the grapevine. Some of the new recruits are girlfriends and sisters of the men but also other girls who, like Anila, have come out of a compulsion to do something proactive rather than wait for someone else to do it for them. After just a month the meetings got too big for the room at the back of St Silas' and the warehouse, known as The Shoe, has become the headquarters for the Handsworth Youth Movement.

To reach The Shoe, Anila walks past the synagogue, Guru Nanak Gurdwara and gaudy Hindu temple which all cluster around the grammar school on Rose Hill Road. Beyond the places of worship, the shops fall out colourfully onto the main high street that is Soho Road. As she passes the first set of shops Anila sucks in the smell of the garam masalas and ripe breadfruit that fill the air. Soho Road is full of life: down-at-heel men fester around pubs, suppressing the desperation of worklessness with cheap whisky and stale crisps, while older white-haired Pakistani men reek of the sharp-smelling beedies they puff in small groups around the benches in front of the library; behind them a group of young black teenagers sit on the library steps drinking Vimto. Older girls of all faiths and races drag younger ones in and out of shops while their mothers prod and sniff plump vegetables, looking one another up and down as they pretend to be checking out the produce. Soho Road is ablaze with colour – bright cotton dresses, shimmering salwar kameez and saris, African print dashiki and head wraps. The sounds of a hundred languages mingle with jangly bhangra and bassy reggae, filling the air with surprisingly congruous sounds. Beyond Soho Road on Grove Lane, the red-brick Edwardian houses look as if they still belong to a more affluent bygone era, but behind the unspoilt facades the affluence has dropped away as the former middle-class, white residents have retreated into the suburbs and smarter areas, wary of the new immigrants with their optimistic, anticipatory smiles, strange sounds and exotic clothing.

'You know...' Marcus says as he meets Anila on the way up to Grove Lane – their chance encounters have now become weekly arranged assignations – '... my mom told me that the year she came to Handsworth the white people marched down Soho Road with banners and shit 'cos Grove Lane school was getting too many 'coloured' kids. They thought all their little white babbies were going to turn black overnight or something, man.'

Each time she approaches The Shoe, Anila imagines it busy with the labour of the immigrant mothers and fathers and other relatives of many of the young people who now attend the meetings alongside her. Now, most of the former footwear packers are on the dole, except for a few lucky ones who have found factory work beyond Handsworth around Hockley and Perry Barr. These days The Shoe is an empty shell, except for the Pentecostal worshippers who hold makeshift church services each weekend and the Handsworth Youth Movement's increasingly regular meetings. Inside, the building is a wide, dim cavernous hall, cheered up with a coat of whitewash by the weekend worshippers. On one side of the large, corrugated doorway is a small table where Anila sits at the beginning of meetings collecting 10-pence pieces, names and telephone numbers from all those that attend. She marks down the information in a foolscap notebook and answers questions about future meeting dates from new recruits.

Mid-way into the long, dull summer the atmosphere at one Wednesday meeting suddenly shifts from the determined, convivial camaraderie to something more urgent. There is a buzz in the room and when Anila enters, Kash catches her eye and smiles a half smile in her direction. Anila lowers her head coyly. Olive Benjamin, one of the few new female recruits touches her elbow. Anila looks up; Olive is almost dancing with excitement.

'They are letting that NF baldhead scum march around here through town and down Constitution Hill next month. It's too close, past Hockley Hill, It's almost to the crossroads with Soho Road,' she says.

Kash begins to speak from the makeshift pulpit.

'Now is our chance, we'll show them we won't put up with this on our doorstep.'

The next day, Anila slips the hairdressing scissors out of Kamela's make-up bag and into the back pocket of her jeans, pulling the bottom of her baggy sweatshirt down to conceal them. She makes her way downstairs to the bathroom, locks the door and stares at herself in the mirror. She begins to snip at the long tresses of hair which fall around her face. The hair falls into the sink in black swirls, cascading down the chipped ceramic bowl towards the plughole. For a moment, Anila has a memory of herself standing behind a three-year-old Billy, catching his fine, curly first hair in a white tea towel as it is systematically shaved off by a fat, jovial priest in his Mundan ceremony. She remembers

Mukesh whispering to her sister Nina that this meant Billy could start a new life, free of previous incarnations, liberating him from the past lives which can remain with us as a burden. Anila chops away more and more of her hair until all that is left is a patchy crown of short cropped hair – a coarse black blanket on the top of her head. She removes the clumps from the sink, throws them in the toilet and pulls the chain before turning on the tap and directing any stray hairs towards the plughole. Then she stares at herself in the mirror; her eyes look wider and her nose is bigger than she'd thought. She is slightly alarmed with this new face that stares back at her. She sits on the closed toilet lid for a few seconds before opening the bathroom door and peering around the corner towards the kitchen.

'Oh my god,' Usha screams, when she sees the cropped head. She drops the saucepan lid she is holding and it bounces on the lino, spinning like a top before coming to standstill.

'What have you done, Anila? You have made my beautiful daughter ugly.'

'Don't be silly, Mom, it's how we have it these days. You've seen Top of the Pops and that. Anyway, it's a political statement.'

Usha calms slightly and recovers the lid from the floor.

'What do you know of these things? Going to meetings doesn't make you a politician, Anila. You are just a follower, like the Hare Krishnas, shaving your hair and following what other people tell you.'

'No, I'm doing something I think is right for once. Anyway, it makes me feel strong, not all weak like I am not expected to do anything for myself, like some housewife. I feel like I can do anything with my hair like this.'

Usha moves towards the sink.

'I have failed to protect you,' she says, 'and now you are all slowly drifting away one by one.'

'I'm not drifting away, Mom. I am trying to change things around here, including myself. You've got to agree it's no good as it is. And now the skinheads are back. We need to make it better or it's all going to get a lot worse.'

Usha turns her back on her daughter and rinses the pan lid under running water.

'You too have become a skinhead, Anila,' she says.

Chapter 20

On Tuesday, the curtains are still drawn in the main bedroom well after 10am. The room is littered with the clothes Mukesh wore to the Black Eagle the night before and the garments smell of beer mingled with stale tobacco. The odour hangs in the air, trapped in by the closed door and windows. Usha enters and flings open the curtains which allow a flood of sunshine into the room. She opens the sash window but the air is warm and still and there is no breeze to dispel the smell so she waves her chunni to create one. The breeze is momentary and not enough to clear away the lingering odours.

'Amrit is on the telephone, you need to get up Mukesh,' she says, shaking her husband gently by the shoulder.

'Go away,' he says in Punjabi and Usha responds in their shared language.

'Get up Mukesh. Speak to Amrit and make it right with work. Then you can start being a father and a husband again and not this thing you have become.'

Mukesh pulls the cover over his head and sighs. Two minutes later he staggers reluctantly downstairs in the underpants and vest he has slept in. Usha stands by the bottom step with the phone receiver held out.

'Huh?' Mukesh grunts into the phone as Usha stands next to him.

'Mukesh, how are you?' The booming voice on the other end says, Listen, I have some good news.'

'Good news?' Mukesh repeats, rubbing his forehead with two fingers – not yet fully awake and his brain still fuzzy from alcohol-induced sleep.

'Well, actually first it is bad news really,' Amrit says more solemnly.

'Huh?' Mukesh says again.

'Colin Boyle died.' Amrit's voice has now reduced to a whisper. 'Heart attack in the Barton Arms last week. Pay day. He drank six pints of Ansells and fell to the floor, but it didn't have anything to do with the drink according to his missus. It was the collection of dust in his lungs, she says, always coughing and complaining of chest pains he was. Anyway, he didn't make it home that night.'

'Colin Boyle?' Mukesh scours his memory for a recollection of this man, but he has none.

'Colin, you know, the big man from rivets. It is very sad. He was due to retire next year and enjoy his life. Always talking about the grandkiddies. You know? Colin – a bit on the racist side – only ever called Johnny sambo and that.'

'Ah yes, I know Colin. That is very sad,' says Mukesh. 'Is this why you are calling me, Amrit? A funeral? I can't go to a funeral, Amrit.'

'No, no Mukesh – not the funeral. The men haven't been invited to that, just a family event it must be. That is not why I am ringing. I am ringing because we have an order from the Continent and Bedford is worried about getting in too many new men who don't know what they are doing. Hardiman has put him in charge while he disappears off to his holiday apartment in Torremol-whatever. Remember, he made us look at the pictures in the brochure?'

'What are you talking about, Amrit? Torrel-whatever?'

'Shush,' Usha says, 'just listen to him won't you?'

'Well the good news is that Bedford has decided to drop the disciplinary.'

'What?'

'I was in the process of talking with the Union to make your case – they were looking into special circumstances because of what happened to your boy. They told me to contact the Indian

Workers Association -I was going to tell you but before I could he called me in and said to tell you to get back to work.'

'Oh, thank god!' Usha exclaims in Punjabi.

'When?' Mukesh asks.

'Tomorrow.'

'Thank you, God,' says Usha again.

'Be quiet,' Mukesh snaps at her.

'Don't be late, Mukesh – eight-thirty okay? A bit earlier so we can talk to Bedford first – settle things and that. It's been a lot of weeks since the suspension and the men, well they won't say anything about the strike or the picket line. They understand you have been under a lot of stress since the accident with your boy last year.'

Usha, still listening, puts her palm against the wall for support at the mention of Billy.

'Is this strike business sorted, Amrit?' asks Mukesh.

'Well, there is still a dispute, it is ongoing, but please just stay at home if we have another day of action, Mukesh. Losing one day's pay is better than having no job at all. It can't have been easy for your wife and children.'

After the phone call Mukesh disappears upstairs and crawls into bed – the sheets are still warm and he quickly slips back into a heavy sleep.

The next morning, Usha opens the curtains in the bedroom at 7am. The day is bright and outside the Church Street houses Errol, the milkman, is doing his rounds. He nods to Usha as she opens the curtains and she nods back expressionless, knowing that he is as fully aware of the family's unpaid bills as she is. Usha looks around the illuminated bedroom, it is tidy now and only the most subtle smell of sleep hangs in the air – the breezes through the open window having cleansed the air during the night. She makes her way over to the bed.

'Come on Mukesh,' she says, 'I have made tea and toast for you downstairs and your lunch sandwich is ready.' Mukesh doesn't stir.

Usha turns on the small radio on the bedside table. The presenter is chatting about Gatport Airwick and it takes her a second or two to realise it is a joke in spite of the presenter chuckling at his own play on words. A familiar tune begins playing, fading in over the chatter of the presenter. Usha turns it up and she tries to place the song but only vaguely recalls the English girls singing it at school and dancing around the playground in pairs. The memory is from way back in her youth when she was barely an adolescent, soon after she had left the bustling, vibrant squares and lanes of Phagwara with her mother and brother to join her father in the drab, rainy streets of Handsworth. It was a time when rock'n'roll had hardly begun and the only songs played in her home were a couple of Hindi soundtracks on chunky, crackly vinyl, bought by her father when he first came to England in the mid-1950s for work. The soundtracks helped alleviate his homesickness at the time and later became a welcome alternative to the others in the house from his own singing as he prepared home-grown coriander and mint for the chutneys he made at weekends. Usha finds herself silently mouthing the words to the song on the radio. The song is romantic, about a boy and a girl dancing and kissing in the moonlight; it is lively but it makes her want to cry. She turns the volume down a little as Mukesh makes a groaning noise from under the sheets and she remembers why she is there.

'Get up Mukesh. Remember what Amrit said? Don't be late.' Mukesh still doesn't respond. 'Please Mukesh. This is not a game. Please get up.'

Mukesh lets out a prolonged but muffled snore from beneath the covers. Usha prods him and he shifts position, the snoring stops but he remains steadfastly asleep. Usha glances at the clock, it is 7.35am.

Usha sits at the kitchen table eating the cold toast and sipping the sweet, tepid tea meant for Mukesh. She tries to remember the first few relatively carefree months of her marriage to him when they lived in a small flat on Archibald Road. It was not much more than a bedsit really, but while living there they both had worked long hours to save for the deposit on the Church Street house before any children came along. Usha worked as a secretary for a local firm of accountants. It was a good job for a young Indian woman, especially with an English firm. The money wasn't very much, even though she had graduated from the technical college with excellent grades in short-hand and touch-typing. She kept working until six weeks before Nina was born. That birth was followed in quick succession by the other four children. She hadn't worked since, but it had crossed her mind more than once as Billy got older that perhaps she could look for work now she no longer had a younger child at home.

Usha and Mukesh had married just a few months after he had arrived in England and soon after he had started at the factory with Usha's older brother, Ravi, who had come home one evening and told their father he had met a nice Punjabi boy from a good caste who would be a perfect match for his sister. Ravi had been married himself for just over a year at that time but still lived in their parent's house where he and his wife Shashi occupied the living room as a bedroom and Shashi did most of the cooking and housework. Usha didn't like the idea of going to live with someone else's family as a housemaid so she was glad to hear that Mukesh had come to England alone, leaving his family back in their village in the Punjab in the same house with the flat roof that had been the setting of the terrible tragedy of their own young son, Naresh. Thinking of it now, Usha connected the two incidents for the first time in her mind – her loss of Billy and the loss of Mukesh's brother, Naresh. Sipping the cold tea and eating the dry toast, she suddenly felt a pang of deep sorrow for her mother-in-law, a woman she never really had time to get to know, even on the two occasions the elder Agarwals had visited England with tickets bought from money Mukesh had sent them. Usha had always found her mother-in-law rather cold and austere, especially towards Mukesh, but she had felt intense pity when the older women had to journey home alone with the dead body of her husband after their second and last visit to England. The sense of that pity returns abruptly in the harsh light of an English morning and Usha wishes she had had the opportunity or the intuition to console the older woman in some meaningful way while she was still alive. At 8am, Usha makes a fresh cup of tea and places it on the bedside table next to Mukesh.

At 8.45am, Mukesh knocks on the glass door of Bedford's office which looks out over the vast factory floor of Hardiman's. Bedford glances up from his paperwork then back down at his wristwatch and beckons Mukesh in with a hand gesture.

'You are late, Agarwal,' he says.

'Yes sorry, Mr Bedford,' Mukesh replies halfheartedly. 'It is hard when you have been off work for so long to get up on time.'

'You could have made an effort, Agarwal. Didn't Amrit tell you to be here for eight-thirty? Do you think I have time to waste waiting for you to turn up?'

'No, Mr Bedford.'

'Mr Bedford, what?'

Mukesh looks perplexed.

'Mr Bedford, sir,' says Bedford and Mukesh repeats it without hiding his contempt.

'You must always call me Sir, right Agarwal?'

Mukesh stares at the top of Bedford's head. He notices that on the crown the hair is thin and greying, although Bedford must be at least ten years younger than himself; his own hair is still the same jet black it has always been, in spite of the last year.

'Yes sir,' he says grudgingly.

'Alright,' says Bedford. This is your one and only chance and only because the others have vouched for you. Have you stopped drinking?'

'No!' says Mukesh.

'No?'

'I only drink in the evening... sir! I am recovered from the daytime drinking now after time off. It was the rest I needed to recover from the daytime drinking.'

Bedford looks up at Agarwal and shakes his head.

'If there is the slightest hint of you having drunk whisky in the factory you'll be out. Understood?' His voice is harsh. 'You can get pissed up as much as you want after work but not on my watch. That stuff you Pakis drink is a lot stronger than a couple of lunchtime pints of mild at the Oak. We'd get shut down if people found out fellas drunk on cheap whisky were operating our heavy machinery. Understand?'

'Yes,' says Mukesh.

'Yes what?'

'Yes sir.'

'Okay, assembly-line! Johnny will show you where. We are two men short so you are going to have to work bloody hard.' Then, after a pause, Bedford looks Mukesh in the eyes and says, 'I didn't want you back, Agarwal, but the men have persuaded me. If you cock up it's them you're letting down, and yourself, not me or Mr Hardiman. Skinny wogs like you are ten a penny in the job centre. I am only doing this to keep the men on side. Do you hear me?'

Mukesh shrugs and moves backwards towards the door.

By the time the bell rings for lunchtime Mukesh craves a drink; not a cup of tea in the canteen but a proper drink in the Barton Arms or the Black Eagle or even the Royal Oak would do. His colleagues on the assembly line have nodded politely to him all morning but none have spoken directly to him. They are all younger men, entry-level school-leavers mostly, and he senses that they know all about Billy and about his suspension even though many of the faces are unfamiliar to him. In the mid-morning tea-break some of the older men from other areas of the factory – welders, galvanisers and shop floor supervisors – came to shake his hand. These are men he has worked alongside for many years but the conversations are stilted, without the familiar camaraderie they once shared. Mukesh feels only disdain for the men, young and old, and it is the thought of a pint of cold beer that keeps him going throughout the morning.

'Come and celebrate my return to work,' Mukesh says to Johnny as they stand side by side in front of the stained urinals just after the bell has rung to signal the beginning of the lunch break.

'Nah, man,' replies Johnny. 'You have to keep your nose clean, Mukesh. I'm not going to the pub with you on your first day back. You know they don't like us going at dinnertime when we have machinery to operate after.'

'Bedford can bugger off,' says Mukesh, 'I am going anyway.'

'Don't be stupid, brother,' says Johnny. 'It's your first day back.'

But Mukesh has already clocked out and is on his way through the door.

'That bloody Bedford can't tell me what to do in my dinnertime,' he shouts back towards Johnny. 'We are not in prison you know. He thinks he can treat me like some low-caste lackey from the Raj days but he goes too far sometimes.'

The men who lurk around the exit turn to stare at Mukesh; some of them rummage about in lockers for packed lunches and cans of pop, trying hard to look uninterested.

'Get back on time at least,' says Johnny but Mukesh is out of earshot.

After a second pint of beer on an empty stomach, Mukesh leans against the bar at the Royal Oak. The ground beneath his feet feels unstable and he holds on to the bar for support.

'Another pint please, barman,' he says, 'and a bag of pork scratchings.'

'Where is Agarwal?' Bedford asks Amrit at 1.35pm. 'He knows dinner is forty-five minutes. He has only been away a few weeks – he can't have forgotten what he has known for nigh-on twenty bloody years.'

'He wasn't feeling well, sir,' pipes up Johnny from a few feet away. 'He might still be in the bogs. Shall I check?'

'Do what you want, boy, but if I don't see him back on the line in ten minutes he is out. Got it?'

As Johnny walks towards the toilets he takes a slight detour to the entrance and scans up and down the street for Mukesh. He spots him further down Lozells Road, meandering towards the factory gates.

'Shit!' Johnny says, running towards him. He pulls Mukesh through the gates, into the main entrance and shoves him towards the men's toilets. He turns on the cold tap and starts splashing cold water into Mukesh's face.

'What the hell...' Mukesh begins to speak but tapers off, unable to articulate the words.

'Tell them you don't feel well and that is why you are wet – tell them you threw up or something otherwise Bedford will have your guts for garters.'

'Guts for garters?' Mukesh repeats and begins to laugh. At first the laugh is just a snigger but it becomes hysterical, like a child unable to control itself. Soon Mukesh is standing by the cubicle shaking with laughter. Johnny stares at him in disbelief.

'Shit, man,' he says, 'you really are messed up, Mukesh. You need the doctor or something. Sort yourself out and I'll cover for you again but I can't do it for long. Bedford will be checking for you in a few minutes. He is on the warpath.'

Mukesh stares back at Johnny. 'Guts for garters' he repeats and begins laughing again. Johnny leaves the toilets shaking his head.

Fifteen minutes later Mukesh walks past Bedford's office and waves at him before walking out the factory door and straight back towards the Royal Oak.

Usha has made lamb curry for dinner, not the cheaper minced keema they are used to having but actual pieces of succulent meat floating in thick, pungent gravy. The children are already eating the dish eagerly when Mukesh staggers through the front door just after 6pm.

'How was the factory?' Usha asks cheerfully. She places two buttered chapattis on a plate which she puts on the table, nudging the other plates out of the way to make space. Mukesh doesn't answer. Instead he opens the cupboard above the cooker, takes down the bottle of Johnny Walker and pours himself a quadruple measure. He knocks it back as Anila, Kamela, Kavi and Usha stare at him. He wipes his mouth.

'What are you all looking at? Bloody hell, can't a man relax for a few minutes after a hard day at work before you throw all these questions at me?'

The children turn back to their meals.

'Come and eat Mukesh, before it goes cold,' Usha says.

Mukesh pours another large measure of the whisky and begins to sip it. He looks at his family in front of him before turning his back on them and leaving the room, gripping the bottle tightly.

The next morning, Usha has to disrupt her morning cleaning to run up the stairs and switch off the alarm clock. The shrill ring has been echoing through the previously silent house for a full two minutes. In the bedroom, Mukesh is fast asleep with his head buried deep under the pillow. Usha sighs as she picks up the empty bottle of whisky from next to the bed. She sets about shaking out the clothes that lie discarded in a crumpled heap on the floor and then she starts gently trying to wake Mukesh for the second day in a row.

'Leave me alone woman,' he says in Punjabi, 'I am not going to the factory. That Bedford treats me like I am a piece of the shit he has scraped off his shoe. I can't take this from a gora any more.'

'Anymore?' Usha says. 'You have only worked one day in months. What is the matter with you?'

Mukesh pulls the cover back over his head and ignores Usha's question. At 9.30am the phone rings. Usha answers it, already knowing it will be from the factory.

'Hello, Mrs Agarwal? Sam Bedford here.'

'Yes, Mr Bedford, he isn't feeling very well. Sorry,' Usha says meekly. 'He should be fine tomorrow after some rest. I will make sure of that.'

'Listen, love, tell him not to bother will you? I'll send one of the boys around with the paperwork. I'll make it so as he can get the dole without any problem and we'll give him a couple of weeks in hand to help you and the kids out, but tell him not to bother coming in again. He sets a bad example for the new men. A lot of them are very young and impressionable, they'll think it's okay to be spending half the working day in the pub if I let your husband back.' He rings off and Usha slides her back down the wall until she hits the floor with a small thud, the phone receiver still held out in her hand.

Chapter 21

Anila rushes down the stairs to reach the ringing phone before anyone else does. She is certain it will be Kash. Just the other day he had placed his hand lightly on her shoulder, touching her neck as she counted up the coins from the donations after the meeting. She had blushed as she turned to face him and he had smiled back at her in a way that made her feel slightly strange. He was about to ask her something important, she was sure of it, but the moment was broken when someone shouted a question across the room about the counter-march which was now just weeks away. Later, she was going to talk to Kamela or Nina about it, but she wasn't sure what exactly she wanted to say – it was hard enough to try and gather her own thoughts about Kash without trying to articulate them, so in the end she didn't bother to mention it after all. Instead of Kash, the voice on the other end of the phone is Brenda.

'Bad news about Kavi,' she says. 'He has been caught shoplifting in Lavery's Newsagents down on Gerrard Street. Frank Lavery is a friend,' she continues, 'and he knows Usha because yous used to have a paper and that, and he knows all about what happened to Billy because, well, it was all over the Handsworth Times, so he didn't call the police. Not this time at least.'

'What was he nicking?' asks Anila.

'Does it matter, bab? Sweets, Coke that sort of stuff. Where's your mom, anyhow?'

Before Anila can answer, Brenda launches into a spiel about how Usha is worn out by Kavi and by the rest of them too.

'Yous all need to think about your poor mom sometimes. A mom never gets over a kid. A year might have passed and you all might have moved on but it has only got worse for her. You lot should all be a bit more considerate instead of giving her more stuff to worry herself about.'

'Moved on?' Anila repeats. 'Really, Brenda? Is that what you think the rest of us have done?'

'Oh, I didn't mean anything by it, bab. I'm just looking out for your mom, that's all. I know yous are good kids really but it's been over a year now and she hasn't gotten over it yet. It's all she talks about still, you know? It's all she really thinks about, besides worrying about your Kavi and you girls. Tell her about the shoplifting, I told Frank I would do, but play it down a bit if you want, bab.'

'Who is on the telephone?' Usha shouts from the kitchen.

'Wrong number, Mom,' Anila replies, as she replaces the receiver.

In the living room, Kamela is watching a Scottish soap opera about country people. Mountains, lochs, wiggly roads that lead to rustic homesteads and accents Anila can barely understand.

'They should have subtitles for this shit,' Kamela says, as if she has read her sister's mind. Anila ignores her. Across the room, Mukesh is slumped in the armchair dozing and snorting in his sleep. Anila glances at him and then leaves the living room and heads for the attic where Nina is laid out across the bed under the open skylight writing a letter to Imran on a torn-out piece of foolscap. She looks up.

'I need to get back to uni – it is so fucking oppressive here and we aren't even halfway through the holidays yet,' Nina says as Anila enters.

'You just wanna get back to your boyfriend,' Anila replies resentfully. 'Escape from reality, from the fact that Billy is still dead and everything is still falling apart here.'

'So what if I do? Wouldn't you feel exactly the same if you were in my position? I don't know how you and Kam stand it.

There is a whole world out there. Not just this shitty depressing little street with its poor people and its issues.'

Anila shrugs her shoulders.

The next day there is another planning meeting at The Shoe, the third in less than a fortnight. Anila has attended them all and is now part of the inner circle that is in charge of making plans and deciding how they will be executed. As she prepares to leave the house, she buttons up her oversized shirt over a khaki vest. Her jeans have been narrowed down the wide legs using Usha's old Singer sewing machine. The seams are wonky but Anila is pleased with the drainpipe effect. She rubs a little Vaseline onto her lips and the rest into her palms before using it to spike up her hair. She checks herself in the narrow wall-mirror, adjusts the seams of her jeans and heads down the stairs to find the old hockey boots she now wears daily.

'Where are you going, beti?' Mukesh asks as Anila sits on the bottom step tying up her laces. Their conversations are strained, never having recovered from the slap incident months before.

'A meeting, Dad,' she says without looking up.

'Meetings? What kind of young girl goes to meetings? What are these meetings you go to all the time?'

Anila licks her fingers and rubs the frayed end of the lace. Mukesh carries on speaking.

'Who goes to these meetings? Amrit tells me they are run by Jamaicans, Muslims, Communists and low-caste people. Is this true, Anila?'

Anila rolls her eyes. An article in the *Handsworth Times* last week had said Kash was an outsider, an agitator, a troublemaker not from Handsworth, stirring up the young people in the area, but she knows he has lived in Handsworth for as long as she has existed.

'We aren't interested in where people are from, Dad, or what religion they are. This is about the situation here – police harassment, politics, the racism and that,' Anila replies, still tying her laces.

'More bloody politics. Politics at the factory and now politics here too. Politics is no use to people like us, Anila. We don't matter to the politicians. Concentrate on your studies instead and stop hanging around with these trouble-makers, Paki bastards and low caste dogs. They are peasants – uncivilised – not like us proper Indians.'

'God, Dad, you are worse than the National Front when you say stuff like that. We are all Pakis to some people you know? The NF don't care where we come from, they only care what colour we are – we're all the same to them.' She takes a breath and continues, 'Do you think skinheads can tell who is a Muslim, Sikh or Hindu? Or what caste people are? Do you think they care? You are worse than them, calling people low caste and that – it's embarrassing. We are trying to change things and then my own dad says the most ignorant things. We are all brothers and sisters here – Muslim or Hindu, black, white, low or high bloody caste. Do you think we still give a shit about that stuff? Honestly!'

'Don't you say that, Anila. This isn't your racism, it is my... our culture. Do you know nothing about our history?'

'Of course I do, I've read Midnight's Children at school – it's all about Indian history and that, partition and stuff. History doesn't explain why you hate people from less than fifty miles from where you were born yourself – it's all divide and rule – you lot just fell for it, just like the British wanted you to. It's just daft, mixed-up shit – you don't even know what you think.'

Mukesh gawps at his daughter.

'Bloody story books aren't history, or the rubbish they teach you at these English schools. I don't want you mixing with these Jamaican jungle-men or these Bangla and Paki hooligans Anila, do you hear me?'

'Junglemen? Pakis? What are you talking about? Sometimes its like you are the most racist person I actually know. It's like you are saying I don't want you hanging around with those weirdos from Dudley or Wolverhampton. Handsworth is my culture, Dad, not some far-off distant imaginary homeland. And you need to realise that this is your community too – black, brown, Sikh, Muslim whatever. Anyhow, you can't actually stop me seeing them. I'm not doing anything wrong – just trying to make things better. You chose this life for us so you better just accept it.'

'Okay, Anila, you think you are very intelligent but at least let me give you this advice – you are a young lady and these are mostly men you are spending time with. It doesn't look respectable and yes, on this thing I can agree – all these men are the same, whatever their colour, don't be fooled by thinking they want you at these meetings for your great intellect. I know what men are like and it is not what you think.'

'Bloody hell, Dad,' Anila sighs, 'I can look after myself. See you later.' She slams the door as she leaves.

The Shoe is empty when Anila arrives. She fumbles in her pocket for her key, lets herself in and leaves the door slightly ajar. The cavernous atrium is dark except for a sliver of light from the gap in the doorway and it takes Anila a few moments to adjust her eyes. She opens her duffle-bag and removes the folded register of members and the donations tin. She places these on the table near the front door. The silence in The Shoe is marred by the white noise of traffic and the faint sounds of Bhangra music from cars whizzing by. The echoey interior has the eerie quality of abandonment; a once busy hive of activity, now a mostly empty shell of what once was.

'You alone?'

A voice in the darkness behind her makes her jump. It is Kash. As he moves closer towards her, her legs begin to shake. She holds on to the edge of the unstable table.

'You're early Anila. That is what I like about you, you are committed. Reliable.' He is right beside her now and she can feel the warmth of his breath across her cheek. 'You understand the cause Anila, and what you need to do. I like that.' He strokes her hair and his hand slides down her cheek and stops just above her breast where it stays for a moment, awkwardly positioned. Kash is staring straight into her eyes now and Anila can feel the blood rush to her face. The burning sensation in her cheeks travels throughout her body which stiffens as his fingers caress the top of her breast. He smirks as his hand moves down her body, travelling towards her hips and to the zip of her jeans. Suddenly, there is a noise at the door. Kash steps away from Anila. 'Wait for me after the end of the meeting,' he whispers. He is still close enough for her to feel his breath on her face.

Before Anila can focus her attention back to the imminent meeting, a small group of men and women bustle in through the door; their voices are loud with banter. Kash greets them from the shadows and they immediately fall into a reverential silence when they become aware of his presence. Anila is shaken, unsure of the feelings careering through her body except a terrible embarrassment – what if these people saw how close to her Kash was standing just seconds before? She tries hard to compose herself and the heat in her body slowly begins to settle and ebb away. Without looking up she holds out the tin towards the queue forming in front of her. Aazim is the first person in the line and he mumbles a greeting and pushes a handful of coppers towards her. She continues to look downwards, trying not to meet anyone's eye. The last of the queue to reach her is Olive.

'What you playing at, Anila?' She says under her breath.

'What do you mean, Olive?' Anila replies.

'Just saying like, we can all see you have a crush on him. Be careful, Anila, some blokes aren't what they seem. I've heard things that you wouldn't want to know.'

'What things? Actually, don't bother, Olive. I'm not interested in gossip.'

'I'm just saying, Anila, be careful. He's older than us. More experienced and that.'

Anila feels heat flush across her face again. From across the room, Kash catches her eye but she turns away quickly, looking around to check if anyone has noticed. Olive is busy in a whispered conversation with Marcus and another girl across the room. Anila feels compelled to slip out of the room but before she has time to do so Kash bangs on a table and the babbling crowd fall into a hush. As he begins to speak, Anila attempts to assess how she will move unnoticed to the exit. She edges a few paces towards it but an elbow nudges her in the ribs.

'Shush can't you? We are trying to listen,' an unfamiliar voice says.

Others turn to look at what is causing the disturbance and Anila stands rigid, staring towards Kash until the others lose interest and return to looking at him. Twenty minutes later Kash concludes his speech in a rallying battle cry, the type he is becoming renowned for amongst the groups of young people that attend the meetings. An enthusiastic applause erupts around the room and Anila takes the opportunity to head towards the door and leave. Outside, two young men sit in a Datsun Estate with all four windows open wide. They gawp at Anila as she exits The Shoe and the driver shouts something suggestive in Punjabi towards her; both men giggle like schoolboys. Their words are only vaguely audible over the loud Bhangra music of Apna Sangeet which blares out from a ghetto blaster balanced on the passenger's knees.

Chapter 22

B renda and Usha sit huddled around the table in Usha's kitchen, their hands wrapped around steaming mugs of stewed tea. It is a dull Wednesday morning, unusually cold for the time of year but there is no distinction between the days or even the seasons for Usha – each one merges into the other as she tries to maintain a semblance of domesticity. Brenda stubs out her cigarette in the ashtray on the table and, as she crushes it into the tin, a barely perceptible cloud of ash scatters and rests on the table top. Usha gets up, grabs the damp dishcloth from the sink caddy and cleans the table, then rinses and squeezes out the cloth and returns it to drip-dry over the tap. Brenda watches her friend as she moves swiftly from table to sink and back again. Before Usha has properly settled into her seat, Brenda has stuck another fag between her lips and she rummages through her bag for her matches. Eventually, Usha speaks.

'I feel like part of me died with Billy.'

Brenda looks up from her bag, alarmed. Just a moment or two earlier the women were speaking of the change in weather, curtain fabric and the rising prices of textiles. Usha sees the pity in Brenda's face – it is the same forced softness that she encounters each time she walks down the street to the small parade of shops on Hunters Road to buy milk or bread or just to break the monotony of grief, or when she ventures further to Lozells Road or even, on rare occasions, to Soho Road for the more exotic vegetables and spices that aren't stocked in the smaller more local concerns. Usha recognises that the way Brenda looks upon her is as if she is a child that has lost her favourite toy or scraped her knee in some misdemeanour or

135

other. *I don't need your pity, I just need my son back* are the words that form in Usha's mind. They are words not meant to be spoken, not meant to upset the very people whose concern keeps her wrapped in a blanket, protected from the real world of harsh, unfamiliar stares of the strangers who populated her life before the death of Billy.

'What do you mean, bab?' Brenda says.

'Like everything around me is carrying on but I am standing still, unable to move,' Usha replies. The words sound clunky, even to herself, as she tries to articulate feelings that she cannot fathom.

'Oh, bab, time is a great healer as they say,' Brenda replies.

Usha smiles weakly; she knows her friend is well-meaning but she also knows that Brenda will not understand how the crushing weight of losing Billy bears down on her every moment of every day, so that even the simplest daily routine – brushing her teeth, making a cup of tea, opening the post – is like wading through a quagmire after prolonged rain.

'I am not sure I believe it, Brenda,' she says. 'The family is falling down around me and I can't do anything about it. Kavi is missing school all the time, Nina never phones or writes when she is away – she hardly comes home and I have no idea what her life is when she is away. Anila is getting too involved with these radical people – I am worried they will lead her the wrong way. Have you seen what she has done to her hair?'

'Aww, it's not so bad, Usha, at least she hasn't dyed it green or orange or some other dreadful colour.'

Usha shrugs her shoulders.

'Kamela is still scared to go out even though the thing with those horrible girls was months ago now, and as for Mukesh...'

'Eugene knows that Bedford one from the factory, you know?' Brenda says. 'They go to the same pub... he could have a word?'

'Oh Brenda, he won't even get out of bed some days except to get a drink – I don't know if he can ever go back to work. Sometimes I don't blame him, I wish I could just go to bed

136

and pull the covers over my head rather than face the world, but I am a mother and the children at least need to know that there will be dinner made and tidying up done. They need this routine, it is all we have got that is stable and a mother has no choice but to provide it.'

Brenda nods, sucking deeply on the cigarette tucked between her fingers.

'How are you coping with nowt coming in? How long has it been? Long enough I expect.'

Usha puts her face in her hands and rubs her eyes. Money is not an issue she was brought up to discuss with outsiders, however close they are. The fact that she had to borrow money from her parents or that the men at the factory had a whip around is a dark secret. She accepted both without choice and felt grateful that it was Johnny who had delivered the money from the men and not Amrit or one of the other men from the community – although they all would have known of course. It wasn't a lot of money, the men didn't have a lot to give, but it was enough to stock up on tins and dried goods. When she told Mukesh about the money he demanded she hand it over.

'It is from my friends for me, a gift to wish me well as I recover from this injustice forced on me by that Bedford bastard.'

When he said this, Usha considered slapping him or shaking him until he became the man she used to know – the patriarch, the breadwinner, the person who took control so she could get on with being a mother and a wife, as was expected of her. Instead she threw the few remaining notes at him before leaving the bedroom, restraining her words and her actions to silence and door slamming.

'They think we are charity cases like these Ugandans and Cambodians?' Usha had heard him shout after she left the room, and she had to stop herself from returning and shouting something unforgivable back at him.

Two weeks later, Usha had to go back to her mother and father to ask for money to feed the children.

'We will pay you back – it is just a loan until Mukesh is back at work,' she had insisted as her father handed her an envelope containing five £10 notes. It was already in his pocket before she had even arrived to ask, and she knew he would have been to the bank to withdraw such a large amount from their meagre savings in anticipation of this moment. She was unable to hide the swell of emotion that arrived with her gratitude and when her father had hugged her and called her his precious puttari she hadn't been able to stop the tears from cascading down her face. Bibi phones her daily now to check they are okay, and most weekends both her mother and father walk through Handsworth Park towards Lozells with a bag of Indian vegetables and Tupperware containers of cooked food and freshly made chutneys. Usha doesn't tell Brenda this.

'Oh we have some savings still,' she says instead. 'Money is not our problem.'

'Okay but you know you can ask anytime, right?'

Usha nods silently, her head hung low. The pregnant pause that follows is broken by the sound of yelling and loud thumps on the stairs.

'Bagsy in the bathroom first.'

'Get off, I'm desperate.'

'Fuck off, Kavi, you can go in the garden if you're desperate. It's easier for boys.'

'Don't stink it out, shitface,' Kavi shouts from the hallway.

'Sorry!' Usha says to her friend, embarrassed. 'I don't know where they get this terrible language... probably school.'

'Oh blimey, Ush, don't worry about it, they probably get it from our lot anyhow!' Brenda laughs and begins to gather up her things. 'I'll let you all get on with it,' she says as she leaves by the back door.

Later that afternoon the house is quiet; Usha knows it is a forced and eerie quiet that comes with emptiness rather than with the fullness of serenity. She has tidied away the vacuum cleaner to the small cupboard under the stairs and has tucked the dusters and other cloths below the sink. The mop and bucket have been squeezed and emptied and placed in the corner behind the bathroom door. She looks around the kitchen at the walls which desperately need a fresh coat of paint. She grabs the scourer from the sink and begins to rub at a yellowish stain on the wall above the cooker before sitting down at the kitchen table to sort through a tray of lentils. The kitchen is silent except for the low white noise of the TV in the next room. The quiet is punctuated by the soothing rain-like sound of the lentils being shifted across the stainless steel plate into sorted and unsorted piles. The quiet of the moment is abruptly broken by a loud bang on the back gate. Usha jumps, inadvertently knocking the tray of lentils with her hand. They scatter across the tray, merging back into one pile and she sighs. A second later, Brenda crashes in through the back door breathless with excitement.

'I've had an idea, Usha,' she says.

Usha moves automatically towards the kettle but Brenda grabs it from her hand and gently guides Usha back towards the kitchen chair.

'Sit down and listen, bab,' she says as she puts the kettle on. She plonks herself on the vacant chair next to Usha, lights up a cigarette and pauses to stare at the flat mustard-coloured lentils in the tray in front of them.

'Are these for eating?' she says, picking a couple in her fingers and scrutinising them. 'You can't be having that for your tea, can you?' She lifts up a handful and lets a stream of lentils spill through her fingers. Both women watch as they cascade satisfactorily back on to the tray.

Usha begins to explain that the lentils will be boiled into a sort of spicy soup when Brenda launches into a garbled monologue,

'We have to do something, Usha, otherwise this community will just explode or whatever the right word is. So, I have done some thinking and I have had an idea, it might sound naff and that but maybe this could work.' Brenda pauses and takes a long drag on her cigarette; she exhales slowly before continuing, 'So, I thought we could get the kids involved in something – you know give them a reason to get up and get out of a morning... keep them off the streets and that and then maybe they would feel a little more motivated, you know what I mean?'

Usha returns to separating the lentils into thin lines, meticulously examining each line for stones before shifting the separated heaps from the left to the right side of the tray.

'Looks like you're checking a babbie's hair for nits,' Brenda observes.

Usha forces a small smile. She concentrates on the lentils and Brenda's words are just a murmur in the background, not dissimilar to the white noise of the television seeping through the wall. She wants Brenda to leave her alone so she can continue her task unperturbed – it is a task which focuses her mind just enough to stop the whys and ifs around Billy's death from dominating her thoughts. Brenda continues to speak.

'As I was saying, I was watching this thing on the telly last night and the kids were all hanging around and doing nothing so their teacher gets them to put on a show, like a performance.'

Usha feels bad about wishing Brenda gone and irritation is replaced with guilt as she remembers the hours of support over cups of tea she has had from this woman sitting opposite her now. Brenda has visited regularly since Billy died – not daily, but at least a couple of times a week and certainly more than any single person that she could call a friend in the Indian community around her. Even the visits from Bibi and her father are not as frequent as Brenda's. Since Mukesh lost his job no-one had offered the kind of the friendship that Brenda had offered – unconditional and constant, unwavering even in more trying moments – the kind of friendship one doesn't realise is needed until it exists and becomes indispensable. Usha rises from the table, reboils the kettle and begins to concentrate on what Brenda is saying.

'That won't be any good around here,' Usha says as she makes tea. 'It isn't America here or even like London. This isn't the sort of area that can be made better with a song and a dance, Brenda.'

'I know that, bab, but the idea of giving them something to do... your lot could lead it, Anila is into all that stuff, she can put it to good use instead of hanging out with those radicals she mixes with. What do you think? We need a project that will bring people together – not just one type of people but everyone around here. We are all facing the same problems after all, aren't we?'

'Well, yes some of the same.'

'Oh hell, I'm sorry Usha, I didn't mean Billy, I meant no jobs and the shops closing down and teenagers with nothing to do and that... sorry.'

'It's okay, Brenda, I know what you meant.'

Usha stirs the tea and places a mug in front of Brenda and then returns to separating the good lentils from the bad.

The next day Brenda comes crashing in again through the back door. This time Usha is scrubbing at a cracked, brown layer of burnt rice on the bottom of a saucepan.

'Horrible noise those Brillos make,' says Brenda, by way of announcing her arrival. 'Make my skin crawl, they do, like nails down a blackboard.'

Usha looks up and smiles weakly at her friend. Brenda's exuberance unsettles her; it is not an emotion she can remember feeling since Billy died and it is strange to be in the presence of it.

'I have written out some notes and Eugene has copied them,' Brenda says enthusiastically. 'I am going to pop them through the letterboxes around here but I thought I better let you know. I have put your address on them inviting people to come to a meeting. It's on a Saturday in the day, like, so no blokes will come – they'll all be watching the football results at that time, dreaming about winning the Pools and that.'

'When?' Usha says panicked. She looks around the kitchen and fixes on a small cobweb in the corner of the ceiling which she has been unable to reach for days. Brenda follows the direction of Usha's eyes, grabs the copy of the *Handsworth Times* from the kitchen table, stands on tiptoes and swipes at the cobweb. Both women watch as it floats down to settle on the edge of the counter top. Usha gathers it up in a dishcloth, shakes it into the sink and washes it away with a running tap.

'The house looks spotless, Usha. Don't worry, it isn't for a week or two anyhow. I just thought it would be better here than mine. Eugene has his tools all over the place all the time. It's just to get some ideas about what we can do, you know, like your Anila, get active and that.'

Usha looks at the words on Brenda's home-made leaflet.

MAKING HANDSWORTH BETTER FOR OUR
CHILDREN – CAN YOU HELP?

The words seem odd together but Usha can't work out why.

'Great,' says Brenda, interpreting Usha's silent contemplation as acceptance.

One week later, Kavi flicks through the *Handsworth Times*, and asks,

'Why is that Brenda woman always here these days?'

'Mom and her are organising a meeting or something,' Kamela replies, even though the question is directed at Usha.

'Bloody meetings!' says Mukesh. As he speaks he sucks up the fumes from a cigarette he holds through a tunnel made by curling his thumb around his index and middle fingers so his whole hand becomes a pipe. Usha waves away the smoke before she speaks.

'Brenda thinks the children around here need to get involved in something positive. She is organising this meeting to get ideas. Young people are bored and that leads to trouble,' she says, repeating Brenda's words from the day before.

'It isn't just boredom,' says Kavi, 'we haven't got anything to look forward to in a shithole like this. No one has got any money to go to a match or see a band or even go to the pictures. There are no jobs for people like us and the police are always on our backs, especially if you are a boy, picking on us for no reason. There's no point in anything when it's like that all around us and Brenda's bright ideas aren't going to change that.'

'You do have a choice, Kavi. I don't like what Anila is doing, I don't even know what she is doing really, except she is trying to change something for the better. Anything has got to be better than this. Brenda will be coming around often. We have a meeting to plan and it feels like a small bit of hope,' Usha says before returning to the kitchen. She picks up empty tea-cups along the way.

'Bloody meetings,' Mukesh mutters again.

The following morning, the contents of the fridge sit neatly on the kitchen table. The inside of the fridge has been wiped down with washing up liquid and the door is propped open to allow it to dry. Usha stands at the sink with the fridge trays and shelves piled in front of her.

'Hey Mom,' says Anila as she stumbles into the kitchen in her nightdress. She picks up one of Benda's photocopied leaflets from the worktop and glances at the details. 'Shit – it's the same day as the march,' she mutters but Usha doesn't hear. 'I can take some of these to The Shoe if you want, Mom,' she says, 'I'm going later. The Youth Movement members can give them to their moms and stuff. Want a hand?' Anila takes a glass shelf from the draining board and a tea towel from the worktop. Her back is towards Usha, who turns from the sink to watch her daughter. Anila is humming a familiar pop tune as she dries the shelf. She stands directly in a shaft of sunlight, intersecting it as it streams across the kitchen and a yellow glow illuminates the top of her jet black hair. The lightness of her presence is strange to Usha and she feels as though she has stepped beyond the heavy familiarity of her own kitchen. She wonders how Anila can be cheerful when any minuscule sign of joy appears incongruous in the weighty atmosphere she has become used to. She stares at her daughter's cropped hair for a moment longer and then turns towards to the sink.

'Thank you, beta,' she says.

Chapter 23

Anila strolls towards Villa Cross with her hands dug deep into the pockets of her sleeveless patterned jumpsuit. She hums a tune that has been stuck in her head for days, irritating her with its catchy refrain and evasive title. The *da-dum* of it swirls around her brain and she tries to shake it loose, actually dislodge it by literally shaking her head from side to side, but the tune is on a loop, stuck fast and the only way to repress it, she realises, is to block it with thoughts of Kash.

Anila is acutely aware that when she reaches The Shoe it will be the first time she's seen Kash since he touched her and her whole being was thrown into a state of confusion. She will have to speak to him but how to approach him is the question that has occupied her for days. She concludes that she will get there early, to arrive before him, and so when he arrives he will have to acknowledge and approach her first. Even so, what will she say without seeming childish and inexperienced? Did she want him to touch her again? She wasn't sure if she did. A hand on her shoulder causes her to jolt.

'Hey, I've been calling you from across the street. Didn't you hear me?' It is Marcus. He walks directly beside her and continues chatting cheerily, 'Are you going to the meeting? I think it will be a good one with that NF march just a couple of weeks away now.'

'Yeah, yeah I'm going. Sorry, I didn't see you.'

The two friends chat about the importance of the imminent meeting. It will be a logistical planning meeting was what Kash had said and Anila had to ask Nina to explain what logistical meant that evening on the phone.

'I like the haircut,' Marcus says, 'I almost didn't recognise you at first. It's pretty cool, man.' Anila touches her own head. She had forgotten just how short her hair was, even though Usha has made constant reference to it with comments which are too earnest to have been made with the intent of spite or malice.

'It will grow out, I suppose,' her mother said, or, 'It looks a little longer today than yesterday, perhaps it will grow quickly,' or, if she was particularly tired and spoke without thinking, 'It is so ugly Anila, you used to be so beautiful before.'

'Actually, I got something for you,' Marcus says, slowing down his step to match her pace.

'For me?' Anila says surprised.

Marcus rummages in the carrier bag he is holding and pulls out a brown package, inside is a thick paperback book.

'Wow, thanks Marcus what's it about ?' Anila asks turning to the blurb.

Before he has time to respond, a young man in a black turban walks towards where they stand chatting on the street. Anila vaguely recognises him from around and about and smiles as he approaches. The man stares back at her: it is a cold stare, direct and unflinching. Anila looks away awkwardly and the man walks on, physically colliding with Marcus as he moves past them. It is more than an accidental brush.

'Oi, watch it will you?' Marcus says, but the man ignores him and walks on a few paces before turning back towards them and spitting on the ground in their direction and casually walking away.

'Oi!' Marcus shouts after him.

'Leave it,' Anila says grabbing his arm, 'he isn't worth it.'

Across the road she catches sight of three sari-clad women lurking in the doorway of Ashoka's. They stare directly at her, and, like the man in the turban, they refuse to look away even when she glares back.

'Fuck him and them, man,' Marcus says. He places his hand in the small of her back and guides her onwards, 'C'mon let's get a cup of tea. We have loads of time before the meeting starts.'

Herbert, the elderly cook at the Acapulco, brings over toast and tea while Anila waves away the pungent smoke of tobacco and marijuana from her face and reads the blurb on the back of the hefty paperback,

'It's about working men,' Marcus says. 'I know it doesn't sound like much and there's hardly any women in it but my history teacher gave it me and well, it's great. I've never read a book like it before, you know about real people, man. I mean they are all white men and stuff but painters and decorators like my dad with the same troubles too, if you know what I mean.'

Anila reads the title out loud: 'Ragged Trousered... Phil – and – throw – pist.'

'I don't know what one of them is. I'll have to look it up in the dictionary.' She sips her tea and continues, 'I don't know much about anything yet.'

'Nor me,' says Marcus.

'We're a bit thick really around here, aren't we?'

'Speak for yourself, man,' Marcus says and they both laugh.

Marcus continues to grin at Anila – it is a warm and familiar smile and Anila suddenly feels a little shy of this boy she seems to have always known.

'Anyway,' she says, 'it's really, really nice of you. I don't think anyone has given me a book before... No, hang on, maybe Nina gave me one for my birthday. Jane Austen or something. I hated it – all about posh women trying to get decent husbands, just like the Indian films our nan used to make us watch at The Elite on Soho Road! But I'm sure this will be better than that if you like it, so ta very much, it's really sweet of you.' The book sounds wholly unappealing but she vows to read it.

Marcus stirs sugar into his tea with his head bowed and Anila wonders if he too feels shy in this moment. She stares at the dark silkiness of his hair and has an urge to reach over the table and touch it to see if it feels as soft and as moist as it looks.

'So,' Marcus says after a moment, 'You and Kash seem to be quite close these days.'

Anila sits back in her seat, she folds her arms and tries not to sound defensive.

'I don't know about close – it's just HYM stuff and that.'

'Really? That's not what Olive Benjamin says. She says you like him, sort of really like him and that.'

'What's it got to do with Olive? So what if I do like him. It isn't a crime is it?' Anila feels annoyed, especially at the thought of Marcus and Olive discussing her in her absence. She can't help but scowl at Marcus as he continues to stir the spoon in his tea.

'You should be careful, Anila. Not everyone is how they seem you know.'

'Olive said that too but what have I got to be careful of?' Anila says, surprised at how irritated she feels. She lights up a cigarette and says, 'I don't need a dad, Marcus, I have already got one of those and besides I can like who the hell I bloody want.'

Herbert appears at the side of the table and asks if they want anything else.

'Nah, man, we'd better get on.' Marcus says to Herbert, who continues to hang about at the side of the table until Anila nods in agreement.

After leaving the cafe, Anila and Marcus head in silence towards The Shoe, exchanging only the occasional verbal observation about the walk. Ten minutes later they approach their destination.

'I liked that,' Marcus says.

'What?'

'You know, having a chat and that in the Acapulco. We should do it again sometime.'

'What?' Anila says again, distractedly. They have entered The Shoe and Kash is standing in the far corner with his back towards them. Marcus is still talking beside her.

'We should have a cup of tea again, I said, it was nice to have a chat,' Marcus repeats.

'What?' says Anila still looking towards Kash.

'You know in the Acapulco.' Anila doesn't answer so he follows her gaze into the distant end of the room where Kash is now looking back towards them. He meets Marcus's eye and nods without a smile. Anila looks down and fumbles in her bag for the stick of chewing gum she spotted earlier. A clap of hands from across the room signals the start of the meeting and Kash promptly turns his gaze away from Marcus and Anila and towards the man standing on the riser on the opposite side of the room. Anila follows his lead.

'Well, I'll leave you to it, man,' says Marcus, moving towards the small crowd gathered around the speaker at the front of the room.

'Oh yeah, see ya. Oh and ta for the book again,' Anila says, also looking ahead towards the man on the riser. She hardly notices as Marcus moves away, instead fixing her gaze ahead but desperately trying to keep Kash in her peripheral vision.

Soon the space left vacant by Marcus is filled with others, most of them familiar strangers, As the meeting begins, Anila finds herself packed into the middle of the crowd and a mild sense of claustrophobia starts to envelop her. She looks around for Marcus, suddenly becoming aware of the gap he has left behind. She spots him leaning on a wall near the exit with his head hung low and she wishes she was still standing with him. She wonders why she hadn't noticed him move away.

'Brothers, sisters, comrades,' the speaker begins, 'we will not allow the scum of fascism to prowl our streets and murder our youth like some rabid dog let off a leash by its hate-fuelled master. Enoch Powell soiled our city with his rhetoric all those years ago and it still continues to poison our streets with its legacy, demonstrated in the sons he spawned who now exist as the National Front. We cannot allow these violent yobs, these murderous imbeciles to march through Handsworth. We have not forgotten our young brother Gurdip Singh Chaggar or Satnam Singh, our neighbour, and we will get justice for these boys and for the other twenty-nine victims of racism slain in the years since Powell made his dangerous speech. We will defend our right to claim this country as our own in retribution for their deaths and for the pillage of our motherlands by the colonialist forefathers of this barbarous scum.'

'Bloody idiots – they need to be educated,' Aazim shouts from the front of the crowd. 'I can teach them a thing or two,' he continues, and there are sniggers all around.

'Alright, alright,' shouts Kash, 'but this is stuff we know already, we don't need firing up we need planning – the march is in a fortnight. What about strategy? That's what we need – banner, chants, a united voice.'

'Strategy? We turn up and kick their fucking heads in – that's what I call strategy,' a younger boy shouts across the crowd.

'Don't be stupid,' says Anila without thinking, 'we can't behave like they do.'

'Anila is right,' says Kash, 'we are more intelligent than that. We're not thugs like them – we'll use the tried and tested non-violent method of restraint and protest. We will be a united wall of strength and that way the police can't touch us.'

'Peaceful protest?' the younger boy says mockingly, 'What good will that do?'

'It will stop one of us getting knifed for starters – you can't put anything past these skinheads, they are out for a ruck – like at the football games,' Aazim replies.

The meeting is long and voices rise and fall as members of the assembly exchange heated debate about the logistics of their approach to the march. After an hour or so the conversations descend into mini squabbles across the floor until finally Kash steps up to the podium and hushes the crowd down.

'This is what is going to happen,' he says. 'We will meet on the corner of Villa Cross and Lozells Road at approximately 10am. Olive, you are in charge of banners – old sheets, that kind of thing. They should say Handsworth Youth Movement plus whatever slogan you want . We want them to know we are organised and not just a random gathering.'

'What about HERE TO STAY, HERE TO FIGHT like before? That's the slogan other groups like us are using, isn't it? None of this peaceful sissy stuff.'

'We have evolved,' says Kash abruptly. 'Fight does not have to mean violence.' He continues reading out a list of instructions and locations, delegating roles to some of the inner circle.

'Anila, you can inform the police that we are planning this demonstration. They can't stop us but if we tell them it might be better.'

'The NF is half made up of off-duty Pigs – we all know that. Telling them in advance – you might as well just phone that NF bastard Tyndall up,' Aazim says.

'Too right,' agree others in unison.

'There will be just a couple more opportunities to get together before the march so we can be unified when we arrive,' Kash says, bringing the meeting to a close. 'Those who don't agree with the tactics come and speak to me after this meeting and we'll see if we can come to some agreement, otherwise don't bother turning up on the day if you are just coming for the aggro.' Finally, he says for all in the room to hear, 'Anila wait for me afterwards so we can discuss what you say to the police.'

From the corner of her eye, Anila sees Marcus heading towards the exit. He is deep in conversation with Olive Benjamin and Anila feels an urge to catch up with them and be in their company. Instead, she stays rooted to the spot as the room empties around her. When the last few men move away from Kash and drift towards the exit a hush fills the room. Anila edges towards the nearest wall and into the shadows; she is uncomfortable in the cavernous empty space and the wall offers solidity. She looks around the room for any remaining people but sees only the silhouette of Kash standing on the opposite side of the room with his back to her. She feels nervous and wonders if she has time to slip out of the exit and catch up with Marcus and Olive or whether she should make some excuse to leave about being needed at home by a certain time, but before she has a chance to weigh up the possibilities Kash appears beside her. Anila is startled by his sudden presence but it is too late to hide her alarm.

'Thanks for staying,' Kash says but she can barely hear him above the loud pounding in her chest.

Kash stands so close she can again feel his breath on her face. This time there is an unsavoury tang to it and she tries to step backwards to distance herself but finds she is already against the wall.

'So what about the police?' she stammers. 'What? Who do I call?'

'We can talk about that later,' Kash says. His face is so close now that she is breathing in his breath. Anila moves her face to the side, away from him. 'C'mon,' Kash says pushing himself against her and shifting her face back to centre with his hand, 'you are an attractive girl, Anila. Even with that short hair.'

'You're hurting me, get off,' Anila says firmly, but Kash pushes his lips onto hers so she cannot speak. She shoves him away with the palms of her hands, but her strength is diminished and he is back up against her almost immediately; his whole body is pressed onto her so she is pinned to the wall. He fumbles with the buttons on her jumpsuit.

'Girls wear such stupid clothes,' he says irritably as Anila tries to shove him away again. 'C'mon, Anila,' he says, 'I know you want this as much as me. I have seen the way you look at me. Don't be a baby now.'

'No!' says Anila firmly. 'I am not ready for this. Not yet, not here.'

Kash laughs and a drop of his saliva lands on her forehead.

'Ahh you want me to take you to dinner first and then book a nice hotel?' Anila tries to turn her face again to avoid his mouth but Kash yanks it back towards him. 'You want this, Anila. Don't deny it,' he says as he unbuckles his belt with one hand whilst keeping her pinned against the wall with the other. Anila struggles to free herself from him but his weight is on her and she can't move. Her stomach churns.

'Please don't,' she pleads but Kash pulls down the side of her jumpsuit and smirks before shoving his hand between her legs. She winces and begins to scream. Kash forces his tongue into her mouth to silence her.

'Don't be stupid, Anila,' he says when she tries to bite down on his tongue, 'this is what happens between men and women. Come, I'll be gentle.' Anila takes in a deep breath of air and tries to steady herself. 'That's better,' Kash says and starts to kiss her mouth again. The sourness of him makes her gag and she pushes at him with all her strength once more but it is still not enough to shift him. She tries to scream again but she is mute. Then, it is too late and he is heaving and panting, his face contorted as he bashes her against the stony wall. The pain is searing, like a blade cutting through her, and she closes her eyes and clenches her fists, desperate for it to be over. When he has finished, Kash steps backwards, spits on the ground beside them and wipes his mouth with the back of his hand. A small whimper escapes from Anila as her voice returns as a puny thing. She pulls her clothes around her body and she begins to weep, trembling uncontrollably. After a minute she dries her tears with her arm, bends over and vomits. Bile stings her throat and the pain between her legs begins to burn as if her whole body is engulfed by fire.

'Sort yourself out,' Kash says roughly, turning away from her. And then, more softly, 'It'll be better next time. You'll get used to it. The first time is always a bit difficult.' He walks away casually and is almost at the exit when he looks over his shoulder and shouts, 'Lock up will you? Oh, and don't wear that stupid thing next time. A skirt or dress would suit you much better, Anila.'

Chapter 24

August is suddenly unbearable as each day becomes more sticky and more humid with no respite from the heat. Days drag on and on for members of the Agarwal household, with each of them acutely aware of the close proximity of the bodies of the others. Heat radiates from them in the small rooms of the Church Street house and intensifies in the areas where they reside most often, collecting as stagnant air in the downstairs rooms where the breezes are more hard to come by. All over the house, windows are wedged open with blocks of wood or rolled up newspapers by Usha at the crack of dawn. She closes them when she is ready for bed late in the evening after all the chores have been done. The attic room is the warmest of all the rooms – cramped with the constant presence of the three teenage sisters, none of whom have ventured out of the house for days in spite of the weather. The piles of worn-once clothes and the dirty-washing basket stuffed with used underwear and sweaty tee-shirts exudes a pervasive odour reminiscent of PE changing rooms.

It is 10.30am and the sun is streaming in through the skylight. All three girls lay on their beds in nighties. Only Anila has a cover on her – a cotton bedspread pulled up high to envelop her head as well as body.

'Not like Nils to sleep late,' says Kamela. 'Do you know what's up with her? She's been properly stroppy these last few days. And just stuck up here the whole time.'

'Perhaps she's worried about her exams. Don't the results come out any day?'

'Nah, she doesn't care about those – not now she is a born-again militant. Wish she'd get over it whatever it is. She is being a right miserable cow.'

'Yeh I know – she is the one that has kept us all going the last few months.'

'What would you know, swanning around your fancy uni with your fancy friends?'

'Fuck off, Kam. Of course I know – why do you think I can't wait to get back?'

'Copping out – that is what you're are doing. Out of sight, out of mind and all that. Anila is right, you don't even think about us once you are away.'

'Why are you picking on me all of a sudden? You've been hanging around the house for months feeling sorry for yourself – you don't have to.'

'Don't be a bitch, Nina. You know what happened to me, and I went back to college for the last couple of days of term because Mom asked me to. It wasn't easy you know, not like for you.'

'You think it's easy for me? At least you lot are together. No one even knows that I had a brother called Billy up there and that is not easy. It's like I am betraying him. Every little Indian lad I see reminds me of him. It's worse if you are far away but I have to get on with it. We all do what we have to do, Kamela, and it isn't the same for everyone.'

'Yeah but you never phone when you are there – don't you think that upsets Mom, and Dad?'

'Don't guilt-trip me, Kam. I am just living my life the best way I can. Not everyone can hang around here being miserable – you and Kavi have been doing enough of that for everyone, not to mention Dad. And now Anila has joined the party. I don't think it will do Mom any good if I phone every time I feel a bit shit.'

'Perhaps you should phone when you don't feel shit then.'

'Fuck off, Kam.'

'Fuck off yourself Miss friggin' clever clogs,' Kamela turns up the volume on the radio and sings along loudly to *Come On Eileen* which is now blaring out.

'I hate this song. They used to be good once,' Nina says grumpily from across the room. She wipes a bead of sweat off her nose and returns to her letter writing.

'La di dah – not much of a student band, eh? Not moody enough or Northern enough I suppose. See, even us thick, ignorant Brummies know what's what in Studentland!'

Nina ignores her.

Anila pulls her pillow taut over her head to muffle the sound of the radio, and the sound of her sisters.

Usha pegs out a row of white sheets on the line and, without a breeze, they hang down rigid, almost touching the ground even though the line has been propped up with an old broomstick on a brick. It is still morning but the sun is beating down hard on the parched garden. Usha looks around at the patchy grass and dehydrated hedges and at the discarded bike wheels and bits of plastic toys salvaged from nearby derelict houses. She recalls a moment of looking on unseen as Billy and Kavi sat together on the grass engrossed in a go-cart building project just a few weeks before the accident. Kavi was taking charge and imparting his previous go-cart building experience to his younger brother who hung onto every word. The memory is ephemeral, drifting away before she can cement it in her mind. A powder-blue butterfly flutters around her face and she waves it away, watching as it fades into the distance and disappears over the unkempt hedgerow that separates this garden from the next.

'You alright, Mom? You look like you are a million miles away.' Nina's voice startles her. 'Is there any bread? I need something to eat.'

Usha looks at her daughter, 'Where are your sisters?' She says. 'We need to talk, all of us, we need to do something.'

'What you on about, Mom?'

'Nina, I am worried about this family,' says Usha. 'It is over a year now since Billy died and there isn't a second when he isn't in my mind but I know that we have to keep on living and moving forwards. I am worried that some of you are not doing that.'

'I just want some toast that's all, Mom. This is all a bit heavy isn't it?'

'Oh Nina, sometimes you are so grown up and other times you are like a small child. It is the same with Kamela and Kavi and I thought Anila would be okay with her new friends and her interest in political things but even she seems to be slipping back down. What is wrong with her, do you know?'

'Oh she'll be fine. Probably nervous about her results. Hey, or maybe she has a crush on someone,' Nina laughs nonchalantly.

Usha scowls at her daughter and for the first time she notices the new way Nina is wearing her eyeliner – in thick black lines below and inside the lower lid as well as a long line out towards her hairline from the edges of her eyes, just like the khol surma Bibi applied to her own eyes when she was a baby.

'So, is there any bread then?' Nina says and then, as if an afterthought adds, 'By the way, I am thinking of going back to Leeds early. Looking for a part-time job before all the other students arrive. Plus they need me to join a house-share as soon as possible. It's in Headingley – a nice area. It will get snapped up if we don't take it.'

Usha continues to look at Nina. She feels as though her eldest daughter has dropped in from another planet. Before she has a chance to respond about the bread or the return to Leeds, Nina has disappeared back into the house.

'You not going to get up today, Anila?' Kamela shouts above the music on the radio. She tries to sound cheerful. 'It's nice outside again. Warm and that.' Anila doesn't respond. Kamela sits on the edge of her sister's bed, 'C'mon Nils. What's going on? It's not like you to stay in bed this long. You've hardly said a word for days. Has something happened to your group? Is it that Jamaican lad, the good looking one? Has something happened between you? I won't tell anyone, promise?'

Anila turns over to face the wall, the pillow still wrapped around her head.

'You ill or something? Shall I get Mom?'

'Leave me alone,' Anila mumbles from under the bedsheet, just audible enough for her sister to hear.

Kamela gets up from the bed to return to her task of applying concealer to the scar which is still visible under the strands of long hair framing her face. As she stands up, a fresh red blood stain is revealed on the crumpled white sheet.

'I think you need a jam-rag,' Kamela says casually before moving back across the room.

Anila sits up and rubs her puffy eyes. She looks at the blood stain on the bed beside her.

"Thank god for that,' she says without thinking.

Kamela stares at her sister.

'What the hell have you been up to, Anila?'

'Go away, Kamela. I was just late... and I wanted it out the way before the march next week that's all.'

Usha collects bits of debris that litter the garden and makes a pile near the tree towards the back wall. Beyond the wall is the state-run nursery school where Billy went for a short while, two or three mornings a week until he was school-age. He had been at home up until that point, and as the others were all at school by then, this was the first time Usha had had the time to play with one of her babies unhindered by the needs of another child. Usha knew at the time that Billy most likely needed some playmates his own age, so she took him to the nursery although she would have preferred to keep him with her. Now she avoids looking at the nursery over the back wall as it reminds her too much of Billy, but she can't prevent the babble and the giggles of the pre-schoolers at playtime reaching her ears, especially in the summer months. She listens in on them like a spy, wishing Billy's was one of the voices she could pick out of the din, just like she used to.

In the summer holidays, the nursery is only open to the little ones in the morning and then, at lunchtimes, it doubles up as a sort of soup kitchen, serving up free school dinners throughout the holidays to local children in workless families to ensure they get at least one proper meal in the day. Usha has noticed that this year the queue for these holiday handouts has grown substantially and when Mukesh first lost his job her fear was this might happen to them too, with all the neighbours seeing her children standing in the queue like waifs. As the weeks passed by, the fear retracted and only Kavi would be eligible now that school was over for Anila, and there was no way Kavi would queue for a meal like that even if they were entitled; he would rather go hungry. This was a consolation to Usha.

Usha takes the yard brush from the small brick outhouse on the exterior side of the bathroom and begins to sweep up the sandy dust that has accumulated on the path of the side-return. The dust rises up in small clouds and she begins to cough.

'You want to damp it down first, you know?' Brenda appears behind her. 'Put water on it so the dust doesn't get all over the place. My nan told me that little trick. Would never have thought of it myself. Anyhow, how are you, bab? Cleaning the garden? That's a good sign. I bet it's a while since anyone has really used this garden, eh?'

Usha smiles at her friend. She has long overcome her irritation with Brenda's unintentional condescending manner.

'Hello Brenda,' she says.

'Alright, bab, got time for a cuppa?'

'Yes, okay. I will put the kettle on.'

'Let's have it out here, it's so nice,' says Brenda, pulling a wooden chair out of the kitchen door onto the uneven pathway of the side-return.

Upstairs in the attic room, Kamela has switched off the radio and put a single on the record player instead to accompany her as she folds the bits of clean washing sent up by Usha in a plastic bag a few days earlier. The lively song is followed by a crackling as the needle gets stuck in the groove. Across the room, Anila is still weeping quietly beneath the sheet.

'What's wrong, Anila?' Kamela asks again with genuine concern.

Silence.

Kamela puts down the tee-shirt she is folding and goes over to Anila's bed.

'Anila, have you had it off with someone?' She asks bluntly. Anila doesn't answer.

'Blimely, that'll be you and Nina with just me left out,' Kamela continues, jokingly. 'Who'd have thought it? Indian girls your age doing that so young – after everything we were told, to not even to look at boys, never mind having it off with them – at just sixteen. They'll never be able to fix you up with a doctor or a dentist now.'

'Go away, Kam,' Anila says.

'Sorry, I'm just kidding you. I didn't mean anything by it. Bravo, I say. It's the modern world and all that, apparently – at least for some people it is anyway, I just wish everyone else agreed. I'm just surprised at you, that's all. Everyone thinks you're the good girl, sensible and that. I think most of them would expect it of me, but you? Funny that I don't even really like boys.'

Anila remains silent even though Kamela has left space for her to speak. After a moment Kamela continues.

'Is it that nice-looking Jamaican guy? Come on Anila, we haven't talked properly for ages... since before... Listen, you can tell me. I won't shout my mouth off, you know. You didn't about me and I won't forget that.'

Silence.

Kamela carries on talking regardless.

'Things have been shit since Billy died but I was just beginning to feel like it could get a bit better, you know? And that is partly to do with you – I was just thinking the other day how brilliant you have been – getting on with stuff and getting involved with politics and that. I wish I could be like you. Don't let some man trouble get in the way of you changing the world, kiddo.'

Anila pokes her head over the sheet.

'It isn't what you think, Kam,' she says softly, wiping the moisture from her face with the corner of the sheet.

'What then?'

'Nothing. It's nothing really.'

Just at that moment Nina crashes into the room with a piece of half-eaten toast in her hand.

'You shouldn't be eating that up here,' Kamela says coldly, 'you know Mom is paranoid about mice coming into the bedroom – nothing with crumbs allowed!'

'Piss off, Kamela.'

Kamela jumps up from the bed.

'C'mon misery guts,' she says to Anila, 'I'll put on one of those rubbish records you like to cheer you up.' She starts flicking through the small pile of seven-inches and settles on one with a black and white two-tone cover.

Anila pulls the sheet back over her head and rolls over towards the wall.

Usha and Brenda are on their second cup of tea as they sit in the sunshine of the side return discussing the meeting they are organising together. It is due to take place in just a few days time.

'I put the leaflet in the window of Lavery's shop,' says Brenda, 'He didn't charge or anything. They usually do – twenty-pence a week, I think.'

'Oh no, maybe too many people will come if you do that. We don't have room for so many.'

'Ah, I wouldn't be worrying about that, bab. We'll be lucky if a handful turn up.'

'Really? Don't you think the other mothers will want to help the children around this area?'

'It's not really about that is it? People can't be bothered. And anyway some won't want to come to an Indian house and that.'

'What do you mean?'

'Well they have funny ideas. They might think something weird will happen.'

Usha is taken aback, puzzled by the thread of conversation.

'She's right,' says Nina through the open kitchen door as she clunks around making more toast.

'People in the area know us,' says Usha, 'they won't have a problem coming into our house.'

'You're expecting white women to come into our house and not turn their noses up at the smell of curry? You live in a bubble, Mom. Out there they think we practice voodoo and eat snakes. Even at university people have some strange views about us.'

'Don't be ridiculous, Nina. Indian people have lived in this country for many years now and English people are not as ignorant as you think.'

'Well she has a point, bab,' chips in Brenda. 'Some of them round here do have some funny ideas about you lot. I say to them, it's just the same you know, same set of problems and worries about money, jobs and the kids, but they seem to think you lot live in a different world from the rest of us.'

'But we have lived here, in Lozells, for almost twenty years, people know us in the community,' Usha says in disbelief. 'I know there is racism from those skinhead types and from the police but the neighbours, well they always smile and say hello to me.'

'Yeah but it's different coming into one of your houses. People don't like what they don't know about around here – they don't like strangeness.'

'We are not exactly strange, Brenda,' says Nina from the kitchen.

'I know that, bab,' says Brenda, 'but there are plenty around here that haven't even been in a Paki shop, never mind one of your houses.'

Nina leans on the door frame eating the slice of toast staring at the two older women.

'We are not Pakis, Brenda. Anyway, that's racist in itself thinking we are all from Pakistan. You white people think we are all the same and all bloody inferior, that's the problem. Pakistan is a different country to India; besides, Paki is a derogatory term you know, whether you are from Pakistan or not.'

'A what term? You use such long words now you are at university, Nina. Anyhow, sorry I didn't mean to sound offensive, I was just saying...'

'Nina,' Usha interjects sternly, 'I am very proud that you are the first in this family, probably even in this community, to go to university. I know you are very clever and you are learning many new things about the world, things we don't know or understand, but that does not mean you can be rude. Please say sorry to Brenda, she is my best friend and she is not a racist like those others you are talking about.'

Brenda blushes when Usha acknowledges the importance of their friendship. Nina shrugs her shoulders, mutters a desultory 'sorry' and heads back inside.

'She is going back to university tomorrow,' says Usha by way of an apology.

Chapter 25

On the day of the skinhead march, thirty or so Handsworth Youth Movement members gather on the corner of Villa Cross and walk in unison towards Hockley Hill where they stand side by side, pushed together so it is difficult to move either one way or another. A caustic smell permeates the air around them and a number of people pull up the necks of their tee-shirts over their mouths and noses or cup their hands over their faces. More members arrive and join the crowd including Aazim, who shouts loudly as he joins the throng.

'Friggin' poison spewing out from that factory. You'd think they'd give it a break on a Saturday,' he says.

Anila's nose and eyes begin to itch. She tries to release a hand so she can rub her face but both arms are pinned to her sides by the bodies leaning against her. She blinks and moves her head from side to side to try and whip up a slight breeze to ease the discomfort. Across the crowd, directly in front of her, Marcus and Olive hold up the red and black banner bearing the words NAZI SCUM OFF OUR STREETS. Around them others hold smaller banners with other slogans which have been hastily taped or tied onto poles and sticks that morning on dusty floor of The Shoe.

Olive had phoned the Agarwal house two or three times in the last week after Anila had not turned up for the last couple of meetings at The Shoe. Anila hadn't told anyone what had happened that day with Kash – what he had done to her – and instead told an inquiring Usha that she had stomach ache when questioned about the hours she was spending in the bath or in bed in daylight hours. Olive had last phoned at 8.30am this very morning and then, when Anila still wouldn't take the call, she had turned up on the doorstep with a couple of the other girls from the group.

'Your commie mates are here, Anila,' Kavi shouts up the stairs. Anila is still in her nightclothes.

'Tell them I'm sick,' she yells back, loud enough for them all to hear.

'She's sick!' Kavi says and closes the door.

'Tell her we'll see her there – at the march. We're meeting at Villa Cross or she can meet us in Hockley, near the flyover. She knows where, and when. Tell her we need her there,' Olive shouts through the letterbox.

A few minutes later Kavi is hovering on the threshold of the attic room.

'Is it that march thingy today?'

'What do you care, Kavi?'

'Aren't you going? You've been planning it for weeks... months, haven't you?'

Anila ignores him but Kavi continues to stand in the doorway. A moment passes before he speaks again.

'Listen, Anila, I know I haven't really said good stuff about what you're doing but I do think it's good that you are doing it. And, well it's helping isn't it? I mean it's bringing people together to fight a common cause – and well, it might make a difference one day.'

Less than two hours later Anila is looking straight into an army clad in Union Jacks marching directly towards her; it is a sea of faces red with anger and hatred. She has never seen a large gathering of white people together like this, standing together as a unit, at least not without police uniform. A lot of the shoppers in the Bull Ring are white people looking for cheap vegetables and cheap clothes in the Rag Market but the crowds in the Bull Ring are whites mingled with black and brown faces too – everyone in it together. The white people marching towards Anila and her group now are different, she recognises this immediately. They identify as the National Front and they are a tribe of tattooed warriors with cerise-coloured faces, shaven heads, black leather boots and Union Jack flags. They have messages of hate daubed across foreheads and knuckles and chests and symbols of fascism proudly displayed across their bodies like an arsenal of weapons. They snarl at the ordinary passers-by and spit directly at sari-clad grandmas who lift up the folds of their skirts and run in the opposite direction away from this menacing group of shorn-haired men whose voices ring out in a football-mob-type chant.

THERE AIN'T NO BLACK IN THE UNION JACK!

Intermingled with this self-styled army is a smattering of more ordinary looking white men in shiny two-piece suits from Burtons or C&A. Anila recognises one of them as the bloke from the estate agents on Villa Road. Then she wonders if the others are the seemingly benign office clerks and showroom salesmen she has walked past on window shopping trips into the city centre or perhaps even closer to home.

Across the wide road there is a smaller group of students who link arms and form themselves into a human barrier. They wave bumble bee flags bearing the words Anti-Nazi League and one or two beckon to the Handsworth Youth members to join them.

'No offence, mate,' shouts Aazim back to them, "we'll fight our own battles. Thanks for the support, though,' he adds, good-naturedly. The students nod approvingly.

Anila snakes her way through her own group and stands close to Aazim. Marcus is a few feet ahead of them and he nods a hello towards Anila through a gap in the crowd and quickly turns away to say something to Olive. As the skinhead army moves closer any gaps between the Handsworth Youth members are closed and they crush together to form a solid, unified mass. Someone grabs Anila's arm and a raspy voice whispers into her ear.

'We can't let these bastards get the better of us, Anila. This is it, sister.' The voice is Kash's and Anila immediately feels nauseous. She struggles to free her arm and turns to stare him in the face but Kash's eyes are fixed ahead. Anila follows his gaze – he is locked in a stare with a particularly ferocious looking skinhead in the front line of the opposition march. Anila is aware that the chanting around them has got suddenly louder and she feels giddy and claustrophobic – as if she might faint. Instead she bows her head, takes a sharp intake of breath and turns to face Kash.

'Don't you call me sister, you bastard,' she says loudly. 'Don't you ever come near me again.'

Kash stares blankly ahead, as if he hasn't heard what she has said.

'Don't ignore me,' Anila demands. People in the crowd around them turn to look, but beyond this immediate circle the chanting heightens in volume. Anila wants to say more, to shout and humiliate Kash but she is dumbstruck. Instead she raises her hand and brings it down in a sharp, hard slap against his cheek. Kash, visibly shocked by the slap, rubs the side of his face. Anila spits at him and turns to walk away down the aisle the stunned onlookers have instinctively created for her. She weaves her way through the crowd to the front row of the protesters without looking back. Around her the chanting grows louder and louder, seemingly heading towards a crescendo.

'Paki bastards.'

'Niggers go home – go back to the jungle where you belong.'

And from her side of the road:

'Fascist scum out of Handsworth.'

Anila joins in the chanting and her voice feels strong and clear. The chanting from both sides of the divide mingles into one loud cacophony which appears to continue rising in pitch until, all of a sudden, the scarlet face of a man from the other side is right up against her, staring straight at her. The man has teeth missing and his eyes are steely blue and appear to bulge out from his skull. Anila is transfixed by his smooth, pink scalp – his breath smells of leather and vomit.

'What you fucking staring at, wog-bitch?'

Anila steps backwards but she is blocked by the wall of bodies behind her. The man grabs hold of her arm and pulls her forward, away from her own frontline and towards that of the NF members in front of her. Others from her own side rush forward too and try to pull her back towards them. Without thinking Anila swings a kick directly between the legs of the man, hitting him straight in his groin and he crumples into a heap on the ground, cupping his crotch with both hands and groaning. Those that have witnessed the kick begin to cheer.

'Good on you, sister,' someone shouts from the back of the group but the voice is drowned out by a roar in front of them.

'That's it,' shouts one of the skinheads, 'we're going in,' and the skinheads begin to charge.

Anila's group is outnumbered, even with the help of the students who have rushed across the road to join in. Her friends scatter, dispersing in all directions, and she runs towards the line of policemen on the far side of the scuffle. Before she can reach them there is a great thump in the small of her back and she stumbles into a bin on the pavement, bent double with pain. The noise around her is now at fever pitch.

'Get out here you Paki bitch.'

A hot and breathy voice is shouting in Anila's ear. She looks around and the man she kicked just moments before is now looming over her. He grabs her neck by the skin and pulls her out from behind the overflowing bin. She tries to struggle free but he has a firm grip and before she can shout out for help he slams her face down onto the hard concrete below. All of a sudden Marcus is in front of her, he pulls the attacker off her and shoves him into the road. Anila's head throbs but she is able to lift it just in time to see two police men stomping towards them. Marcus has disappeared into the crowd – she can just make him out ahead of her, mingled in with others of their group who are fighting off two burly men, laying into them with punches and kicks. A police officer pulls her up and a trickle of warm blood seeps down her forehead, dripping from her chin onto her tee-shirt.

'Ow, watch out, you're hurting me,' she says as the police officer drags her roughly across the road. Again, she struggles to free herself but she is too weak and battered, and before she can muster any strength to release herself she is bundled into a waiting police van. Inside the van, Kash, Olive, Aazim, Marcus and others are squeezed into the tight space. Each of them is bruised or bleeding and no-one speaks. Through the tinted windows Anila watches as the police officers steer the skinheads back into line and the remaining Handsworth Youth members are shooed away with truncheons and shoves in the back. Meanwhile, a mixture of skinheads and their suited fellow-marchers circle the van, sneering at the occupants and raising one and two finger salutes. Anila puts her head on Marcus's shoulder and closes her eyes.

At two o'clock that afternoon the sun begins to break through a thin mist of white cloud above the zig-zag houses on Church Street. Usha is cleaning the kitchen windows with a ragged Silver Jubilee tea-towel and a spray can of Windolene in preparation for the meeting later that afternoon. An abrupt knock at the door makes her drop her cloth. She edges open the front door – this is her second visit from the police in little over a year.

'Mrs Agarwal, nothing to worry about but I'm afraid your daughter has managed to get herself into a bit of trouble,' the police officer says.

Usha dries her hands on her thighs, removes her apron and grabs her handbag from the end of the banister. She follows the policeman out of the house. On the other side of the road Elsie Meeson stands with Marie O'Connell and they stare at Usha, nodding their heads in an ambiguous gesture as she steps into the waiting police car.

Anila leaves Thornhill Road Police station hand in hand with her mother. She looks around for other members of the Movement on the street and catches a glimpse of the back of Marcus's head being pushed into an orange Cortina by a thunder-faced man who can only be his father. A frumpy woman sits in the front passenger seat staring stonily ahead. A few paces ahead of Anila and Usha, Kash Ram walks alongside a young woman in a purple tie-dye headscarf and a simple lilac salwar kameez. She is as slight as Kash except for the small, neat bump jutting out beneath her tunic. The couple walk with their arms interlocked. Anila takes a couple of seconds to absorb the scene in front of her. Kash looks across at her and nods in a matter-of fact way.

'See you at the next meeting, sister,' he says, just as he does after every meeting. His young wife turns briefly and glances at Anila. She tucks loose strands of glossy black hair into her casually worn chunni then turns away without a glimmer of expression. Anila grips her mother's hand tightly.

Chapter 26

At five o'clock, Brenda and Usha stand side by side next to the living room window. They peer out from behind the net curtains into the street, craning their necks to see if anyone may be heading in the direction of the house from further up the road or beyond.

'It's like that time before you have a party and you start doubting your friends – whether they are real mates or not – thinking no one will come. Do you know what I mean, bab?' Brenda says jovially.

'I don't think so,' says Usha.

'I remember at my twenty-first, waiting and watching the clock and thinking no-one liked me and then suddenly, after a couple of Babychams loads of people were in my mom's kitchen dancing to Chubby Checker and having a ball. I don't think I knew half of them.'

Usha looks at her friend blankly.

'Brenda, I was married at nineteen,' she says. 'Indian girls didn't go to these sorts of parties.'

'Suppose not, bab.'

They watch as a woman that neither of them recognises tentatively approaches Usha's front door. The woman hesitates before she knocks.

'Here we go,' says Brenda as Usha heads out the room to answer the door.

Five minutes later three more women, all strangers, congregate in the small hallway waiting to be shown where to go. They have arrived together and chit-chat amongst themselves, ignoring Usha.

'This way please,' Usha says, and points them through the nearest doorway into the living room where the first arrival stands awkwardly near the fireplace.

Bibi arrives next carrying a package of freshly cooked pakora wrapped in tin-foil. More women begin arriving soon after and of the half dozen or so new faces that have turned up most are white or black. Other than Usha's own mother, the only other Asian person is a pleasant, squat woman with a moon-shaped face. She is dressed in a traditional beige-coloured Punjabi suit and introduces herself as Shilly. Usha tries to guess her age but finds it difficult, especially as her plump, reddened cheeks make her seem younger than she probably is. It takes Usha a few minutes to place her as the woman from Surjeet Singh's General Stores, a shop on Lozells Road. As Shilly enters the living room, a couple of the other women nod in mutual recognition. Shilly stands next to Bibi and the two women exchange pleasantries in Punjabi.

Kamela and Kavi sit behind the banister at the top of the stairs watching the arrivals,

'Who the hell are they all?' Kamela whispers.

'There's that O'Connell one from across the road,' says Kavi. 'I didn't think she'd come – she always seems to be looking down her nose at us, silly cow.'

'Shush, Kavi, she'll hear you.'

'I don't give a shit,' says Kavi.

'You have such a dirty gob, Kavi – you should learn to control it.'

'Fuck off, Kamela. I speak how I want. Besides, you're always swearing and that too. Anyway, it's true, the O'Connells do look down on us. However low they are, we are lower to them so they can be all snooty with us. They are the scum for most people but we are their scum.'

The living room door is still ajar and Kavi and Kamela listen as Usha directs some of the guests towards the settee. Before they arrived she had tried to spruce the old settee up with a bright orange batik-print. The throw has retained the aroma of the Indian marketplace from which it originated, even after many years stored in a suitcase under Usha's bed, and that slightly musky smell now permeates the room. Some of the women sniff to place the smell and rub their noses as if averting a sneeze.

Usha pokes her head out of the living room door and looks up towards the place where Kavi and Kamela sit concealed from view.

'Come and make tea please you two. I know you are just there.'

The siblings drag themselves down the stairs.

'Where is Anila?' Usha asks in a soft voice when they reach the bottom step, 'Is she okay?' She directs the question to Kamela, who shrugs her shoulders and heads towards the kitchen. 'And your father? Is he back yet? He went out hours ago.' This time she addresses Kavi but he also shrugs and turns to follow Kamela down the hallway. Usha whispers after him, 'Keep your eyes open for him, Kavi, please. He may have been in the pub again and I don't want to be shamed with his drunkenness in front of these strangers.' Kavi doesn't respond. 'Bring the biscuits too please,' Usha calls after him a bit louder.

'Blimey, she's pushing the boat out isn't she?' Kavi announces, pointing at the two packets of Custard Creams and a packet of Ginger Nuts on the worktop.

'Brenda bought the biscuits,' says Kamela.

Upstairs in the attic bedroom, Anila lies on her bed flicking through the pages of the book Marcus gave her. Her face and shoulder throb with pain despite the aspirin and the bag of frozen peas wrapped in a tea-towel given to her by Usha when they returned from the police station. She daren't look in the mirror, knowing her face to be a bruised mess. She tries to focus on the words in the book but the print is too small and hurts her eyes. The descriptions of plasterers and carpenters bring to mind the men that work alongside her father at Hardiman's. The book holds no interest for her and its sheer size is overwhelming. On the radio, Shalimar sing *I Can Make You Feel Good* and Anila tries hard to order the thoughts that race around her head.

In the kitchen, Kavi and Kamela are buoyed by the activity in the house and they chat in a way that has become a rarity amongst the family members.

'So, do you know who any of them actually are? Except the obvious ones of course,' Kavi asks, picking up their conversation from earlier.

'Just people from round and about. Brenda probably bought them all a drink in the Royal Oak to get them here.'

'Not people, just ladies Kamela. All, you know, mostly well… not Indians are they? There's Bibi but she doesn't even speak enough English to know what we're on about never mind Brenda and the like. You know, I think Brenda is the only white grown-up that's ever been in the house before and now look, there's loads of them. And black ones too. And all ladies.'

'Women, Kavi, not ladies. That's like some Victorian shit, like Dickens or George Eliot or whatever. Old fashioned shit.'

'Who? Okay, women then. But it's all good isn't it? I mean, seeing Mom all excited about having these ladies here and all those others coming here trying to do something,' says Kavi.

'You've changed your tune. I thought you said it was all a waste of time before, to Anila.'

'Yeah, but those lot she hangs around with are just full of it. They think they are some kind of revolutionaries or something but as far as I can see they just hang around that piss-smelly warehouse talking bollocks.'

'Nina says they are part of something bigger – a youth movement across the country, you know like CND or the civil rights stuff in America but young people – young black people like us. She said there is another group like them in Bradford.'

'We aren't black, Kam, in case you hadn't noticed. Last time I looked I was still "cup of tea" brown.'

'Nina says we are, politically and that – black I mean. That group in Bradford is mostly Pakis and Bengalis and that but they call themselves Black. I don't really get it but she says we have to define ourselves and not let the establishment do it for us.'

'Bollocks! Calling ourselves a different colour and going on marches isn't going to stop kids like us being treated like we don't belong here and don't deserve a future. And look at the state of Anila today – that isn't what I thought would happen when I persuaded her to go this morning.'

'You persuaded her?'

'Yeah, well she didn't need much persuading really. It's just that she seems so miserable these days and then I realised that I kind of missed that enthusiasm that she's had these last few months for her group. She's been sort of positive when everything else has been so negative. But after she got smashed about today I don't think it will do much good for kids like us – Indian kids and that. I mean the mommy-jis and daddy-jis aren't going to let their Bimlas and Sanjays get involved now, are they?'

'It's not just about Indian kids, Kavi. That's the whole point. Kids in London, or Bristol or Manchester, black, white or Indian, don't have work or money or anything. Mrs Thatcher and her government are making sure of that. That's why there's all these riots and stuff. That's what Nina says anyway. I suppose she knows better than we do now she goes go to an actual university! At least Anila is trying to change things. Getting beaten up is just a setback – she'll get over it.'

'What, like you did?'

'Fuck off, Kavi.'

'Well, they can't change the fact that we are stuck here in Lozells, the arse-end of Handsworth which is the arse-end of Birmingham itself. We don't have much of a chance to get out or be something better.'

'Nina has,' says Kamela.

'Maybe, but they are only going to let one or two Ninas into the universities before they find a way to shut those doors on us too. At least we're not in India,' continues Kavi after a pause, 'I suppose we might have even less chance than fuck-all there.'

'Bloody hell, Kavi, I thought I was finding it hard but you definitely need to sort yourself out. It's not healthy being that negative about everything.'

Five minutes later, Kavi and Kamela are standing by the living room door with the tray of tea and biscuits. The conversation in the room is stilted – small talk about streets and schools. The siblings enter the room and hand out the refreshments. Four women sit like sardines on the settee, pushed up together so close it is hard for them to release their arms and hands to take the cups from the tray. A large white woman sits in the only armchair available and the remaining women stand around awkwardly, not quite knowing what to do with themselves.

Marie O'Connell is staring at a calendar above the mantelpiece: the image depicted is a scene of a pale blue adolescent Krishna reclining by a lake watching buxom, semi naked courtesans frolic in the water. Marie is transfixed by the image and does not avert her eyes even when she reaches out to take a cup from the tray in front of her. Next to Marie stands Violet Murray, a stout Jamaican woman about the same age as Usha and Brenda. Violet has a kind but tired face and she breaks the small talk by declaring a sense of purpose in her high pitched crystal-clear tone.

'So, we is all here for a reason, Mrs Agarwal, shall we get on with it then?' She pronounces Agarwal as though the A is preceded with an H so it sounds like 'Hugarwal'. This amuses Usha and she smiles as she responds, nervously at first, looking towards Brenda for reassurance.

'I am worried about my children. Not just my children, our children, all the children around here. They have nowhere to go and nothing to do and this isn't good.' Usha's voice quivers as she speaks but the other women smack their teeth with tongues in agreement and she is encouraged to go on. 'This is a generation of young people that is currently without hope and we need to change that or there will be problems in the future. Already we have seen riots in our streets and people say there will be more. The teenagers have nothing to look forward to and a government that is ignoring them. This is the problem we are seeing all around us – not just in Handsworth and Lozells but all over the country. Maybe we can at least do something to help our neighbourhood, a small thing maybe but something at least so there are no more riots here.'

Kamela takes a seat on the arm of the settee, transfixed by her own mother. Kavi hovers around the edges of the room like a curious fly.

'I agree,' says Marie, 'but there are no jobs for any of us. My hubby has been on the dole for ten months now, and not for want of trying, mind, but plenty of us are in that boat, eh Mrs Agarwal?' Usha feels shame at the thought of all these strangers knowing that Mukesh is without a job and hanging about the pubs spending what little money he has managed to cling on to from his severance pay on beer and cigarettes. Marie continues to speak: 'So what the kiddies going to do when even the grown men don't have jobs? It's a crying shame the way this country is going.' She stares at Usha as she speaks.

'Well, that's why we wanted to have a meeting,' Brenda says, 'to come up with a plan to busy the teenagers so they have a sense of purpose, especially the ones that have left school and have nothing to do.'

'What are you suggesting, ladies?' Violet Murray says.

'They should all join the bloody army,' pipes up the large woman in the armchair. 'At least that way they could learn a few manners. Send them to the Falklands, that's what I say. They still need people out there to keep the Argies out. National Service is what they need, then they'll be able to give a bit back to the country instead of waiting for it to be handed on a plate to them.' She too addresses her comments directly to Usha.

Violet Murray sucks her teeth in response before speaking.

'Sending our young men to fights wars in far off lands we haven't even heard of, that don't make any sense.'

'If they are not prepared to fight for this country,' the woman says, 'then they shouldn't be here, they should go back to where they belong!'

'And where exactly do you think they should go? These young people were born in this country. We are part of the Commonwealth in case you hadn't noticed.'

'No point falling out, ladies,' Brenda says. 'We are talking about all the kiddies, not just the black ones or the white ones. We are all here for the same reason – to think of solutions, not to scrap.'

'Shame,' says Kavi from the corner of the room, 'I like a good lady-fight.' Usha, Kamela and Brenda all turn to scowl at him and Kavi grins back at them cheekily.

Anila switches off her music and sits on the steps outside the attic room straining to hear what is going on downstairs. After a few minutes she heads down the first flight and takes a seat at the top of the main stairs where she can hear much better. The voices downstairs are all unfamiliar except those of Brenda and Usha and there is a charge in the air that she recognises as similar to the atmosphere of the first meetings at The Shoe. After a few moments, Anila is distracted from the excited tones emanating from the women by a commotion in the kitchen – a clatter of something hitting the floor. She slips down the stairs and hallway, catching Kavi's eye in the opening of the living room doorway.

'It's a cat I think,' she says as her brother pulls a 'so what?' face at her.

In the kitchen, Mukesh is drinking a glass of water by the sink. There is an upturned saucepan on the floor beside him and thick orange liquid seeps from it, spreading out into a wide, coagulated puddle.

'What is that, Dad?' Anila asks as Mukesh turns to look at her. His shirt front is wet and his flies are open – a damp stain snakes around his thigh and down towards his knee. 'Bloody hell, Dad. You need to clean yourself up before all those women in the front room see you.'

'What women?' Mukesh mumbles.

Anila heads to the bathroom to look for a cloth to clean up the spillage. As she opens the bathroom door the strong waft of newly sprayed urine escapes into the air around her and she covers her nose and mouth with a cupped hand. It takes a moment for her to notice the wet splashes across the bathroom floor, on the toilet seat and in a small pool at the base of the toilet. She quickly closes the door.

'You're disgusting,' she says to Mukesh as he leans into the side of the sink to steady himself.

Anila runs down the hallway, grabs Kavi's arm and drags him towards the kitchen. 'You'll have to help me clean up, Dad has pissed all over the bathroom and there is dhal all over the floor,' she says. She pushes Kavi towards Mukesh and he attempts to usher his father out of the kitchen towards the bathroom at the back of the house.

'Those ladies will be coming in here soon,' Kavi says, 'and you don't want them to see you like this do you?'

'Who are these bloody ladies and women you are all talking about? This is my kitchen, why are you and your sister trying to remove me from it?'

'Just get out of here won't you, Dad? You're a bloody state. It's embarrassing,' Anila pleads.

'C'mon Dad,' Kavi adds, 'Mom is having a meeting and there are lots of strangers in the house. You really don't want them to see you like this,'

Mukesh seems oblivious to what his children are saying, instead he stares intently at Anila's face. Anila touches her cheek and recoils.

'Have you been fighting?' Mukesh asks.

Anila knows the purple bruising and the black eye look as terrible as they feel but she ignores the question.

'C'mon Dad, at least go upstairs and lie down,' she says.

Mukesh swipes his arm across the worktop and knocks two unopened packets of biscuits to the floor; one splits open and the biscuit crumbs scatter across the floor, adding to the mess.

'Fucking hell,' says Kavi.

'Don't you tell me what to do, Anila, or you Kavi. You children are the shameful ones here, fighting and swearing and hanging around with low-caste Chamar hooligans and Jamaicans with daggers.'

Kavi grabs his father's arm and pushes him towards the door. He is taller and stronger than Mukesh.

'You are pissed, Dad. You don't know what you are talking about. You're not making any sense. You had better go and sleep it off before you cause a scene.'

Mukesh struggles to release himself but cannot and the two of them stumble into the sink, knocking Anila out of the way as they fall.

'Let me go you bloody stupid boy,' Mukesh shouts as Kavi pulls him up from the floor.

'Sssh,' Kavi says abruptly, 'they'll hear you!' He claps one hand over his father's mouth and restrains him in a clinch from behind with the other. 'Go and close the living room door,' he says to Anila and she does as she is told. Kavi shoves Mukesh along the hallway and up the stairs towards the front bedroom, keeping one hand still firmly clasped over his mouth. Anila follows.

'Perhaps we should lock him in,' Anila suggests, taking the room key from the inside lock.

'Yep, good idea, sis. Soz, Dad but you need to sober up before we let you out. Why don't you get some sleep?'

Mukesh sits on the edge of the bed with his head in his hands. He mumbles something in Punjabi but the only word decipherable to Kavi and Anila is 'respect', muttered in English.

'I'll bring you a glass of water,' Anila says kindly as she leaves the room. Before she closes the door she glances back at her father and he looks up towards her with eyes that are glassy and distant. Anila locks the door behind herself and slips the key into the front pocket of her jeans.

In the living room, the women have agreed that something must be done to occupy the local young people to stop them 'going astray' as the armchair woman puts it. Suggestions as to what this may be have still not been discussed, superseded by tittle-tattle and local gossip. A couple of the women are already getting ready to leave, in time to get 'the tea on' they say.

'Shit,' says Anila to Kavi, 'we'd better go and clean up that mess in the kitchen before they all want another brew – it's been a while. You can wipe the bathroom down, Kavi.'

'Fuck off,' says Kavi, 'I'm not wiping up his piss.'

'Someone has to,' Anila insists and Kavi reluctantly follows her towards the kitchen. They close the kitchen door just as the living room door opens and Usha leads three of the women out of the front of the house.

'So,' says Shilly to the remaining women in the room, 'what exactly will be our plan to help the young people?'

'Well,' responds Brenda as Usha reenters the room, 'Usha has an idea about the Bomb Peck at the back of Wills Street, don't you, bab?'

'Um, yes,' says Usha quietly as she sits down in a vacated seat next to Bibi. 'I thought that the only thing they have to do around here is play at the Bomb Peck but it is just a collection of abandoned rubbish really. It isn't safe, I don't think, just remains of houses and bricks and metal and things. Perhaps we can get some of the businesses to give wood and other things and the young people can try and build a proper adventure playground, like the one in Newtown that the Council built. There was a picture in the Handsworth Times, did you see it? It can't be too difficult and maybe the Council people will help if they see we have a strong support from ordinary people in our communities.'

Kamela looks at her mother proudly, she has never heard her speak so eloquently to strangers before this day. Marie O'Connell speaks next.

'Well I think that could work. Some of the men could help too. My Derek would be up for it I reckon, and it will get him out from under me feet.'

'Yes, it is a good idea,' says Violet, 'but how will we convince the young people to do it? Many of them don't even go to that place or if they do it is only to smoke bad things away from their parents. They are too old for playgrounds.'

'Yes, but we could put up a basketball net, they all watch them Harlem Globetrotters don't they? And all ages play football. Plus we could have some benches so the girls would have a place to meet up and chat and that, a place to get together,' Brenda says.

'Maybe,' says Violet. 'We need a committee or something to make plans. I will be on it. We can't do it all in one meeting.'

'Yes you are right, bab,' Brenda says to Violet. 'This is just the start to see if people are interested. That's what me and Usha thought, didn't we Ush?'

Usha nods but she is distracted by a banging on the ceiling above their heads.

'What's that noise? Your hubby doing some DIY?' Marie asks.

Usha doesn't respond directly but instead says to Kamela,

'Go and see what this noise is, beta. Please tell whoever it is to stop until our meeting is finished. It won't be long.'

Anila and Kavi are already outside their parents' bedroom when Kamela arrives to join them just as the banging stops as unexpectedly as it started.

'Mom is really good down there – she has this great idea about the Bomb Peck and that. I've never heard her speak like that,' Kamela says before adding, 'Anyhow, what is going on up here?'

'Dad pissed himself so me and Anila locked him in the bedroom.'

'What?'

'He's drunk,' explains Anila. 'We didn't want him to spoil Mom's meeting so we locked him in. Do you think we should open it?'

'Nah,' says Kamela and before any of them can speak again they hear the sound of glass smashing in the room.

'Shit, he's broken the window,' Kavi says as Anila fumbles with the lock. When they open the door they see the window is wide open but seemingly intact. Instead, a whisky bottle lies smashed in glass shards across the floor under the open window and Mukesh is nowhere to be seen.

In the living-room, the women have agreed to meet the following week and Brenda has offered to phone the women that left early to let them know the plan and to encourage them to bring along others.

'Bloody hell!' Marie says suddenly and the others all turn to look at her. She is staring at the window towards the street. 'There's legs in your window, Mrs Agarwal, brown legs, look!'

Kavi, Anila and Kamela rush into the room just as the women turn towards the window where a pair of bare skinny legs dangle down from the frame, flanked at the top by white Y-fronts. As more of the body begins to appear and a torso is seen slowly edging downwards, the women gasp and Usha covers her face with her hands, peeping through slightly parted fingers.

'Kavi,' says Brenda taking control, 'go and help your dad so he doesn't hurt himself.' She then turns to the other women and says, 'Ladies, perhaps we should go into the kitchen to finish the meeting?'

'No way,' says Marie, 'this is bostin. I'm staying put.'

Mukesh is hanging down precariously with both hands gripping the narrow tiled shelf above the window frame. His white vest is tucked into his underpants and his stunned face stares directly in at the occupants of the room.

'Lord have mercy, it is him,' declares Violet Murray who stands at the back of the group. The women all turn away from the window and look at her quizzically.

'It is who?' Shilly asks.

'The man from the riot,' Violet says, not making much sense to the others in the room until she continues to explain. 'The man who saved the life of that poor boy who was burning to death when the riots happened last year on Lozells Road. This Indian man put out the flames with the shirt off his back when the rest of us were too shocked to move. He is a hero – the boy would surely have perished if he hadn't stepped forward.'

'Oh yes,' says Shilly, 'my husband, Surjeet is his friend. They were together that night. He told me all about the bravery of this man, your husband, Mrs Agarwal?'

'Darren, that's the boy – he's my neighbour's kid.' The woman who says this is the large woman occupying the armchair. She continues, 'He would have died for certain if your hubby hadn't of stepped in. That's what the doctors at the hospital told her anyhow.' Usha gawps at her and then at Mukesh in the window as he hangs down like a rag-doll in underwear.

Kavi is outside now and standing beneath his father with his hands clasped together to create a landing step of his palms. Mukesh steps safely into his son's hands and Kavi carries him like a child in his arms through the open house towards the kitchen. He closes the door behind them, away from the women in the living room who all stand in stunned silence staring at the now empty window-frame and beyond it to the small crowd of curious onlookers who have gathered on the street to watch the goings-on.

Chapter 27

Kavi runs the cold tap into the sink for a few seconds before putting a pint glass beneath it. He lets the water run until the glass brims over the sides and soaks his hand. Soon the cloudiness of the tap water disperses. Behind him Mukesh sits at the table, his expression is blank and Kavi wonders if he even realises how stupid he looks sitting there staring into space in his baggy vest and Y-fronts.

'Get me my cigarettes,' Mukesh says in monotone. Kavi does as requested, sprinting up the stairs to fetch the half-empty box of B&H from its usual resting place on the bedside cabinet in his parents' bedroom. The broken shards of the whisky bottle lay scattered across the floor and Kavi edges them towards the wall with the side of his foot. He grabs Usha's dressing gown from the back of the door before he leaves the room.

The kitchen is empty when he returns but he glimpses Mukesh in the side return through the window and he watches for a second as his father flicks a ladybird off his arm. Kavi then drags a chair out of the back door, hands over the cigarettes to Mukesh, places the dressing gown on the back of the chair and returns to the kitchen to search for some matches and pull out another chair.

'I killed Billy,' Mukesh says when Kavi hands him the matches.

Kavi catches his breath and places the dressing gown across his father's shoulders.

'I killed Billy by helping the boy on fire,' Mukesh continues. 'The way of the ambulance was blocked by me helping that boy, if it was a minute earlier or a minute later, Billy would be alive.'

Kavi, who had left the front room before Violet Murray's revelation, has no idea what his father is talking about.

'You're not making any sense, Dad. I think you need help, like mental stuff – to help you cope and that. Maybe you should visit All Saints for a bit.'

'You think I am mental, Kavi?'

'Well, let's face it, you have been a bit of a mess these last few months with the drink and that.'

'You think I am a drunk too?'

'I just mean I know it has been hard since Billy died, for all of us. The drinking has been worse, you've got to admit it.'

'Hard? You don't know just how hard it is losing your child, Kavi. I hope you never find out.'

'He was my brother – it has been hard for me too,' Kavi says angrily. 'The girls have got each other to talk to and Mom has Brenda but you haven't really got anyone and nor have I, that's why we are finding it harder.'

Mukesh looks at Kavi as though he has only just become aware of his presence. He holds the open cigarette packet out towards his son and Kavi takes one willingly, taken aback by the gesture.

'Thanks,' he mutters as Mukesh offers the matches.

Father and son smoke in silence, blowing sharp plumes in the direction of the dusty garden ahead. They continue to sit quietly until Mukesh's cigarette has burnt down to the filter. He drops it to floor and begins to speak again.

'I am responsible for the death of your brother and also the death of Naresh. I am the maker of my own tragedies.'

Kavi drags on the cigarette, trying hard to keep up with Mukesh's stream of consciousness.

'What are you talking about, Dad? You're not making any sense again.'

'Naresh and Billy were just eleven years old,' Mukesh continues, 'and if I wasn't dreaming of ras malai and cricket maybe Naresh would be alive... maybe I would have stayed in

India and not have come to this stupid country where I don't really belong, where there is no respect for elders and the children do as they please. Maybe, Billy too would be playing cricket in the sunshine, eating mangos and coconuts straight from the tree.'

'Who the hell is Naresh, Dad? What the hell are you on about?'

'He was my brother, Kavi. My beloved brother who left me, just like Billy left you. They were both too young and I should have stopped it happening both times.'

'What?'

Mukesh tells Billy about Naresh. It is a condensed version of the same story Usha shared with Brenda a few months after Billy died.

'Shit,' said Kavi, 'that is bad.'

'So you see Kavi, these things follow me. I bring bad luck.'

'Don't be silly,' says Kavi, 'how can either of those things be your fault? You were just a kid when your brother died and as for Billy, how could you have changed that? You aren't making sense. Besides, if you hadn't have come to this country none of us would be here anyway. I mean, you and Mom would, but not together like.'

The buttons on Usha's cerise pink dressing gown sparkle in the sunlight and Kavi stares at the strands of light that reflect from them and dance about on Mukesh's face. He looks on his father with overwhelming pity as Mukesh lights up another cigarette.

'I need whisky,' Mukesh says. There is desperation in his voice.

'You drink too much, Dad. Anyway, you broke the bottle, remember?'

'My flask is by the bed, get it for me.'

'You didn't kill anyone, Dad. You are mixing up grief with feeling sorry for yourself and instead of helping us all cope you are making a fool of yourself by drinking too much.'

Mukesh doesn't respond and instead covers his face with his hands. Kavi knows his father has started to cry.

'I'll get your whisky,' Kavi says. When he returns with the hip-flask, his father is blowing his nose loudly on the arm of Usha's dressing gown; streaks of snot cover the sleeve as it falls back into Mukesh's lap.

'Listen Kavi,' he says, grabbing the hip-flask from his son, 'I may be a drunk but I am not mental. I should have saved Naresh that night and maybe everything would have been different... better.'

'Why don't you tell me what happened?' Kavi says with genuine curiosity, 'I mean everything, before he fell off the roof?'

'Alright,' says Mukesh and he does, taking gulps of whisky as he speaks. Kavi listens patiently as his father describes the carefree childhood he shared with his peers before his life was shattered by tragedy. He tells stories of hot summers and the tree-climbing and the endless games of cricket. When he finishes speaking he closes his eyes and leans back in the chair, sighing out a long and audible breath. Kavi takes the hip-flask from his father's lap and shakes the remains into his own mouth, he then slumps back into his chair and allows the burning liquor to seep down his throat in small trickles. He continues to watch as Mukesh slips into sleep and he fixes on the black hairs on his father's undulating chest as they glisten in the fading sunlight. It has been a long day.

Chapter 28

In the dead of night, Anila awakes soaked in sweat. She kicks off the blankets and tries to get back to sleep. Her body and mind are exhausted by the day's events but sleep only returns in sporadic bursts, full of vivid images of Kash and the jeering face of the thug who beat her up the day before. Soon it would be morning and a creeping sense of panic begins to take hold of her at the thought of facing another day.

Dawn arrives unexpectedly, filling the room with a hazy pink light. Anila sits upright, giving up on sleep and wondering whether the creaking of the stairs might disturb the others if she creeps down to make herself a cup of tea. She decides not to bother and instead tentatively begins to draft a letter on a sheet of paper torn from an exercise book.

Dear Nina,

Something happened a few weeks ago and I need to tell someone. You are not here so it will be easier for me to tell you rather than anyone else (meaning Kamela and Mom of course).

I know you are going to think I am a stupid little girl when you have finished reading this but I hope you will give me more credit than that and understand that the reason I got myself in this situation was not because I am daft or a slut but rather because I am trying to make something good come out of the bad that is all around Lozells and Handsworth – the racism and the boredom and

*the hopelessness that we have to live with around
here. By joining the Handsworth Youth Movement I
really thought I could be part of changing all that
or at least drawing attention to it so people like us
(the ones that don't get a chance to go away like
you – you don't know how lucky you are!) and the
other kids around here aren't forgotten. Anyway,
I am sorry I couldn't tell you this when you were
here but I think you will understand how difficult
that would have been for me – we don't really talk
in this house about anything important since Billy.
Plus my period hadn't started by then so that was
an extra massive worry. Thank god I don't have to
think about that anymore...'*

Once Anila starts writing she finds she cannot stop and the
words keep flowing out of her until all is said and there are no
words left. She ends the letter by describing the incidents at
the march, the way she had slapped Kash in front of the crowd,
getting beaten and arrested, and finally about Mukesh hanging
in the window in his underwear in full view of the women at
Usha's meeting on the same day. She reads back over the pages
she has written, too exhausted to change anything, and seals the
letter in an envelope before she has time to reconsider. Finally,
she throws on some clothes and creeps down the stairs to the
front-room where she knows Usha keeps her address book and
some postage stamps in the drawer of the sideboard.

A few minutes later, Anila sits on the wall of St Silas' Church
next to the post-box which now contains her letter to Nina. The
day is just beginning but already she feels worn out from the
catharsis of the letter writing. She stays seated on the wall for an
immeasurable amount of time and only returns home when the
households around her begin to stir; windows are flung open to
let in the morning breeze and new light of day as Church Street
awakes to a quiet Sunday morning.

Anila flicks through the copy of Saturday's *Handsworth Times* which was delivered to the house by mistake the evening before. The Agarwals still owe money to Frank Lavery for unpaid newspaper bills but the paperboy, used to delivering to the house, sometimes forgets and still posts the paper through the letterbox on his rounds. The headline on the late edition looks promising, *Yobs clash with peaceful protesters* it says. Reading on, however, Anila struggles to suppress her growing anger with the paper's reporting. *Local West Indian and Asian youths disrupt planned peaceful protest opposing immigration at a time when jobs are scarce for English men and women,* the article reads. Anila tosses the paper to the floor. She, alongside Kash, Marcus, Aazim and others are named the main perpetrators of what the paper calls an *unofficial radical group called Handsworth Youth Movement supported by militants.* It describes Anila, more sympathetically than the others, as... *one member who is the sister of riot-tragedy schoolboy Billy Agarwal.*

After discarding the newspaper, Anila listens to the sound of Usha moving around the kitchen, already embroiled in her domestic tasks. The rest of the household is still in bed and, besides the occasional shuffling noises from the kitchen, the house is silent. Anila imagines her letter arriving with Nina, at a house she cannot picture. She feels repulsed as images of Kash in The Shoe whirr through her head; his contorted, convulsed face makes her want to throw up and she has to distract her mind by picking the newspaper up from the floor. For a moment, she wishes she hadn't sent the letter and just tried to forget what happened that day but it is too late, the letter is sent and, regardless of all her misgivings, she is relieved to have shared the burden. Anila paces the room as quietly as she can, overwhelmed by tiredness. She picks up objects randomly, looks at them fleetingly and then replaces them. For the first time she notices a pale square on the wall where a group picture of the Agarwal children used to hang. She tries to recall when it may have been removed but can't. She wonders if Usha removed it before the women came for the meeting yesterday to prevent any references to Billy that might cause her to rush out of the room without explanation.

Anila's restlessness is interrupted by the sound of something dropping through the letterbox. The envelope is handwritten and addressed to her and she slips it into her back pocket to read in the bathroom, the only private space in the house. The note is from Marcus.

Hi Anila,

I just wanted to know you were okay after yesterday. I haven't seen much of you at the meetings recently and we didn't get a chance to talk yesterday, obviously, but, well, I have been thinking about you. I will be at the Bomb Peck at 11am this morning if you want to talk – it's quiet there on Sundays. It would be good to see you.

Anila slips the note into the envelope, folds it and returns it to her back pocket. She brushes her teeth, washes her face, careful to avoid the bruising, and returns to the living room to wait for 11am to draw near.

Two hours later, Marcus and Anila sit on a concrete slab in the shade of a derelict house that edges the Bomb Peck. They share a can of coke and talk intermittently, throwing stones at a pile of bricks in front of them. Anila is aware of how comfortable she feels in Marcus's presence.

'Your parents didn't look too pleased yesterday,' she says.

'They think I am going to fuck up – ruin my chances of going to university if I get in trouble with the Pigs.'

'You want to go to university? Anila says, surprised.

'Well, it isn't just for white people and you Indians you know, Anila?' Marcus replies. 'It's a long shot – what with coming from around here and being black as well. I'd be the first in my family, man, and probably the first West Indian in Lozells, if I ever did go.' Marcus talks with his head tilted slightly downwards and Anila watches the contours of his profile as he speaks.

'Nina was the first in our family. It's not impossible,' she says and then, after a pause, 'What about the Handsworth Youth Movement?'

'What about it? It'll be over a year if I do go, and one clash with a few idiots isn't going to put me off, man.'

'Suppose so.'

'What about you? You haven't been at the meetings lately. I thought maybe you'd fallen out with Kash or something – quite a few people seem to be recently.'

'What do you mean? '

'Well, he can be an arrogant tosser sometimes,' Marcus says and Anila smiles wryly. 'It pisses people off,' Marcus continues, 'I mean he is a good leader, inspiring and that but he is a bit full of himself, man. Did you even know he was married? About to have his second kid by the looks of it.'

'His wife was there yesterday, at Thornhill Road... I don't know if I will go back,' says Anila. She pulls her feet up onto the slab and hugs her knees. She is keen to move the conversation away from Kash; even the sound of his name makes her feel nauseous. 'I'll be busy with college and that soon,' she says.

A couple of much younger children arrive at the Bomb Peck and start to kick a football to each other. They shout and laugh as they play, encouraging each other to kick the ball this way or that with mis-used expletives.

'I'll have to get home,' Anila says, stretching out her legs.

Marcus gets up first and holds out his hand to help her up. As she rises to standing position he pulls her gently towards him and moves his mouth towards hers. As he gets closer, the face Anila sees coming towards her is Kash's not Marcus's, and in alarm she jolts her head backwards and pulls her hand free. Marcus doesn't resist.

'Shit!' he says, shocked by her response. 'Sorry, I just thought...' but Anila doesn't hear as she begins to run in the direction of Church Street. The two young boys who are playing just a few metres away stop their game and stand watching silently as Marcus shouts after Anila and she continues to run. She doesn't look back.

Chapter 29

In the few days that follow, an uneasy silence returns to the house. The mood is not unfamiliar but is in contrast to the slightly charged atmosphere that had arisen in anticipation of Usha's and Brenda's first meeting, with its promise to bring a gathering of strangers and the intention to discuss the future instead of the past. The atmosphere is different now – from the shadowy back bedroom where Kavi's stuff lies strewn across Billy's bed to the pokey attic room where Anila and Kamela spend long days holed up away from the world, barely speaking to each other or doing very much of anything. That muted excitement, brought about by the suggestion of hope, has all but completely dissipated and instead shame and disgust have replaced emerging glimmers of optimism for Usha. She now can hardly bring herself to look at Mukesh never mind talk to him, or anyone else in fact. She refuses to answer the phone when it rings. She knows it is Brenda. The doorbell has rung a few times since the meeting but the callers have remained ignored, including Bibi. The back door leading from the kitchen to the garden has been locked and the back gate secured with a small pile of old house bricks. The house is quiet but it is not peaceful.

Early on Wednesday morning, Usha sits in the kitchen mentally constructing a list of all the jobs that need doing in the house and berating herself for getting distracted from the housework these last few weeks. She wears old brown slacks and a long discoloured tunic she acquired the year Billy was born. She examines the pencil-line cracks in the tiles that make up the splashback to the sink. She searches underneath the sink for the pine disinfectant she uses to wipe down the worktops and fridge and once she recovers the bottle she pours a glug of the thick neat liquid into a glass. Then, with an old toothbrush, she begins to scrub at the cracks, loosening the dirt and diluting it into a wash of thin grey water which drips down the tiles towards the back of the sink. Once this is done, Usha rinses out a dish-cloth, wipes down the tiled surface and steps back to look at her work. Not completely satisfied, she begins the whole process again. As she contemplates her next task, Usha becomes aware of Anila hovering in the kitchen doorway.

'There is so much cleaning to do in this house,' Usha says without looking at her daughter. 'All those people walking around on our carpets without taking off their shoes. I felt too embarrassed to ask them, but goodness knows what they have brought into this house from the filthy pavements outside: pigeon and dog mess and the spit of the old men which might carry TB or goodness knows what else.'

'The house is okay, Mom, just leave it. Let's not do this again.' Anila's voice is frail and resigned. There is no danger of her shouting in frustration or screaming to the skies this time. From a distance, Usha scrutinises the bruises on Anila's face with concern.

'No,' she says firmly after a moment, 'the house is too filthy. I have neglected to keep it as clean as I should have. I haven't got up to mop the carpets since before the stupid meeting on Saturday. Mice run around spreading germs whilst we sleep and then you and the others lie across the dirty carpets putting your bodies, and even your faces, where they urinate.'

Anila turns and leaves the kitchen. She goes upstairs and gets back into bed.

When she is alone again Usha looks around the kitchen. It seems unusually drab, despite the sunlight streaming in through the window which, instead of cheering up the space, highlights the grease stains which cover the out-of-reach parts of the walls and ceiling in a sticky, yellow film. Usha sits down, overwhelmed by her growing list of tasks. Instead, she imagines what Billy would have looked like if he had reached another year older. This was the age at which Kavi grew quickly – sudden spurts of growth which transformed him into an elongated version of himself, stretched out of recognition. She wonders if this is what would have happened to Billy too, although he was always thin and waif-like, more like Anila and Kamela rather than Kavi and Nina, who both hung on to the puppy-fat right up to adolescence, and beyond in Nina's case.

The phone rings. Usha ignores it until it rings off. It rings again but Usha continues to ignore it. Once again it rings off and immediately begins to ring a third time. Kavi comes crashing down the stairs, cursing as he yanks the phone off the hook. He yells down the receiver without waiting to find out who is on the other end.

'What the hell do you want? Can't you take a bloody hint and go away?'

It is Nina on the other end.

'Calm down, Kavi. It sounds like chaos there. Go back to bed but tell Anila I just got her letter this morning and I'm coming home at the weekend, right?'

Kavi puts down the receiver and turns towards the stairs. The phone rings again and he grabs the receiver.

'What now, Nina?'

The voice on the other end isn't Nina.

'About time, I have been calling all morning.' It is Brenda. She continues to speak before Kavi can get a word in edgeways. 'Actually, I have been calling for the last few days. Tell your mom I am coming round and she better open the door – she can't hide away from the world. We've started something now and we have to carry on however embarrassed she is about what happened with your dad. Tell her I am coming around, okay? Tell her to get the kettle on, I am on my way.'

'What am I a bloody messenger-boy?' Kavi mumbles before heading up the stairs. When he reaches the top he turns round and shouts back down the stairs, 'Brenda is coming round now.

Do us all a favour, close the curtains and hide if you can't face her.'

Usha hears Kavi's relayed message and retreats to the bathroom, emerging a minute later with her face washed and her hair tied back. She returns to her seat and resolves to ignore Brenda when she knocks on the door. Five minutes later the doorbell rings and Usha sits and twists her wedding ring in circles around her finger. Within seconds there is banging on the back gate. Again, Usha ignores the noise but it gets louder and louder, culminating in a crash that makes her rush to the window just in time to see a pink leg appear over the top of the back gate. A moment later, Brenda is standing at the kitchen window, looking in at Usha whilst smoothing down her floral-print dress and dishevelled hair.

'You have to let me in now,' she shouts through the glass.

Usha begins to laugh, unable to help herself, and by the time she opens the back door both women fall into each other giggling.

'You didn't see my knickers did you?' Brenda says.

Usha, blushing at such a question, shakes her head.

Ten minutes later both women sit at the table, cups of tea in hand.

'How will I face those women again?' Usha asks. 'It is so shameful for them to have seen Mukesh in that way.'

Brenda shrugs her shoulders, 'I am sure we have all seen worse in our time. It wasn't that bad, Usha.'

'He was drunk and in vest and pants, climbing out the window in front of my mother – how bad can it be? I didn't even know the children had locked him in the room. At least there was only one other community member there and that Shilly, well she didn't seem like the gossiping type.'

'One member of the community?' Brenda repeats. 'Aren't we all part of a community here?'

'Yes, but you know what I mean, the Indian community where this kind of behaviour would be judged very badly.'

'I think this would be seen as unusual by any standards,' says Brenda mockingly. 'Even us goras, as you call us, don't go swinging around out of windows in our underwear, bab.'

'It is bad enough that we haven't been to the temple since the accident,' Usha continues, despite Brenda's gentle mockery. 'Mukesh says he hasn't believed in god since he was a child and I can't make the children go with me anymore. I don't want to go on my own. My father has told me the community is concerned, and that we have neglected certain rituals that are important to do after a death. This will only make it worse.'

'Forget what people think, Usha. All communities have a bit of that going on – not just you Indians. Blimey, us Catholics can't talk – you should hear some of the gossip after Sunday mass.'

'I don't know,' says Usha, 'I don't care about the rituals. Perhaps, like Mukesh, my belief is now being questioned too.'

'Well, all the more reason to get on with something else – something important for now, for everyone. Your Bomb Peck idea was bostin and whatever those ladies think about what happened with Mukesh, that will soon be forgotten when we start making some progress. That coloured lady, Veronica, was it?... no, hang on, Violet... the one who was at the riot, and the fat one who knew the lad who got burnt, well I think they are going to be talking about a bit more than Mukesh's pants, don't you? C'mon, bab, let's carry on with it.'

'I don't know, Brenda, I am very behind on the housework and the children will be going back to school and college in a few weeks – I need to concentrate on these things. Anila is mixed up in all sorts of things I don't understand and Kamela and Kavi hardly leave the house. They are my priority. As for Mukesh...'

'Listen Usha, Mukesh isn't the only fella with a UB40 around here – there are hundreds in case you haven't noticed, thousands probably. You only have to walk past the dole office on a morning to realise how bad it's getting. And as for the young ones, didn't we agree that by helping all the young people we will be helping our own? Isn't that what a community does? I bet if we organise another meeting, those ladies and more will turn up and there will be no mention of Mukesh's underpants.'

'Stop saying that, Brenda. I don't know – I can't bear another shameful episode like that. Maybe, if we do it we can have the meeting somewhere else?'

'That's the spirit, bab. I'll ask at St Silas' – that would be better. You can't just give up because of one setback. Remember this is for your Billy, in his memory and that.'

Usha winces at the mention of Billy.

'Okay, maybe,' she says.

The next morning, Brenda is at the front door again with some crudely made notices.

'I spoke to the vicar at St Silas' after I left here yesterday and I have just done a few of these,' she says handing half of the notices to Usha.

HELP MAKE LOZELLS BETTER FOR OUR KIDS

MEETING TO DISCUSS IMPROVING THE
BOMB PECK

SATURDAY 3PM, ST SILAS CHURCH HALL.

ALL WELCOME – ESPECIALLY MOTHERS.

'Saturday? So soon?' Usha says reading the leaflet.

'Yes – strike while the iron is hot and that. C'mon, let's write a list.'

Usha wipes her damp hands on her apron, removes it, hangs it on the back of the kitchen door and takes a deep breath.

'Okay, where do we start?' she says as she grabs her list-book and pencil from the worktop. She takes a seat next to Brenda, veering around the mop bucket she was about to fill at the sink.

Chapter 30

As Usha clears the breakfast dishes from the kitchen table, Nina arrives at the back gate. She stands on tiptoes to reach over and unbolt the lock at the top of the wooden door and enters the kitchen with a holdall slung over her shoulder.

'Hi Mom!'

Usha jumps – the saucer she is rinsing under the tap drops in the sink and smashes into pieces.

'Nina, what has happened? Why are you back so soon? You only left last week, are you okay? We weren't expecting you until your term has finished.' Usha picks up the broken bits of crockery from the sink as she speaks.

'Nothing happened,' Nina replies casually. She drops her holdall in the middle of the room and flicks on the kettle switch. 'Just nothing has started properly yet so I decided to get the first coach this morning. It left just after seven so here I am. Not bad, eh? Leeds isn't as far as it seems and I was missing you, Mom.' She kisses the back of Usha's head, sits down at the table and babbles on about the journey while the kettle begins to boil in the background. Usha makes the tea, puts a mug in front of her daughter and sits down beside her. 'Could you make me some toast, Mom? I'm starving,' Nina asks.

'Yes, beta,' says Usha, getting back up.

Upstairs in the bedroom, Anila is lying on her bed staring at the ceiling and listening to the latest album she borrowed from the music library. It was due back over a week ago.

'Turn it down a bit, Anila,' Kamela says from the other bed, 'I mean, I like The Jam and that but it's a bit early isn't it?'

Anila turns it down and returns to her bed.

'Are you going to Mom's meeting later today?'

'I don't know. I'm sick of meetings to be honest. I just want some quiet time.'

'Quiet time? Bloody hell, Anila, I mean, I know it's horrible getting your head kicked in but you can't let something like that rule your life. You need to straighten your fizzog, bab – I have to move on and so will you. I know it's different – I mean the reasons for it but at the end of the day it's about people trying to tell you what you can or can't be, even though you can't actually help what you are.' Kamela pencils over her eyebrows as she speaks.

'It isn't just what happened last week, Kam. There is something else before that. Something I should have told you.'

Kamela stops applying her make-up and looks towards her sister.

'I knew there was something, you've been miserable for weeks. You were going to tell me before, remember? But Nina came in. I know you have been seeing that Jamaican lad, Marcus is it? I won't tell – you probably think it will be the end of the world if Dad and Mom found out but it's not the worst thing that can happen, believe me – and if you like him, well does it really matter that he is black?'

'It's not a simple as that.'

'Nothing is bloody simple. I know that – life would be very different if it was!'

Anila doesn't know how to tell Kamela about what happened. She doesn't have the words or the stomach for it so instead she says, 'Kam... I know we said we wouldn't talk about what happened that day in the underpass... but... well...'

Kamela ignores her and returns to her eyebrows. Anila had intended to say that she'd read something about that sort of thing in the 'Dear Jenny' section of the magazine, that there was a phone number you could call to talk about it, but before she can say anything else the door flings open and Nina walks in.

'Alright?' she says, looking from Kamela to Anila.

'Friggin' hell, not again, you only went five minutes ago,' Kamela says.

'Blimey,' says Nina, 'that's no way to greet your sister. You should be pleased to see me.'

'What you doing here?' Anila asks meekly.

'I got your letter, stupidface. Did you think I wouldn't come after that?'

Anila feels exposed.

'What letter?' Kamela says from across the room. 'What bloody letter?' she repeats when there is no response.

By now Nina is sitting on Anila's bed with her arms around her younger sister's shoulders. Anila begins to cry.

'What is going on?' Kamela asks again. 'Is this about your spat with that Marcus?'

'Marcus?' says Nina, still holding the trembling Anila to her shoulder, 'Who is he?' And then turning to look at Kamela she says quite solemnly, 'This is about something else, Kamela.'

Anila's crying begins to subside and Nina gently pushes her away. She grabs a tee-shirt from the floor and wipes away the secretions from her shoulder.

'Listen you two,' she says, 'maybe the three of us should get out of here. Let's go into town, do a bit of shopping – I just got my grant cheque – I could treat you both. We can have a look around the Oasis market, I need some new jeans anyhow, and then go to Drucker's for a sarnie or something. What'd you reckon? My treat.'

'I'm up for it,' says Kamela jumping up. 'Drucker's, blimey, it's not even our birthdays or anything. Better not tell Mom, she'll go mad with you for spending your grant money on stuff like that.'

'Mom'll be okay, I've already put five quid in her money jam-jar. That'll help a bit at least. Anyway, I think I might have got a part-time job at Chelsea Girl in the Merrion Centre from next week. I went to an interview and I can probably do a couple of shifts with my timetable this year, plus Saturdays.'

Kamela begins to choose some clothes from her drawer. 'Will you get a discount?' she asks.

'Come on, our kid, how about you?' Nina says to Anila.

'Okay,' Anila says in a small voice. She rubs her face with her hands before easing her legs from lotus position to a full stretch.

The downstairs hallway is filled with the delicate tones of Lata Mangeshkar playing out from the cassette player in the kitchen. Usha sings quietly along to the *Kora Kagaz* soundtrack. The tape was a present from Mukesh several years earlier when the children were still at primary school. He had asked the shop assistant at Mr Ali's Music Emporium on Soho Road to put it aside until pay-day and when he finally handed it to Usha he did so like an excited child, knowing she loved that film almost as much as *Pakeezah*. As the girls descend the stairs they turn to look at each other, lifting their palms upwards and shrugging their shoulders in gestures of surprise. It has been a long time since Usha has played any of her beloved cassette tapes.

Nina pops her head around the kitchen door,

'Me and the girls are going into town. We'll be back later, alright?'

Usha quickly presses pause on the cassette player.

'Okay,' she nods guiltily.

'It's alright, Mom,' Nina says. 'Put it back on, it's good to have a bit of music around. It makes everything seem okay.' And then she adds, 'Listening to your tape isn't betraying anyone, Mom – it's like fresh air to hear that on in this house.'

Usha depresses the pause button but turns the volume right down so Lata's voice is just a thin background whistle against the white noise of the kitchen appliances – the fridge and the twin-tub dominate the domestic soundscape once again.

On the bus, Nina and Kamela sit next to each other on the only empty double seat upstairs. Anila sits further forwards next to a well-dressed white man in his twenties. He wears a Walkman and has the volume up loud so the Phil Collins album he is listening to is clearly audible. Anila turns around and looks for another empty seat nearby but there aren't any. All three girls light up cigarettes simultaneously and, together with almost all the occupants of the upper deck, blow out streams of smoke to add to the thick haze of tobacco which hangs in the rooftop space above their heads.

'What was in this letter, then?' Kamela asks discreetly, once the bus begins to pull off. Nina tells her and by the time she has finished they have passed Great Hampton Street and are almost in town.

'Shit,' says Kamela after digesting Nina's words.

'She says she feels dirty all the time, poor thing.'

'Why didn't she tell me?'

'No offence, Kam, but you're a bit close to home, literally and that. Sometimes it's easier if there is a bit of distance.'

'The daft bugger. I knew that group was trouble. She should have known better, the silly fool.'

'She is just a kid, how was she to know that bastard would do that. If I get hold of him, I'll bloody kill him.'

'Yeah, but if people find out they'll say it was her fault. She hasn't stopped talking about that bloody group for months – everyone knows she went to all those meetings by herself. Shit, if people in the community found out we'd be the talk of the town again. And if Dad found out...'

'For god's sake Kamela, this is Anila we are talking about. I think there are more important things to worry about than what other people might think, including Dad. She is a woman who has been attacked, for fuck's sake.'

'Calm down. What are we going to do? We can't go to the police.'

'I don't know, part of me thinks she should. What happened to Anila is about men like that Kash thinking they can do what they like 'cos they have a bit of power. It doesn't just happen around here you know?'

'I know, but we can't go to the police – everyone will find out and I don't think Mom, or Dad, can take anymore. Anila won't want that either – everyone blaming her and talking about her behind her back – you can't do anything except what is acceptable around here, even if it isn't your fault – and we can't just escape somewhere else like you – I wish we could.'

A few hours later the girls make their way back from Birmingham city centre towards Handsworth and home. They are worn out by the talking, crying, advice-giving and window shopping. As they alight at Villa Cross, they automatically link arms and walk towards Church Street in a chain of three – Nina in the middle holding on to her sisters firmly by their arms. They walk past the Acapulco cafe where Marcus is sitting at a window table reading a paperback. He looks up as the girls pass. Anila feels the hairs on her arm rising at the sight of him. She shyly lifts her free hand in a greeting, Marcus raises his hand too and quickly turns back to his book. Nina and Kamela exchange a brief smile and the girls continue on.

At the top of Church Street on the junction with Lozells Road a huddle of five or six women becomes noticeable. They walk a few metres ahead of the girls and disappear around the corner into Church Street. As the girls also turn into Church Street they stop and watch the women as they enter the grounds of St Silas' to join a queue which snakes its way around the main church building, down the side and towards the church hall at the back.

'Bloody hell,' says Kamela, 'look at that.'

'What?' Anila and Nina say in unison.

'They're here for Mom's meeting. I forgot it was today. Shit, I told her I'd help out.'

'No way,' says Anila.

'What meeting?' Nina says.

Kamela pulls her arm free and sprints on ahead towards the church while Anila explains to Nina that the meeting is

206

the follow up to the event the week before, where Mukesh had appeared in the window in his underwear.

'Blimey,' says Nina, 'even Mom is becoming some kind of political activist now.'

'Not political but a community activist I think you'll find,' Anila says proudly.

'Well good for her!'

As they near the church, Kavi walks past with some plastic cups tucked under his arm and two jugs of orange squash gripped in his hands.

'Oh, you're here as well, again,' he says looking at Nina. 'Well help out then – there are more jugs of juice at the house and some biscuits.'

'Sure thing, kiddo,' Nina says in a faux-American accent and both Anila and Kavi shake their heads.

Nina and Anila stop for a second to look at the queue before moving on. It is made up mostly of women – middle-aged in the majority but also a few younger and older ones too – altogether they number around twenty-five or possibly thirty. There are black, white and brown women including Bibi, Violet Murray, Marie O'Connell and even old Elsie Meeson. The group of women is interspersed by a small scattering of men, no more than three or four that the girls can see.

Chapter 31

Kamela rises early, much earlier than she has for many months. She dresses for the warm weather immediately, checks through her bag and before leaving the room she pokes Anila in the back.

'What? Can't you see I'm asleep.'

'I'm going to the library – d'ya want me to take those records back? You'll get a fine again if you don't watch it.'

'Yes, please, I've taped them already. Ta very much,' Anila replies dozily before rolling over and going back to sleep.

Downstairs, Kamela butters two slices of bread and spreads one with Shippams sardine paste. She wraps up her sandwich in foil and searches the cupboards for more items to add to her packed lunch as Usha cleans up around her.

'Hey, I haven't finished yet,' Kamela says, grabbing the bread from her mother's hand. She spreads another slice thick with fish paste and eats it for her breakfast whilst pushing the sandwich and the remains of an opened packet of Custard Creams into her bag. 'Has the Pop-man been, or have we not paid that bill yet, either?' she asks dismissively.

'Where are you going, Kamela?'

"Town, Central Library. I need to get some books – catch up on college before we go back – I missed a lot last term.'

Usha puts the opened jar of fish paste in the fridge and gives Kamela a hug,

'Good girl,' she says.

'Ta-ra, Mom. I'll be back in a bit.'

Kamela stops at the entrance of the alley and glances around before pulling Anila's old magazine out of her bag. She leans against the wall at the threshold of the archway and flips through the pages of the magazine, past the fashion section and photo-loves to the 'Dear Jenny' section on the penultimate page. She re-reads the short letter from a reader which describes a situation that resonates deeply, it begins with the words, *Please help me, I think I am a freak.* Following the short letter there is a response from the agony aunt that is both practical and non-judgmental and Kamela sighs as she reads it over and over again. She searches for a biro in her handbag, copies out the printed advice-line number onto the palm of her hand and tosses the magazine on the bag of rubbish left out for the binmen by Usha that morning. She then steps out of the shadows and into the glaring sunshine of the morning.

'Oi, Kamela,' a voice shouts.

Kamela looks up and down Church Street but it is deserted.

'Up here,' the voice says and Kamela look up across the street to see Debbie O'Connell leaning out of an upstairs window of the house opposite.

'You going up town?' Debbie shouts. 'Hang on if you are, I'm going too. I'll only be a tick, we can go together and have a natter on the bus, like.'

When Debbie disappears from the window, Kamela walks on hurriedly towards Lozells Road, hoping to reach it and continue her journey alone but as she passes by St Silas' Church, Debbie comes charging up beside her.

'Wait up a bit,' she says and Kamela shrugs her shoulders. 'How are you, Kam?' Debbie continues, trying to keep up the pace, 'I haven't seen you properly for ages. My Mom came over to your house and to the other meeting over there,' she says pointing back towards St Silas'. 'She said it was alright and that. That your mom and her mate are going to fix up the Bomb Peck. Is that right?'

'Yes!'

'So, you coming back to college this term? You hardly came before the holidays. I know you got smashed in and that but it was ages ago now. Someone said you'd copped off with a Jamaican boy – that's why they did it; one of them fancied him for herself or something. Is that what happened?'

'Bollocks!' Kamela says. 'Sod off, Debbie.'

'Charming! I was only asking. Our Gary said someone told him you were a lezza and that's why they knifed you but he can be a right yampy sometimes and I told him not to be so friggin' stupid. I don't have pervy mates, I told him – I stuck up for you. Anyway, he was still pissed off with you and your sisters when he said it, for showing him up at the Bomb Peck in front of his idiot skinhead mates, yonks ago. He doesn't hang around with them anymore anyhow – he's trying to grow his hair and that now.'

Kamela lights up a cigarette without offering the packet to Debbie.

'Can't get rid of that bloody ugly tattoo though. Dad went mad when he saw it – clipped our Gary around the head – said his dad, our granda fought against the Nazis, said he'd be turning in his grave and that. Anyway, you don't need to worry 'cos those ones that got you in the underpass have been thrown out of the college now – you won't see them again.' Debbie stops in her tracks all of a sudden, 'Oh fuck,' she says, 'I've forgotten me bag. Hang on here and I'll run back and get it.'

Kamela breathes a sigh of relief and quickens her pace towards Lozells Road. When she reaches the junction she dashes across the main road instead of turning left. She makes a detour up Mayfield Road, heading towards town via a longer route.

Forty minutes later, the bus pulls up by the side of Chamberlain Square. Kamela alights and heads straight into a phone box outside the library entrance. She dials a number from memory, waits for her call to be answered and then pushes coins into the slot.

'Is Jeanette there?' Kamela asks and she holds the receiver away from her ear as the man on the other end yells out

Jeanette's name. Kamela lights a cigarette, takes a deep drag on it, exhales slowly through pursed lips and waits once more.

'You bitch,' she says when she hears a girl's voice down the phone line, the words already planned in her head. 'You bloody left me in that subway and you haven't bothered to even find out if I was dead or alive all this time. You're a fucking bitch for that, Jeanette Dooling, and when I come back to college, if you come within two yards of me, you won't know what's hit you!'

Kamela slams the phone down, retrieves her change from the slot, looks around outside the phone box, breathes in and out slowly and picks up the receiver again. This time she dials the number written on the palm of her hand and waits impatiently for her call to be answered.

'I think I need some advice, and I'd better tell you that I'm Indian first because it'll make a difference whether you think so or not...' Kamela says when someone finally picks up on the other end.

A few minutes later, Kamela leaves the phone box with an address for somewhere called The Nightingale on Thorp Street, not far from the city centre, scrawled on a piece of paper.

'Fuck it,' she says to herself defiantly, 'I am going to have to live with this one way or another – at least I'm in Birmingham and not the back streets of the Punjab.' Then she strides towards the Central Library with albums by The Jam and Black Uhuru neatly tucked under her arm.

Chapter 32

The Bomb Peck is the remnants of Alexandra Terrace, a small and squalid set of dwellings between Brougham Street and Villa Street, cut across by Wills Street at the top end. It is accessed through the alleyways and gardens behind Church Street as a shortcut, or the long way down to Nursery Road and around the back way to avoid overgrown bushes and brambles. This is the way that the small group of women from the St Silas' meeting walk now. Other than Usha and Brenda there are five or six of them – those that expressed an interest in getting more involved. Brenda leads the group and speaks to whoever is listening as they walk.

'You know, my Eugene's nan lived on Alex. Terrace when he was little? He used to go and stay with her when his mom was having more babbies. He remembers that Meesons' had a sweet shop on Villa Street and his nan used to let him walk there himself with a penny if she had one. It was owned by the sister or aunt or something of the old dear on your street.'

'There's nothing dear about Elsie Meeson,' Marie O'Connell says. Brenda ignores her and carries on speaking.

'There was only one house left properly standing after the bombing – an old man named Mr Kelman lived there. Eugene says he used to chase the kiddies with his walking stick and if he caught them he'd give them a right walloping.'

The large woman from the first meeting in the Agarwals' living room is also amongst the group. Her name is Jean Noakes.

'I remember Mr Kelman,' she says. 'We lived next door to The Vine then, on Villa Street and that was the only place he'd go other than his own house. They called him Gypsy Kelman 'cos he blacked his 'tache with a burnt matchstick. The rest of his hair was as white as chalk. He was terrifying if you were a kiddy. His name wasn't even Kelman, I don't think. It was Kel -something-Ski or summut.'

Usha listens to the conversation without hearing what the women are saying until Violet sidles up to her and speaks in hushed tones.

'You know, Mrs A., your husband was very brave that night of the riot last year. I will never get the picture out of my head of the boy on fire – the look in his eyes. My boy Leroy was out there too, getting involved and behaving badly. I slapped his ears when he came home but I was grateful to the lord above that he wasn't the poor soul who was burnt almost to death. I made Leroy pray in gratitude too that night, before we had even heard about your son, Mrs A. The other boy surely would have perished if it wasn't for your husband – don't be too hard on him Mrs A., you and him, well you need each other.'

Usha doesn't have time to respond before Jean Noakes joins them.

'She's right. It would have been two kiddies dead that night if your fella hadn't stepped in. Strange bloke isn't he?'

Usha doesn't know what to say so she doesn't say anything and instead tries to block out the bad thoughts that invade her mind; thoughts about wishing the other boy dead instead of her Billy. A wave of nausea takes hold of her and she steadies herself with a deep breath.

'So, what are we going to do at this Bomb Peck?' Marie asks, filling the pause with chatter whilst sucking on her cigarette – of the group of eight women, only Usha and Violet Murray are not smoking.

'That's what we need to decide,' Usha says bluntly.

When the women turn into Nursery Road, they see two groups of older teenage boys ahead of them standing at bus-stops on either side of the road. One group is made up almost entirely of black kids, the other white kids from the estates towards Newtown. The two groups are involved in some kind of verbal stand-off. The exchange is light-hearted, or so it seems – banter about football and clothes mostly – but an atmosphere of precariousness hangs around them, as if a 'nignog' or 'raasclaat' too far may push things over the edge and cause an eruption into something more unpredictable.

'Keithy Bowler, your mom will be wondering where you are,' Jean Noakes shouts across the road towards the white boys.

'And you, Walter Ross,' Violet shouts at the other group.

The boys all glower at the women and then turn away so their faces are no longer visible except to their own separate gangs.

'It's terrible them not having anything to do once they leave school,' Brenda says. 'It's no wonder they hang around getting themselves into trouble. I blame the government myself, they don't care about kids around here. That Maggie Thatcher has a lot to answer for.'

'They could go on one of those YOP things, you know, youth opportunities and that? Too bloody lazy, that's the problem,' Jean Noakes says.

'Slave labour, my Derek says,' Marie O'Connell chips in. 'Just a way of pretending there's jobs when there isn't really.'

Jean Noakes sucks her teeth and drops her pace so she is no longer walking alongside Marie.

'It's worse than I remember,' one of the women declares as they catch sight of the Bomb Peck ahead.

'It's a bloody dump,' says another.

They enter the site by clambering up a small bank of rubble. Then they veer around a stained and stinking mattress before standing on the perimeter of the Bomb Peck and looking at the expanse of waste ground in front of them: it is populated with the remains of walls and random items of dumped furniture and industrial waste; old bits of rope hang from sturdy tree branches, some with tyres attached, others with bits of wood or just a large knot; more old mattresses lie beneath the windowless ruins of a dilapidated house.

'The kids jump from the upstairs windows on to those mattresses,' Marie says. 'I've seen them do it,' she adds.

Usha gasps at the thought of this and covers her face with her hands so as to avoid being a witness to such a scene, as if a young person might leap from the empty window frame any second.

'It'll take some work but we can do it if there's enough of us,' Brenda says, putting her arm around Usha's shoulders. 'I'm not saying it'll be easy, mind, but think how great it would be to have a proper space for them to go to. We can have real swings and maybe a climbing frame or something.'

'Perhaps we can have a small place to grow vegetables, like we do on the allotments on Trinity Road? The young people can take responsibility and learn how things grow too,' Violet says.

'That's going a bit far isn't it?' Jean Noakes says. 'Kids don't even want to eat bloody vegetables, never mind grow them. Half of them around here only ever see a carrot in a tin. Anyhow, I thought the idea was to make this a place they want to be in, not a bloody labour-camp.'

Violet sighs, her enthusiasm dampened.

'I'll make a list of ideas,' says Brenda, pulling out a small notebook and pencil from her handbag. 'Swings, climbing-frame, somewhere to sit and chat, veg-patch. Anything else?'

When the list is compiled Brenda puts the notebook away and says, 'Right then, anyone fancy a cuppa at mine before the kids get in from school?'

Usha, Violet and Marie follow Brenda back towards Brougham Street away from the Bomb Peck. As they pass by one of the decrepit houses they hear creaks and rustling from beyond the tumbledown walls of the building. A moment later a middle-aged man appears in a gap in the wall where the front door would have once stood. As he emerges he wipes away the rubble-dust from his face and clothes before adjusting his turban. Usha stares at the man and, when he catches sight of the four women, he screens his face with his hand and shuffles off in the opposite direction. A moment later a girl also emerges from the broken-down building; her hair is unkempt and she is covered in a film of grey-brown dust but her lipstick is bright and intact. She stares with glazed eyes at the women before briefly brushing the dust off her clothes and lighting up a cigarette. The girl blows the first puff of smoke directly at the women and stomps off.

'She's no older than our Debbie,' Marie says. 'She'd be better off at the back of Rackhams. What a slapper!'

'Poor bab,' says Brenda.

Later, as Brenda sees Marie and Violet off, Usha sits in her friend's kitchen with her head in her hands.

'C'mon, Usha, cheer up. We'll have our work cut out but the women are keen and, well there's loads more of them too from the St Silas' meeting. And the fellas will help, there's plenty out of work with nothing else useful to do, and the others can muck in on the weekends. I know it looks like a lot to take on but I'll ring around some of the factories and that tomorrow and see if they can give us anything useful. Tell you what, we can divvy it up. I'll go through the Yellow Pages in front of the telly tonight and do a list with numbers and that and drop half off to you tomorrow. C'mon, bab, we can do it.'

'I'm tired, Brenda.'

'Well, get yourself home and get an early night.'

'Not tired like that, Brenda. Really tired. Worn-out. Exhausted. Don't know if I can go on.'

'We've started something now, bab. We can't just leave it.'

'I know, but I just want it all to be how it was before: Mukesh being grumpy and drinking too much but not so much he can't work or look after us, and the children listening to their music too loud and bickering with each other about which side to watch on the television and me just taking care of them all, and, well, Billy being with us. Him being alive and riding down the street on his bicycle and leaving dirty cups and plates with crumbs on in his bedroom and moaning about school with the others.'

'We can't turn back time, Usha. We have to look forwards, it's the only way.'

'I know, but at least if I look into the past Billy is there.'

The two women sit in silence for a moment and when Usha stands up to leave, Brenda touches her hand gently.

'Ta-ra a bit, Usha,' she says, 'and listen, bablin, you'll be alright you know. I promise.'

Chapter 33

During the weeks after the meeting at St Silas', the phone in the Church Street house rings at least three or four times a day. The callers are mostly strangers asking what time they should be at the Bomb Peck the next weekend, what should they bring? Can a sister-in-law or an aunty, or less frequently a husband, come along? Usha keeps a list next to the telephone so she can recall who is who and what they have offered to do to help the project. Brenda arrives most mornings with the scrapbook that the two women fill together with plans and drawings and the occasional newspaper or magazine cutting. The distraction is welcomed into the house by all except Mukesh, who is silently acquiescent – as though he cannot be bothered to care either way. For the rest of them this renewed busy-ness in the household begins to mirror a normality that has long disappeared.

By the time September begins to draw to an end, the mornings are becoming increasingly chilly. However, in spite of the cold, Kavi is the first up besides Usha most days, going to school with a regularity that begins to indicate the re-establishment of routine. Usha makes him Ready Brek, keeping the milk on a simmer until she hears him moving around the bedroom above the kitchen. When he comes downstairs she hugs him tight and clings to him for a few seconds, until he breaks free and rushes to the bathroom; she then breathes a sigh of relief and waits for Kamela and Anila to appear downstairs for their breakfast.

The girls now travel to and from college together, even on the days when one or the other's lessons start later or finish earlier. They wait in the refectory or the library for one another at the end of the day so they can get the same bus through town on the way home.

When the children have left the house for the day, Usha opens the curtains in the master bedroom in an effort to stir Mukesh out of bed before midday. Since the window incident he has become more and more reclusive, only venturing out of the house every other Tuesday to collect and cash in his dole cheque and buy cigarettes and whisky with the money he receives. On rare occasions, he will pay off some of his tab in the Black Eagle and the Barton Arms. He avoids the Royal Oak since leaving the factory, even though it is closer to home than the other pubs, as this is where the Hardiman's workers are most likely to drink.

'I don't know what to do,' Usha confesses to Brenda one morning.

The children are out and Mukesh is dozing, slumped in the armchair in the living room with the television on in the background. Brenda and Usha sit in front of their scrapbook and as Usha begins to speak, the mood in the room quickly reverts to a familiar gloom.

'He just lies around all day and I have to step over him to clean the house. At least he doesn't have the money to drink every day any more. If it wasn't for my Child Benefit I don't know what we would do.'

'Well, that's a good thing isn't it?' Brenda says.

'What is?'

'Him not drinking so much, I mean, not the other things about the Family Allowance and that.'

'Yes, but Mukesh's problems aren't just to do with how much he drinks. They are deeper than that and I don't know what to do about it. If it goes on any longer we won't have enough money for food. I feel ashamed that he isn't working and feeding the family. Nina is giving me money from her grant – it should be the other way around. I can't keep going to my parents.'

'Something will work out, bab,' says Brenda sympathetically. 'Lots of fellas are on the dole now and lots of people are struggling. It isn't shameful to be in this position. It is hard for men to go from being the breadwinners to more or less useless because the factories or shops or whatever have closed down.'

'Yes, but Mukesh lost his job. He had a job and he threw it away. The thing is, I think maybe he is sick, more than just a drunk and on the dole but really sick in a way that he can't get better.'

'Mental sick?' Brenda says crudely.

'Well depression maybe,' says Usha, 'I have been reading about it in Reader's Digest and well, I thought maybe this was something I had at first but now maybe not. I mean, I miss Billy so much and not a moment goes by when I don't think about him or see his beautiful face in my head. I can't bear that he is not here and I couldn't protect him. Some days I feel that I am in a shipwreck with big waves coming over me – that everything is destroyed and there is nothing to cling onto. But then I see the others – Kavi and the girls – and they are like bits of wreckage from the big ship and I can hold on to these and survive. And now, well there is more to hold on to, like with the Bomb Peck. It gives me something to focus on, especially because it is helping the children. The waves keep coming but they won't drown me because I have to survive for the other children.'

'Bloody hell, bab, you are so poetic sometimes. Nobody would ever think you grew up speaking Indian and that.'

'I think I might have read something about grief being like a shipwreck once, or maybe it was a dream? Anyway, it's true for me but the thing is, Brenda, I don't think it is the same for Mukesh. He has no wreckage to hold onto, he has let it all float away and he is allowing the big waves to throw him about, pulling him deeper into the ocean – to drown him.'

'Bloody hell!' Brenda says again. 'Maybe you should take him to the doctor. Get some Valium or something.'

'He had some of that already. I did too. I still do, but these medicines are not to be taken with alcohol so I had to hide the tablets away from Mukesh. He will never go to the doctor. I can hardly get him to get out of bed these days.'

'You'll have to send him to the looney bin at All Saints, Usha. I know it is difficult to imagine, but when someone gets that bad some of that electric shock stuff they do there is the only thing that will work. My Aunty Patty had it once, after she went through the change. She started hearing people in her head telling her to bash her husband with the frying pan. She actually did it once, bash him I mean, and then they came for her. Anyhow, it worked – all calm and that afterwards. Not the fiery old cow she used to be.' Brenda takes a breath and continues, 'I'm not saying he is mental or anything but it's not normal sitting around the house all day in your pyjamas and climbing out of the window in your Y-fronts for everyone to see, is it?'

'Don't you think I know that?' Usha sighs and rubs her face with her knuckles. After a moment she changes the subject and says more cheerily, 'Look I found this picture,' and she rummages around in the drawer next to the cooker until she finds what she is looking for. 'It's of a climbing frame in London. It is made out of wood and pallets from local factories. We could make something like this, or at least we could get the teenage boys to build it.'

Ten minutes later the phone rings and Usha heads into the hallway to answer it. Brenda follows her.

'Yes, this is she. Who is calling please?' Usha says in her most formal voice. She cups her hand over the receiver and whispers to Brenda, 'It is the Handsworth Times – they want to know about the Bomb Peck.' She returns to the caller and says, 'How did you get my phone number?' She repeats the response, 'Oh, you had it on your records from before, I see.'

'What's he saying?'

Usha lifts her finger to her lips, gesturing to Brenda to be quiet.

'Yes,' she says into the phone, 'I think we would like you to come and see what we are doing... yes you can interview myself and my friend, Brenda... yes okay, two o'clock at the Bomb Peck tomorrow. We will see you there.'

'They want to do a story about us?'

'Yes!' Usha says excitedly. 'Somebody called them. A young man they said but they didn't get his name. Anyway, they said that we were examples of good community citizens and they want to feature us in the newspaper this week. They want to meet us tomorrow.'

'Ooo, we'll be famous like. Perhaps we'll get stopped and asked for our autographs. What you going to wear, Usha? I expect they'll want to take our picture. I wonder if Carol Mckenna has time to do my hair this afternoon.'

'I don't care about that Brenda, but maybe if the people at Birmingham Council see it they might give us money to help finish the Bomb Peck.'

'Yes, of course, but we want to look good too, don't we? C'mon, bab, admit it.'

A few days later, Brenda arrives carrying half a dozen copies of the *Handsworth Times*.

'Frank Lavery told me we were in there,' she says. 'He gave me two copies for free, one for each of us, and I bought the rest.'

'I should have worn English clothes,' Usha says to Brenda as the stare at the newspaper. Anila and Kamela have joined them as they gather in the kitchen looking at the open copy on the table. 'I look like I have only recently arrived from India,' she continues, pointing at the grainy monochrome image.

'You look like you, Mom. You look great – you both do,' says Kamela. 'Anyhow, well done for getting something positive in the Handsworth Times about our family for once – it's been a long time coming,' she adds light-heartedly. They all laugh.

'What's all this then?' Kavi asks, bursting into the kitchen and grabbing a copy of the paper. 'Oh bostin, they actually listened then. They didn't sound too convinced when I phoned them last week.'

Usha puts her arm around Kavi and squeezes him.

'Get off, Mom, you're so embarrassing,' he says, freeing himself, and the group all laugh again.

Chapter 34

The following Monday, Kavi is sitting on his bed flicking through his school library copy of *Of Mice and Men* when Mukesh comes into the room.

'Shit,' says Kavi, 'you never come in here.'

Mukesh doesn't answer and instead goes over to Billy's bed and, with a sweep of his arm, he clears Kavi's guitar and discarded clothes off the bed and onto the floor.

'What the bloody hell are you doing, Dad? That's my stuff!' says Kavi.

Mukesh still doesn't answer and instead he sits on the edge of the bed and begins to cradle the uncovered pillow that once belonged to Billy. He rocks the pillow to and fro, as if it is a small baby in his arms, and begins to sing a lullaby in Hindi.

> *'Come one, come all and have a look,*
> *The baby is swinging in his crib.*
> *Maasi Aunt has come from Meerut with a suit and*
> *a bonnet.*
> *Let us dress our baby in these.*
> *Come one, come all and have a look,*
> *The baby is swinging in his crib.'*

The sound of his father singing this vaguely familiar song makes Kavi want to cry. Instead, he stares, transfixed, at Mukesh.

'Dad, are you alright?'

Mukesh falls forward off the bed and lands on his knees. He begins to weep. At first it is a gentle sobbing but soon it becomes a full blown howl that bounces off the walls and fills the room with the terrible sound of anguish. Kavi gets on the floor beside his father and puts his arms around him but Mukesh pushes him away. Between the bawling, he mumbles Billy's name over and over again and continues to squeeze the pillow, rocking back and forth uncontrollably.

'I killed them,' he says.

'No you didn't!' Kavi responds. 'You are getting all mixed up, you just tried to help someone. You kept someone alive – we all know about the boy on fire in the riot. We had to find out from someone else, from a stranger – why didn't you tell us?'

'I let Naresh walk off the roof. I let him break into a thousand pieces. I killed him.'

'No you didn't,' Kavi says again, shaking his father by the shoulder. 'Stop this Dad, please stop it. Shall I get you some whisky?'

'Whisky can't help me, I am going to hell. I am going to hell.' Mukesh begins to knock the side of his head against the wall next to Billy's bed. The sound becomes a monotonous drum beat which gets louder and louder. Kavi looks on helplessly.

'Stop it, Dad. Stop doing that, you are scaring me.'

Mukesh stops for a moment and looks blankly ahead.

'Where is my baby boy? Where has Billy gone?' he says and then the wailing begins again.

Kavi runs to the top of the stairs and shouts for help. Straight away Usha is charging up the stairs from the kitchen and Anila and Kamela are heading across the landing. They all cram into the little bedroom at the back of the house and watch Mukesh rocking to and fro, cradling the pillow and humming the old Hindi lullaby.

'What we going to do?' Anila says.

'What can we do?' Kamela says.

Usha goes over to Mukesh and gently prises him up to a standing position. As she does so he buries his face into her shoulder and whispers, 'Usha, where is our Billy?'

Usha takes Mukesh by the hand and leads him along the landing to the bedroom at the front of the house. The curtains are still drawn and Usha helps Mukesh into the bed. She lifts up his legs and pulls the covers over him, tucking him in like a young child.

'Where is he?' Mukesh asks again and this time Usha answers.

'He is safe,' she says.

Anila links arms with Kamela and they both begin to quietly weep. Kavi turns and walks towards the bedroom he once shared with Billy. He closes the door behind him.

'Do you think he might be having a nervous breakdown?' Brenda asks Usha.

'I think it might have already happened,' says Usha. 'I have spoken to the doctor and he is going to come himself later today. I told him that since this has happened Mukesh has hardly got out of bed. I have to take food up to him and he only comes down to use the bathroom.' She pauses and then says sternly, 'Brenda, please don't speak to anyone about these things that are happening to us, not even Eugene. The children have started to live their lives again after many, many months and Mukesh, well he seems to be going backwards rather than forwards. Maybe he will recover from this one day but I can't cope if everyone is pointing at us and talking about us all the time.'

'Listen, Usha, I don't talk about private stuff to anyone,' replies Brenda sounding slightly offended. 'Anyhow, you Indians get so worried about what other people think all the time – shouldn't you just focus on getting your hubby sorted? Does it really matter what other people think? Perhaps once he has some new tablets from the doctor he can go back to work. Do you want Eugene to speak to Sam Bedford?'

'Let's talk about the Bomb Peck,' Usha says.

'If you like, bablin,' says Brenda more gently. 'Why don't we go for a walk around there? We can see how the young lads are getting on with the climbing frame. Didn't they make a start at the weekend?'

Ten minutes later, just after 9am, Usha and Brenda leave the house.

'Blimey, it's a bit parky isn't it?' Brenda says when they get outside.

'Yes, it is cold,' replies Usha as she rolls the ends of her scarf around her hands like an old-fashioned muff. 'I think it will be another long winter.'

The two women walk through the alleyway which leads to the back garden of the derelict house behind the O'Connells'. The navigate their way through the overgrown garden and onto Wills Street via a broken back gate.

'Look Brenda,' Usha exclaims excitedly as they turn into Brougham Street.

'Bloody hell,' says Brenda and the two women walk faster to get a closer view of the huge wood and rope structure being erected ahead of them.

'Alright, Mom?' A voice says from behind a small, half-built wooden tower. 'What you doing here so early?'

'Kavi, I thought you were still in bed,' says Usha.

'Nah, couldn't sleep so got up to come here. Some of the other lads, Clive and Joey and that, are over there making the rope-ladder. Good, isn't it?'

'Oh yes!' Usha and Brenda say in unison.

Chapter 35

By the beginning of December there is snow in Birmingham. For over a week the people of Handsworth awake to streets that appear clean and brightened by the fresh flurries. Beneath the surface, however, sludged ice is compacted and perilous and the few people with regular work in the area trudge through it without proper footwear or adequate clothing. The older Asian women are the least prepared – they layer thin saris with hand-knitted cardigans and tank tops and continue to struggle through the bitter cold wearing low-heeled court shoes and mules that suffice for the other seasons but are useless for snow and ice.

'Handsworth looks better in the snow.' Anila remarks to Kamela as she stares out of the grimy bus window on the way to the city centre. 'It's like it's all clean and fresh, pretending to have got rid of the filth but we all know it's still there underneath. By lunchtime it'll all be a nasty, dirty slush. It's literally a whitewash.'

'What you on about, Anila?' Kamela says.

Anila doesn't answer but continues to stare out the window. As they pull into the bus-stop outside Taj and Co. butchers, Anila spots Kash crossing the junction of Hamstead Road and Villa Road. A few paces behind him is the woman she recognises from the police station in the summer. The woman pushes a pram with one hand and holds on to a small child with the other. She walks tentatively on the ice, attempting to catch up with Kash as he strides ahead. Anila turns away from the window.

'What's wrong Anila? You don't look right,' Kamela says.

'It's him,' Anila replies, pointing towards Kash as he nears the bus.

'What? That bastard from your meetings?'

'Oh shit, Kamela, he won't get on the bus will he?'

'Not if I have anything to bloody do with it,' replies Kamela.

When Kash is almost at the bus-stop he glances up and catches Anila's eye. She quickly turns her face away again just as Kamela jumps up on to the seat behind.

'Kamela, what are you doing?'

Kamela slides open the narrow window above her and hollers out onto the street below.

'Oi, you, wanker,' she yells.

The other passengers on the top deck all turn to observe the commotion; some tut in obvious scorn, others look on amusedly, glad of the disruption to an otherwise slow and dreary bus journey. Kamela continues to shout out of the window,.

'Don't you come anywhere near my sister again, you fucking bastard.'

Kash looks away in the other direction, pretending to be oblivious to the shouting above him. His wife and small son stare up at Kamela and they are joined by the small crowd of people shivering in the bus-stop queue.

'You, I'm talking to you, Kash bloody Ram. Don't turn away and pretend you can't hear me. You touch my sister again, you bastard and I'll make sure everyone knows exactly what you are like. It will be all over the front page of the bleeding Handsworth Times believe me. Now fuck off and crawl under your stone and don't even think about getting on this bus, scum!'

'Shssh now, Kam,' pleads Anila and Kamela climbs down from the seat and calmly takes her place next to Anila. She leans across to look out the window and both sisters watch as Kash scurries away past the bus-stop with his wife and son in tow. Just as the bus engine fires up and begins to pull off, Kash slips on the ice and falls in an undignified heap on the grey mush of sullied snow at the side of the pavement.

'Serves him bloody right,' Kamela says, laughing.

'Shut the friggin' window,' one of the other passengers shouts from the back of the bus. 'It's bloody freezing up here.'

That evening, Kavi and the girls sit in front of the television watching *Game For A Laugh* and eating anda bhurji with their dinner plates on their knees.

'I don't think I can eat any more of these scrambled eggs. We seem to have them every other bloody day.'

'Cheap, that's why,' says Anila as she pushes the food from one side of the plate to the other.

'There's not even any butter on the chapattis. It's like eating a bit of cardboard,' Kavi complains.

'Beggars cannot be choosers,' Kamela sings the line to the tune of *Handsworth Revolution*. 'Mom does her best,' she continues, 'and it can't be easy feeding us lot without any wages coming into the house. At least we don't have to eat all that nasty bland frozen rubbish skint white people eat.'

'I quite like some of that actually,' Kavi replies. 'You can't beat a beef burger with Smash. It's better than all that dhal and shit that makes you fart.'

The phone rings. Anila looks around at the others but they don't even seem to notice the noise from the hallway. Kavi is chuckling at the TV programme and Kamela is carefully heaping spoonfuls of anda bhurji on to her chapatti and rolling up the edges of the flatbread to make a filled cone. In the corner of the room, Mukesh is snoring in the armchair under a copy of the *Handsworth Times*. Eventually, Anila gets up and heads for the telephone, avoiding her father's outstretched legs as she leaves the room.

'Is that you Anila?' the voice on the other end says.

'Yes, who is it?' Anila replies. She doesn't recognise the voice on the other end.

'It's me, Olive, from the Handsworth Youth Movement. How are you? I haven't seen you for ages.'

'Okay,' Anila says flatly.

'Okay – is that it?'

'Well, yeah! Just trying to get on with my studies and that.'

'You don't come to the meetings anymore, why not?'

'I just said. I have to study and that.'

'You sure it isn't something else too? A few people have had some disagreements since that march back in August and well, people are leaving. It's all breaking up, like. Some are saying there are too many of your lot now, others that there are too many West Indians. We are saying we should stand together – whatever our colour – that's what Handsworth is.'

Anila continues to listen without responding.

'Anyway, some have gone off to make their own groups – just black kids or just Pakis like, and others have signed up to join bigger things like the Socialist Workers and Militant and other groups like that.'

'What are they?'

'White people's groups I think – communists maybe. I don't really know but someone said they are always at the factory when there is a strike on. They have a newspaper which they sell, looks like the Daily Mirror. Anyhow, it's only a few that have done that, most of us want to stick together.'

'So, what are you calling me for?' asks Anila.

'Well, Kash is going. I don't know whether you heard or not?'

'Going? What, to join one of those bigger movements?'

'No, don't think so. He is moving to Bradford or something. Marcus and some of the others fell out with him.'

'Marcus?' asks Anila, surprising herself with her own sudden interest.

'Yes. Marcus, Aazim and some of the others said Kash was not being democratic and was behaving like some kind of totalitarian dictator.' Olive veers off her point to add, 'Oh, Anila, I was so ashamed, I didn't even know what they meant – I had to go home and look it up in the dictionary but I'm still not completely sure. Honestly, they didn't teach us very much at that bloody school we went to. It was like they wrote us off before we even started just because we didn't pass our Eleven-Plusses.'

'What is your point, Olive?'

'Well, I know you fell out with him too. We all saw you slap him one at the march. There was some gossip that you fancied him and stuff and that's why you stopped coming but I think it was something else. I know you probably don't want to talk about it and it's ages ago now anyway but that isn't the reason I am phoning. Some of us met up at the Acapulco the other day and we all agreed you were one of the best members, reliable and that. You are great at organising and at talking. Some people said maybe you should take Kash's place as the sort of spokesperson.'

'Who said that? They must be bloody daft,' says Anila. 'Who was there, at the Acapulco?' She wants to know if it is Marcus who has said these complimentary things about her.

'Oh, there were a few of us,' Olive replies. 'We want to carry on but be more sort of balanced so it's not just one or two blokes telling everyone else what to do. The fellas who came to the Acapulco agree – they want that too. There is talk that there might be more riots before Christmas. People are really pissed off with the police and SUS and all that, especially the black kids and then our dads are all out of work, plus the NF are supposed to be marching again in a few weeks, in the new year, so we need to get organised.'

'Maybe we should try and get something in the Handsworth Times about it,' says Anila. 'Like about why everyone should be opposed to them coming to an area like this full of different kinds of people living side by side, and how they are just coming to cause trouble when we all get on alright really. That the real problems are boredom and not having jobs and stuff.'

'That is a great idea, Anila. Will you do it – like write it and send it to them?'

'I could do. I am pissed off about it all, it's just that I have had a lot on with starting college and the Bomb Peck stuff that my mom is doing.'

'Will you come to the next meeting then? Go on say you will. We haven't set a date yet so we can do it for whenever you are free. We don't have The Shoe anymore, it's getting pulled down so it could be at St Silas', not far for you to go. Tell you what, if you come to the next meeting we can get some of our lot to help your mom with her project thing.'

'Will he be there?'

'What, Kash? Nah, he's off next week. I don't think we'll be seeing much of him anymore.'

'What about Marcus?'

'Oh yes, he'll be there. He is sort of the leader now, although he won't say he is. You haven't had a ruck with him too have you?'

'No,' says Anila, 'nothing like that. I just wanted to know who was still involved that's all.'

'Who was that on the phone?' asks Kavi when Anila returns to the living-room.

'No-one,' replies Anila.

'Well you were ages considering it was no-one,' continues Kavi, still watching the television as he speaks, 'so I ate your anda stuff – it was stone cold so I thought you wouldn't want it.'

'You're a greedy bastard, you are Kavi,' Kamela says from across the room.

As Anila gets ready for bed she says to Kamela, 'I think I am going to the next Handsworth Youth Movement meeting.'

'What?' Kamela shouts over the voice of John Peel chatting through the transistor radio.

Anila repeats her intention a bit louder and Kamela sits up from her horizontal reading position.

'You are not!'

'I am. He won't be there though. He's leaving Brum and going to Bradford to live or something so hopefully I will never have to see him again.'

'What? Really? Since I gave him a bollocking from the number sixteen?'

'No, don't be daft. It's been planned for a while apparently.' Anila pauses and after a few moments says, 'Hey Kam, will you come with me? To the meeting I mean. Will you?'

'Yeah okay,' Kamela says, 'if you want me to. Turn the big light off, will you? And turn the radio up a bit, I love this song.'

Chapter 36

On the morning of 10 July, Usha walks from room to room in the Church Street house opening the windows and curtains to let in the fresh air and bright sunshine of the new day. It is only 8am and she has already swept and mopped the floors, cleaned the bathroom and dusted the mantelpiece, picture rails and door frames. When she has put away the dusters and other cleaning tools, she stretches her arm down the back of the settee and pulls up the framed school photograph of the children. It was taken the year Billy joined Lozells Primary School, the same year Nina was preparing to leave it – it is the only formal portrait of all the children together. Usha dusts the frame, gently kisses the face of each child, wipes the glass and places the photo back on the hook above the settee where it used to hang. She fiddles with the positioning until it exactly fills the pale square exposed by its temporary absence, and then she places a garland of fresh marigolds around the frame. She stands back, a foot or two away from the settee, to regard the image for a few moments before heading to the kitchen and switching on the kettle.

'Amrit phoned from the factory yesterday,' Usha says to Brenda a couple of hours later as they sit over tea and toast in the kitchen, waiting for the children to wake up.

'What did he say – are they looking for men?'

'Actually, he wanted to ask me if I would like to work in the office part-time. The secretary is having a baby and he seemed to know I could do touch-typing and shorthand.'

'Bloody hell, bab, that's bostin. I know plenty of people who would love that job – or any job actually. I hope you said yes.'

'I said yes – I think they have only thought of me because of all the things that happened with Mukesh last year. I think they feel pity for me but we can't afford to have pride these days. I have to do whatever I can and this is a blessing. I haven't told Mukesh yet.'

'How is Mukesh since he got out of All Saints?' Brenda asks.

'He is a bit better,' Usha replies. 'He gets up and gets dressed more often.'

'Oh that is great,' says Brenda. 'They do seem to work wonders up there.'

'Yes, but half the time it is like he isn't really here, if you know what I mean.'

'Not really, bab.'

'He is quieter… different.' Usha says.

'Well maybe he is calming down a bit. Time is a healer and all that. Perhaps he'll go down the job centre or maybe even go back to Hardiman's. If you're there you can try and convince them – and they have a new manager now – Bedford has moved on, I heard. A promotion to the Northfield site or something.'

'Maybe,' Usha says, unconvinced. Then she adds, 'Today it is exactly two years since Billy died. I'm not sure Mukesh even knows what month it is.'

'Oh blimey. I didn't realise. I am sorry Usha. Are you doing something?'

'Doing something? You mean at the temple? No, I don't think so. This is a private thing.'

'Maybe we could all walk down to the Bomb Peck if your kids ever get up. We could plant some flowers or something. I've got some pansy seeds left over. It might be too late – in the year I mean – but it would be a nice thing to do with the children and as it's Sunday they are probably all around aren't they? What do you think?'

When Brenda has gone home and the flowers for Billy have been planted at the Bomb Peck, Usha looks for Mukesh in the house. She finds him sitting in front of the photo of the children in the living-room. He reeks strongly of tobacco and faintly of whisky and when Usha speaks he sighs at the disruption and continues to stare blankly into the distance.

'I want to go home,' he says after a short while.

'You are home,' Usha says and Mukesh shakes his head.

'This has never been my home. Handsworth is no good to me. I don't belong here, I don't belong anywhere. I was destroyed before I came here and this place has made it worse.'

'Mukesh,' Usha says, 'we are your home – me and the children. Can't you see that?'

'You will all leave me one day,' Mukesh says and he takes a swig of his whisky straight from the bottle. 'Go away, Usha.'

Usha calls the children downstairs to eat the beans on toast she has made for their tea. Nina, back from university for the summer holidays, hands out the plates of food to Kamela, Anila and Kavi as they all squeeze in around the kitchen table waiting to be fed.

'Don't finish all the tomato sauce,' says Kavi, grabbing the bottle from Anila.

'Sod off, Kavi,' his sister replies grabbing the bottle back.

'Give it here, you git.'

'Bog off, Kavi, you always take too much and I want some too. Give it here after you've finished, Anila.'

A glass of orange squash gets knocked over in the scuffle.

'Grow up you lot,' Nina says as she looks for a tea-towel to mop up the spillage.

Usha leaves the children to their bickering and walks out into the garden. The late afternoon air is fresh and warm, but the ground is still muddy from the rainfall the night before. Usha smooths down the folds of the sari she wears and lifts up the bottom edges so they don't get spoiled by the mud. She makes her way to the far end of the garden where she knows there is an old stool, and where she won't be able to hear the noises from the kitchen or smell the tobacco odours which are strong enough to drift down the hallway and seep into the rest of the ground floor of the house. Usha wipes the moisture off the stool with the train of her sari and sits down. She listens to the sounds of children playing in the gardens around her: the thuds of balls being thrown at walls and the whoops after goals are scored between makeshift goal posts. In the distance there is the scream of a siren, perhaps a police car or perhaps an ambulance.

Acknowledgements

For support along the way thank you to: Dr Sue Roe, University of Sussex, Eva Lewin at Spread The Word, Chris Taylor at New Writing South, Karen Costelloe for her unwavering belief and Cynthia Rogerson via The Literary Consultancy, who will be unaware of how her feedback spurred me on.

Thank you to Selwyn Brown and David Hinds of Steel Pulse for the use of lyrics from the brilliant *Handsworth Revolution*, and to Dr. Vanley Burke for his evocative photograph of Lozells Road.

Special thanks to Kevin Duffy for his energy and enthusiasm in making this and other books happen, and to the whole of the Bluemoose team, in particular, Hetha Duffy and my editor, Leonora Rustamova.

Love and gratitude to my mother, Brij Bala Duggal, my late father, Sarbjit Duggal, my siblings, Parveen, Shine, Simon, Diamond and Peter, and my extended family – Duggals, Traynors and others. Thank you also to my friends for their invaluable encouragement and support. Finally, to Joe, of course, and to our children, Ruben, Milan and Varsha.